LUMEN

LUMEN

and the Thistle

EJ Wozniak

Table of Contents

Prologue

Crusty eyelids and shivers were aplenty on an early morning in a bustling park in the middle of an ordinary town. The sky was cloudy, and it was breezy. The clouds loomed overhead, as though they were an ominous threat to the people below. Winter was on the horizon. The men and women walking to work bundled themselves up with their scarves and trench coats to protect their bodies from brisk gusts of wind. The working class in this town cut through the park to avoid the crowded morning streets. Freshly brewed coffee stands were sprinkled throughout the park, which provided a collective, early-morning aroma of roasted beans. The men and women darted quickly to different carts, grabbing cups of coffee as they went and immediately returning to their path. It was almost mechanical, automatic. Nearly everybody clutched their briefcase or purse in one hand, and an unopened umbrella and a coffee in the other. Even one man wore a full suit with a plastic poncho over it as he scurried to work.

Everyone kept their heads down, seemingly unable to look up to say hello or acknowledge the fellow working class individuals that made this town go. This was unusual as it was a tight knit town, one where everyone seemed to know everyone. The sun shined on most days here. But not today. No one here seemed to be happy to be walking to work on a day like this. Men and women alike had a grim expression on their face as they strode through the park. Some glanced up to the clouds as if they could read them, as if they could tell when the rain would start.

One man walking through the park appeared to be in no hurry at all. Nor did he carry a briefcase or an umbrella. He wore thick black-brimmed glasses which rested upon a freshly shaven face, a rather thick nose, bushy salt and pepper eyebrows. He wore a black Homburg hat and a grey trench coat like most the others, but he seemed to have difficulty with it as he scavenged for money in the large, bulky pockets to pay for a cup of coffee. He was finally able to muster up change and took his steamy cup of coffee to a nearby bench with a smile. One lady passed by the man with the thick, black-rimmed glasses and gave him an odd look, a gaze that said, "Why are you so happy on a day like this?" The man held a newspaper under his arm. When he took a seat on an old wooden bench, he crossed a leg over the other and opened the paper. He skimmed over the stories on the front page, but not one of them caught his eye, nothing except the excerpt on the top right of the newspaper.

Today's Forecast, Page 5.

The man instantly turned to page five and found the weather portion toward the bottom.

Today's Forecast: 100% chance of rain. Bring an umbrella!

A large grin stretched across the man's face, picking up his coffee as he folded his newspaper. He smiled as he took a deep breath. He could smell it coming now: the dew aroma just before a big rain. He looked up to the sky as a single raindrop fell onto his glasses and slid down the lens, leaving a small trail of water droplets.

The man looked back down with a grin.

"Job well done, J, a job well done," he said to himself. He buttoned up his coat and tucked a black bead necklace he had been wearing carefully inside of the coat.

The man left the park as abruptly as he entered, never to be seen again. Nobody knew who he was, so nobody noticed one less man coming through the park in the mornings.

It rained heavily for the next three days.

Chapter 1 - Lumen

Lumen wasn't like the other kids in his small town. He didn't have many friends and was considered different in the eyes of others. Some kids called him that freak without a dad. Although Lumen had never met his father, it didn't bother him. He thought his mother did a great job as a single parent. His mother, Alice, always told him he was the man of the house, anyway, so she didn't need another man around there. Truth be told, Lumen didn't think he may ever be the man of the house, of any house for that matter. Ever since he was a young boy, he had always been unlike other children. Lumen used to stare off into space for long periods, often times in class. There was no telling when exactly his eyes would glaze over. Sometimes it happened when he was walking, eating, even during a test. Other children picked on Lumen for his unsettling gaze and often called him crazy or weird.

Most parents in town also thought there was something off about Lumen. That was, of course, until he was diagnosed and their judgments had been confirmed. From the looks of it, Lumen often appeared to be staring at empty space. The rumors surrounding his gaze ranged from magical beings to angels and demons. But to Lumen, he wasn't just staring off into space. There weren't any magical creatures, no voices, and indeed no demons. It was much more than that. He was actually looking at something, something only he could see. He was staring at the lights.

Lumen was a fair boy of average height for his age. He had dark brown hair and thin, lanky legs and arms—but wasn't unathletic though; he loved to run. Running made Lumen forget about all the problems in his life. He felt like he was at his freest. He was on the cross-country team as a freshman in high school but eventually quit because several of his teammates picked on him too much. Despite the name calling and cruelty, Lumen never wanted to get any of the other kids in trouble. He kept quiet, hoping the kids would just leave him alone. Unfortunately, things didn't quite go his way.

He once won the "Prettiest Eyes" award in middle school—Lumen had eyes that were the same color as a green tree frog—but even when he won that award, it turned for the worse. The day he was to take a picture for the award, his mother dressed him up in his best looking green and white striped polo shirt with his nice black khakis. He combed his hair to the side with some gel and wore his favorite black and white sneakers. However, before Lumen could so much as a smile for the yearbook photo, the yearbook photographers dragged him into a bathroom to give him a cold, wet swirly.

"Crazy kids should appear crazy in their pictures," said one photographer as he pushed Lumen into the stall.

"Yeah, you skitzo, you can't look nice. You would be lying to the whole school. My parents said it isn't fair for kids like you to be up for school awards. People just voted for you because they feel bad for you," said the photographer's partner, Blake, as he proceeded to force Lumen's head into the toilet and flush it a few times. Lumen didn't put up a fight. He figured he should have known this would happen. Instead, he focused on breathing between dunks in the dimly lit middle school bathroom.

Incidents like that were why Lumen tried not to draw attention to himself. Lumen won the award again his freshman year of high school but asked to be withdrawn from consideration. It was easier this way for Lumen. The more he was able to hide in plain sight, the less he had to worry about all the bullies. He had been called crazy all his life, but Lumen never felt mentally unstable. Sure, he didn't quite know what normal meant per se, but he was sure he wasn't crazy. He only saw lights. They were distracting at times, but there were no voices in his head; he didn't talk to imaginary figures; it was just the lights. Lumen believed he wasn't the first and only human in existence to see these lights. They stuck out like a sore thumb and were as real as the bullies who held his head in a toilet. They sometimes were so overwhelming that he couldn't help but to look at them, no matter how much he tried not to.

During the last week of middle school, Lumen came home four consecutive days with his clothes torn, dirtied, or missing. After the fourth day, he went to the doctor for a routine check-up, and his mother found out that Lumen had an ear infection, presumably from the dirty water in the toilets at school. As she was unaware as to the extent of the bullying, she pushed Lumen to find out what he had been doing that would have caused this, and he eventually confessed to the extreme bullying. That was the last straw for Alice. She demanded to know what was wrong with her only son; she wanted him to live a healthy life.

The doctor came into the room with a chart in hand.

"You tell me what is wrong with my son, right now." Alice whispered harshly.

The doctor looked at Alice, then at Lumen, and took a deep breath. He spoke loud enough for them both to hear.

"After some preliminary tests, well. . . it looks like your son may be showing signs of schizophrenia, ma'am. Very, very minor at this point, but nonetheless, schizophrenia."

"Call me Alice, please . . . Are you sure, doctor?" Alice put her hand on her forehead to process what the doctor had just said. Tears filled her eyes and she took deep breaths.

"We still need to run a few tests to confirm, but the signs are pointing to that diagnosis. It is minor at this point in time but could, and most likely will get worse," the doctor said.

"What does this mean for my son?"

"Well, schizophrenics usually experience hallucinations. They may hear voices, they may have thought and movement disorders . . ."

"My son doesn't experience voices. All he said is he sees are something along the lines of panels of light. . . something like that. Couldn't his eyes just be bad? I have worked with patients who have schizophrenia, and they differ greatly from Lumen. I could tell you stories . . ." Alice's eyes bulged as she held her hands clasped together in front of her pale face.

"I am afraid not, Alice. These lights may be just the beginning. Chances are it will get worse over time. Medicine can help with controlling symptoms, which we will administer to Lumen today. Does schizophrenia run in the family?"

"No, no one in my family has it."

"What about the father's side?" the doctor asked. Alice looked down.

"Lumen's father has never been around," Alice said, looking slightly uncomfortable.

"Genetics are not biased to which parent is or is not present."

"Well, no, I hardly knew him myself. I suppose it could run on his side, but I'm not sure," she said with an acerbic tone.

"Any chance you can give him a call to find out? It would help to be familiar with the severity on his side. It will help us administer the correct dosage of medicine."

"No," she snapped.

"No?"

"I don't know where he is. Nor do I want to know."

The doctor did not push further and instead prescribed a low dosage to start, assuring Alice that Lumen could lead a traditional life as long as he took his medicine. Lumen did not like the idea of being medicated, even if it helped. All he thought about was what the other kids at school would say if they saw him taking pills every day.

Lumen sometimes pondered about his father's identity and why he had left them. He tried not to think about it too much, though, his mom did more than enough to take care of them both. Lumen was an only child. Alice was a nurse at a mental health facility, which meant she worked long, hard, and varied hours. She always did her best to make it home for dinner to see Lumen at least once a day, however, that was hardly the case. She often worked double shifts and wasn't able to leave the hospital.

On his many lonely lights, Lumen often visited the restaurant across the street from his house called La Dernière Pièce. On one particular night, Lumen's mom left him money on the kitchen table of their two-bedroom house, and Lumen knew that meant she would not be coming home until late that night or early the next morning. Sometimes, she left a note, but he didn't see one. *She must have been in a rush*, Lumen thought. Lumen walked across Inventa Way, where he resided, to the restaurant. It was a little run down, family-owned place that had excellent chicken pot pie. Lumen couldn't figure out why the restaurant had a French name, he was positive they didn't serve French cuisine. He figured they were just trying to make it sound fancier than it really was. He remembered one of the bus boy's name was Henry, only remembering because he learned about King Henry II of France in class. Lumen concluded that even Henry didn't know his name was French.

Lumen walked in and found a booth. All the booths were red with glitter and had plastic covers. There was single seating near the kitchen with red swivel bar stools, but those were uncomfortable to Lumen. He chose a booth toward the back and smiled when he saw his favorite waitress, Shari, approaching. Shari was a plump, red-headed woman with a gaping space between her front teeth. She wore big hoop earrings and had long, painted fingernails. She wore black jeans that were seemingly too tight and an oversized white button down shirt that was always dirtied with food. She was always kind to Lumen.

servers were acquainted with Lumen and knew his
_r. His typical order consisted of chicken pot pie with
ᴊate shake on the side. It was his absolute favorite. He
ᴊs thought the chicken pot pie ingredients meshed
ᴊether perfectly, all the right ingredients together in one. He
didn't have to think about what went together, it just did.

"How's it going, Lumen? The usual?" asked Shari, smiling.

"Yes, please. Thank you."

"Not a problem, sweetheart. You want the shake before or
after your meal today?" Shari asked as she set down ice water
with lemon on the table.

"I will take it after please."

"You got it."

Lumen felt comfortable there; no one judged him when he
stared off into space, which wasn't often there. For some
reason, the lights were not as present in the restaurant. There
was the occasional light panel, but nothing overwhelming for
Lumen. He once noticed how the few panels he saw there
were red. He figured it had to do with the reddish glow from
all the glittered booths inside.

Kids his own age never ate at this restaurant by themselves.
Lumen remembered the one time Blake came in. He thought
he wouldn't be able to come back now that Blake realized he
dined there, but Blake didn't even glance Lumen's way that
night. Lumen got a good kick at how his parents ordered him
around and made him sit and eat properly; he was used to
seeing Blake walk around the cafeteria and push other kids
around. He often threw his food at the Study Club instead of
eating it. Lumen wondered how he could go all day without
eating.

Blake's parents noticed Lumen almost at once that night,
and they took great care to sit across the restaurant, away from
the *off* child, even if it meant sitting next to the bathroom. He
heard them tell Blake to leave him alone and not to bother
him—not because they didn't want Blake to bully him, but
because they were not sure what would trigger him. Lumen

thought a lot of the parents in town had some backwa
thinking.

Lumen ate his chicken pot pie and slurped down his chocolate shake. He left money on the counter, waved goodbye to Shari, and headed back home across Inventa Way. He strolled across the street. Lumen crossed his arms and immediately felt goosebumps rise as iIt was a bit colder than he expected, a chilly signal that fall was fast approaching. He noticed more light panels as he made his way home. Looking up at the electrical wires, he observed more colors than just red but tried not to pay attention to them. He remembered how his mom told him he was sick and that, with hard work, it could be defeated.

"You can't stare at them all the time, honey, especially in public," she had told him after they left the doctor's office.

"I can't help it sometimes, Mom."

"I know, I know. I just don't want people staring at you. Please don't point and try to grab them like you used to. The more you pay attention to them, the worse your sickness will get. The doctor says you need to stay occupied. I got you another puzzle . . . And take your medicine."

"I hate the medicine, it just makes me tired."

"I know honey, but it's for your own safety."

"Fine."

They are just lights, he thought. What harm could they be doing? Aren't schizophrenics supposed to be seeing monsters and other terrifying things? Aren't they supposed to hear voices and make irrational decisions? He thought he should do more research on the disease before coming to conclusions on his own, but it didn't seem right. He supposed it wouldn't seem right to anyone.

Lumen walked across the street, trying his hardest to neglect the lights. He walked athwart his cracked driveway, through the half-dead lawn, and into his cozy home. The house was never entirely clean, but it was never a mess either. His mom often left the laundry on the plush blue couch for Lumen to fold. He didn't feel much like doing it right then. Instead, he moved the clothes over and plopped onto the

9

...ouch is the best, he thought. He sank in, turned the
...ched some cartoons. He enjoyed his time away
There were no bullies, no mundane classes, and
...ung at him wherever he went.

...en watched a couple episodes of his favorite cartoon
...egan to focus on the lights. There were more panels than
...ual. All different colors: blue, green, yellow, a red panel here
and there. They appeared unorganized and sporadic to Lumen.
If only he could move them around into place, he would feel
much better. The paper-thin panels of light that were floating
all around him were overwhelming him. They were
everywhere.

The phone rang. Lumen snapped out of it and walked over
to the phone hanging next to the kitchen.

"Hello?" Lumen asked, his voice aloof and unfocused.

"Hi, hun, how you doing?"

"I'm all right, Mom. How's work?" He said with more
interest this time.

"It's going to be a late one again. Did you eat?"

"Yes, Mom."

Sometimes he thought his mom babied him. He was 15 for
heaven's sake. He wasn't a child anymore.

"Okay good, can you please fold the clothes on the couch?
How are you feeling tonight? Are you seeing a lot of them?
Did you take your medicine?"

"I will, I'm fine, and no not really. I took my medicine," he
lied to Alice. Lumen didn't usually lie, but when it came to
taking his medicine, he had started lying more often. He had
become a pro at not taking his pills. Lumen told himself the
lies were justified as long as he kept his grades up in school.

"Good, good. Well, I got you a couple of new puzzles just
in case you get overwhelmed. I put them on the kitchen table.
I got to run. Please go to bed at a decent hour tonight. I know
it's Friday, but I would like to have breakfast with you in the
morning before I have to go to work."

"Okay, Mom, I will. Love you."

"Love you too, hun."

Lumen sighed, trying to decide on what to do. He thought
about calling his one good friend, Alec, but he always had to

babysit his siblings on Friday nights. Alec was the only perso in the town who didn't judge him.

Lumen walked back over to the couch and almost tripped over a dog toy. He hadn't seen his dog, Wrigley, since he got home. This was strange since Wrigley usually came running to the door when Lumen returned.

Lumen instantly started to worry

"Wrigley? Where are ya, boy?" Lumen whistled for him.

No answer.

Lumen felt the panic run up and down his spine almost instantly. He darted to the back door, but it was closed. *Did Mom let him out and forget he was out there when she left?* She hadn't done that before. Lumen frantically walked to his room and felt a wave of instant relief wash over him. Wrigley sat in the middle of the room with his back to Lumen, wagging his tail. There were papers on the ground all around him. Lumen thought he must have knocked them off his desk. Wrigley was looking up at nothing.

"Wrigley?"

Wrigley turned around and finally noticed Lumen. He wagged his tail so hard that he knocked over Lumen's lamp; he was overly excited per usual. Wrigley was part German Shepherd, part Labrador Retriever. He was a fairly large dog, so when he jumped on Lumen, Lumen usually fell over. They wrestled on the ground for a few moments before Lumen got up and called for Wrigley to leave with him to the living room. Lumen picked up the papers and put them back on his desk.

As they left the room, Lumen looked at the spot where Wrigley was looking and noticed a glut of blue light panels. He shrugged it off and closed the door. "Maybe I should take the meds tonight . . ." he said aloud to himself.

They walked back down the hall to the living room. He looked at the pile of clothes and sighed. Lumen had hoped they would somehow fold themselves. He walked over to the blue couch, turned the TV back on, and folded the clothes. He never enjoyed folding his mom's clothes; he didn't want to know what his mom's undergarments looked like.

"Yuck," as he tossed those to the side.

Wrigley sat beside the couch, chewing on something. Lumen looked down and didn't recognize the toy in Wrigley's

11

`lmost looked like a block of ice. His mom must
`ew toy for him.

    `inished folding the clothes and relaxed back on the
`hortly after, he went over to the kitchen and opened
`ridge to see if there was any food. There was plenty of
`od there, but not anything Lumen wanted; he was looking
more because he was bored. He decided he would check out
the two new puzzles his mom had bought him and went over
to the kitchen table.

    Lumen was incredibly fast at completing puzzles. Ever
since he had been diagnosed his doctor recommended puzzles
to make him think and stay occupied, away from the lights.
Even before the diagnosis, he loved doing puzzles. He loved
piecing them together. In the first grade, while all the students
were doing simple 25-piece puzzles, Lumen completed 500-
piece puzzles with ease. As a teenager, he finished complicated
puzzles faster than most adults. It was one reason he never fell
behind in school. He had always been a great problem solver,
not just with puzzles, but in every aspect.

    If he hadn't been diagnosed, Lumen probably would have
been able to skip a few grades. He thought about that
sometimes. He figured he must have more purpose. He felt he
should be on his way to college already, with some Ivy League
schools begging him to attend their schools. He could be one
of the youngest doctors in the country, or work on space
shuttles that could reach Mars, or solving world hunger. His
doctors once mentioned that he could possibly be a genius.
That was of course, overshadowed by the fact he was a
diagnosed schizophrenic and he could only stay in the general
classes as long as his grades stayed up. Keeping his grades up
was never the hard part. Taking his medication and avoiding
the lights, however, was a different story. Lumen had to go to
the nurse's office after his second class every day so the nurse
could watch him take his medicine. The nurse, Mrs. Goebbel,
was an older woman who had terrible eyesight. She wore
glasses that enlarged her gray eyes so much that Lumen had a
hard time looking at her directly. Each day she requested that
Lumen open his mouth to show that the pill had been

swallowed. Lumen became skilled at hiding the pill under his tongue and spitting it out in the bathroom after Mrs. Goebbel turned her back to him.

He learned that he should no longer do puzzles in school because it became yet another reason to be picked on. Blake and his friends hunted Lumen in the library during lunch and throw the puzzle pieces about, leaving Lumen to clean them up and start from scratch. From then on, he decided to stick to doing them in the comfort of his home, on the kitchen table.

He grabbed the dark blue box. It was a 2000-piece of Van Gogh's *Starry Night*. He picked up the other box, which was maroon and featured a picture of Paris, France with the Eiffel Tower on the left side. He jokingly wondered if he could find La Dernière Pièce somewhere in the picture among all the cafes.

Lumen ripped the plastic of the Paris puzzle, opened the box, took a deep breath, and dumped the pieces out. He checked his watch for the time, 8:27. His mind raced. He completely forgot about the lights.

Wrigley trotted back to Lumen's room.

Chapter 2 - Alec

Lumen put the last piece of the puzzle into place. He exhaled and then took a deep breath. He checked his watch. *11:13 PM*. Lumen rolled his eyes. It took him 2 minutes longer to finish this puzzle than the last 2,000 piece puzzle he completed. He was frustrated with himself. Lumen strived to beat himself each time he did a puzzle.

"Are you kidding me? Get it together, Lu," Lumen said bitterly to himself. Lumen decided to go for a run around the block to blow off some steam. His neighborhood was quiet, and he never worried about being robbed or jumped because they lived in a fairly small town. Everyone knew everyone. Word would get around about who did it eventually.

Lumen put on some gym shorts, laced up his running shoes, and left. He thought about taking Wrigley as he was walking out the door, but he didn't see him. When he stepped out, he took a deep breath of the brisk fall air. Lumen loved the feeling of the cold air filling his lungs. He smiled and took off.

His neighborhood was well lit, and there were hardly any cars driving up and down the street. There were a lot of trees, most of which were almost leafless as winter approached. He ran by *La Dernier Place* and saw Shari getting into her car. She must have just gotten off for the night. Lumen waved.

He ran down the block and turned the corner. His neighborhood was one big loop, and perfect for a brief run. If he stayed left, he would end up at home eventually. Lumen started to breathe heavily as he passed one of his mom's co-worker's home. The house was dark, with no car in the driveway. *The hospital must be short staffed tonight.* Lumen wondered if his mom would even get up early enough to have breakfast with him the next day. He also remembered how his mom would not be happy about him going for a run this late.

"I don't like you running this late. What if you get caught up in your lights and no one is there to snap you out of it? It's dark out there, you could get lost, hun!"

"It won't happen, Mom, running helps. I will take the medicine before I go if that makes you feel better."

"I would feel better if you ran when it was light outside."

"Fine, Mom." He thought about the lights being present day and night, *it doesn't make a difference*, he thought.

Lumen didn't put up a fight with his mom ever. He didn't want to make her worry or work harder than she already did.

Lumen began to sweat. He felt a cramp on his side. He didn't let it slow him down as he passed Blake's house. Lumen increased his speed slightly stretch of his run as he didn't want Blake to see him. He could turn around and head back home the way he came, but the best part was coming. Most of the run was flat except for the end stretch. He reached the big, steep hill, looked up, and pushed himself up as fast as possible. There weren't any homes up at the top of the hill, nor were there streetlights. It was perfect for stargazing. For others, it was an ideal spot to bring a date. Friday night was prime time for that. When he finally reached the top, he slowed down. No one was around. He was surprised and relieved to have this moment alone. He tried to catch his breath while he looked up, noticing the cloudy night.

"Dangit! There was supposed to be a full moon tonight. . ." Lumen said to himself out loud. He looked around to make sure nobody was around to hear him. He was still alone. The last thing he needed was for someone to find him talking to himself.

Lumen took a deep breath and started making his way down the other side of the hill where houses and street lights appeared again on both sides of him. He reached the bottom of the hill and ran another block and a half or so to his house.

He slowed down at his driveway and put his hands on his head. He tripped over the crack in the driveway. He looked around to make sure no one was around to see and hurried into his house. As he walked toward the kitchen to get a glass of water, he stepped in a big wet spot on the carpet. He stopped and looked down.

"Wrigley, did you pee in the house?" Lumen realized he should have taken him out before he left for his run.

He went and grabbed some paper towels and dabbed the wet spot. The towels did not appear yellow. He got down to smell the spot, and it didn't smell like anything. Lumen thought it must just be water or Wrigley's slobber.

"What kind of toy did mom give you?"

Again, Wrigley didn't come to the door to greet Lumen as he usually did. Lumen was worried but figured he was distracted with a toy in his room.

Lumen wiped up the rest of the water, or slobber, and headed to the bathroom to take a shower. He brushed his teeth while the water heated as he didn't like wasting time. When the water was hot enough, Lumen finished brushing his teeth in the shower. He cleaned himself and got out as fast as he could. He wrapped a towel around himself and walked to his room. Wrigley wasn't there.

Lumen turned around back down the hall calling for Wrigley. He went back to the living room and into the kitchen. No sign of him there either.

Lumen felt that familiar sense of panic he had experienced just hours before. Did he somehow let out Wrigley before he left for his run? He hurried back to his room to put some clothes on to go and look for him outside.

He reached his room to find Wrigley staring at nothing.

"Wrig, where were you? You scared the heck out of me."

"Hey, Lumen."

Lumen jumped back, and his towel almost fell off.

"What the . . . how did you get in here, Alec?"

Alec took a moment to answer.

"Uh, you left the door open, obviously . . ."

"You scared me half to death. Get out of here, I need to change. I'll meet you in the living room."

Alec walked out of the room. This was the first time Alec had shown up without asking Lumen beforehand.

"You too, Wrig."

Wrigley trotted out of the room. Lumen looked up while putting on his socks, noticing how many blue panels were in there, all bunched together where Wrigley was sitting. Lumen ignored them and got changed so that he could find out why Alec decided to show up out of the blue.

Lumen walked into the living room to find Alec sitting and watching TV, sweating profusely as usual. Wrigley sat beside him on the couch, apparently chewing on something again. It looked like another block of ice, or something similar.

"Where did you get that, Wrig?" half expecting him to answer.

"Don't start talking to animals now, you'll give people the wrong idea . . ." Alec said with a smile.

"Shut up, Alec."

Alec laughed to himself as Lumen sat on the chair beside the couch. He sat down and looked at Alec. Alec wore his typical outfit: gym shorts and a white t-shirt with some black sneakers and long socks. Alec was an athlete. He could run, jump, lift weights, and play any sport better than the average person. If it was related to physical activity, Alec could do it and do it well. He was also a good looking young man. He was muscular, tan skinned with slicked, brown hair and blue eyes. Lumen always thought that Alec should be one of the "popular" kids. There was one thing holding Alec back from prominent high school status: he sweated like crazy, so much so you could see sweat stains at all times. It even gave him a constant stench of stale sweat. The sweating didn't seem to bother Alec. But, like Lumen, he got picked on the minute he transferred to Bromide High. Unlike Lumen, Alec was well-versed in sticking up for himself. Alec was more of a lone wolf until he met Lumen.

They first met in the bathroom, an unfortunate and familiar spot for Lumen. He never thought it would be the place to meet a new friend.

"Bathroom is clear. Blake, grab Lumen and get him into the bathroom. Let's give him a little surprise." Blake and his crew had all snickered together.

"He's coming around the corner, hold on . . ."

Blake waited and grabbed Lumen on the shoulders and threw him into the bathroom. He locked the door.

"It has been a while since you got a swirly, skitzo, I think you're due." Blake sneered.

Lumen stayed silent as usual. Blake and his friend grabbed him and shoved him into a stall. They pushed Lumen to his knees and put their hands on the back of his head.

"Hope you can hold your breath better than last time." They proceeded to shove Lumen's head into the toilet; Lumen braced himself when suddenly the hands on the back of his head and shoulders were gone. Lumen came up, thankful for the brief moment of fresh air.

"How'd you get in here, smelly?" Lumen heard Blake say.

"You leave him alone, or you'll have to deal with me," said another voice that Lumen did not recognize.

"What are you gonna do, faucet-pits? We would throw you in the toilet as well but you already look and smell like you've been in there," Blake laughed.

Alec grabbed Blake by his collar and pushed him against the wall. He raised his fist. Blake tried to squirm away, but he could barely move.

"Alright, alright. Let go of me . . . please. . . let go . . ."

Alec hesitated but let him go. Blake and his friend unlocked the door and left quickly.

"Thanks, you didn't have to do that," Lumen said relieved.

"It looked like you needed the help."

"I'm used to it," Lumen shrugged.

18

"It won't happen again if I can help it. . .I'm Alec by the way."

"I'm Lumen."

"I know, the crazy kid, right?" Alec said with a smirk.

Lumen turned red. He strongly disliked his reputation as the crazy kid.

"Wow, you're a new kid, right? And you have already heard that? It's not as bad as everyone says," Lumen said defensively.

"I know, I'm just giving you a hard time. Don't worry, I, uh, sweat a lot, as you can see,"

Alec lifted his arms to show the sweat stains.

"So I used to get bullied like you. Learned how to stick up for myself at my last school."

"Well then, maybe we should stick together. Did you just move here?"

"Yeah, maybe we should. And yeah, just moved in last week," Alec said with a smile and stuck out his hand. Lumen grabbed it and shook it, immediately noticing how moist the hand was.

They were best friends from that point forward and hung out nearly every day for the past year. They hung out during breaks at school and usually spent weekends playing video games and watching movies. The only day of the week they would not spend together was Friday; Alec had to babysit on Friday nights. Aside from that, Alec rescued Lumen from plenty of swirlies over the course of the school year. He always seemed to be there at the right time--except for that night.

"You can't just walk into my house, Alec."

"Sorry, I wanted to make sure you were okay . . ."

"Why wouldn't I be? Aren't you supposed to be babysitting?"

"Oh, right, it's Friday. Uh, yeah, my parents came home early. . .So, are you seeing a lot of the lights lately?"

"Did my mom call you?" Lumen said abrasively.

"No. . ."

19

"Then why are you asking? You hardly ever bring that up, and now you show up to my house super late, unannounced, and start asking about the lights. What gives?"

"It's 12 o'clock on a Friday, Lu. I just want you to know I am here to help. I've been thinking and I just don't want you to feel alone. . ."

"What?"

"Nothing, I should probably go."

Lumen was perturbed by the way Alec was acting.

"What? Are you okay?" Lumen asked.

Alec nodded his head.

"Yeah, yeah, don't worry about me."

"You want me to walk with you home?" Just then, Lumen realized he had never been to Alec's house. Or met his parents. Or siblings. He didn't even know their names. Alec always had a reason to not go to his house, from his siblings napping to the house flooded, and Lumen never thought anything of it until now.

"No, I'm alright. Just remember what I said."

Lumen was very confused but felt relieved to see Alec walk out the door. He looked out the window and didn't see him. He must have started running home. Lumen thought his parents must be worried that he left so late.

Lumen turned around and saw Wrigley still chewing on the block.

"Give me that, you're making a mess."

Lumen picked it up and realized it was a small block of ice, larger than a cube from the freezer though.

"Where did you get this?" again half expecting Wrigley to answer. Wrigley just stared at him. Lumen went to the kitchen to check the refrigerator. The freezer wasn't open. He looked underneath the fridge to see if somehow ice was falling down.

Nothing. Lumen scratched his head in confusion but figured his mom must have given it to him.

Lumen decided to go to bed. He wanted to make sure he could get up for his mom before she went to work.

"C'mon, Wrig, bedtime." Lumen took him outside to go to the bathroom and headed back to his room afterwards. Wrigley slept with Lumen most nights.

Lumen got to his room, jumped into his pajamas, and slid into bed. He felt restless and began processing the strange events from the evening. The blue lights still lingered. He looked at them intently for a few moments and then tried to ignore them to fall asleep. He did this over and over for some time. The light wasn't coming from anywhere and moved slowly in random directions. They were just windows of light, present at all times, and Lumen wasn't sure why his mind would make these up. But there was something incomplete about the lights. He became frustrated and decided that he should take his medicine. It would help him sleep. He got up, and as he passed his desk, he knocked over some papers. He turned on his desk lamp. Lumen looked down at them and didn't remember leaving any papers out. He knelt down to pick them up and noticed some odd drawings.

"What the . . ."

There was a remarkably realistic drawing of an older gentleman with long graying hair and a long beard to match. He wore a ragged, long green trench coat with a lot of pockets and buttons. He appeared to be wearing an odd gown underneath the trench coat, and black pants underneath. The man wore what appeared to be goggles with a brown leather strap on top of his head, holding his hair back. A wooden pipe hung from his mouth. Lumen saw that the man had large graying eyebrows and had an older-looking face. His nose was fairly large. He was leaning on a cane and beside the cane was a large, black cat--not a fat cat, but an abnormally large cat. The cat was sitting next to the man and had a red vest on. The cat also had goggles on top of its head.

"What a weird drawing . . ."

Lumen figured he had accidentally picked up someone else's papers when he left class that day. He tried to think if there were any artists in his classes. He couldn't think of anyone he had seen drawing before.

Lumen left his room and went to the kitchen. He grabbed his pills from the medicine cabinet, took a pill, and headed back to his room. He laid around Wrigley and looked out his window. The clouds had cleared, and he could see the full moon. Consoled by the moon, Lumen smiled and drifted off to sleep.

Lumen awoke the next morning just in time to catch his mom for breakfast. He noticed that his mom looked exhausted. She had heavy bags under her eyes, her mascara was smeared and her shoulders slumped. She was attempting to make breakfast but had burnt the toast, and she didn't even turn on the stove to cook the eggs.

"Mom, don't worry about it. I'll just have some cereal."

"Huh? Oh, I'm sorry, hun. I am drained. They kept me for six hours of overtime last night and expect me to come back in by 9 this morning. We need to bring some other nurses on; I cannot keep doing this forever," Alice said, her voice rasping.

Lumen scratched his chin.

"When was the last time you called in sick?"

"Well, there was that one time you had a doctor's appointment for your, you know, and I called in that day." Alice didn't like addressing Lumen's diagnosis directly.

"That was over a year ago, Mom."

"Was it really?" Alice stared off into space, thinking about the last time and also trying to stay awake. Lumen turned on the coffee maker.

"Why don't you call in today? You can catch up on some sleep and we can hang out after you nap."

"I don't know, hun…" Alice appeared to be thinking hard about it. She never wanted to do anything that would put her job in jeopardy.

"Mom, you never miss work, never call in sick, always work overtime. I think you will be okay. If they get mad at you for taking a day, they don't deserve you," Lumen stated.

She smiled.

"Okay. It sounds like a date. You're feeling okay today, right?" Alice said with a look of concern etched into her face.

"Yes, Mom," Lumen said slightly agitated as he was sick of always having to answer the same question.

"Okay, good. Well, let me make a call, and I will head to bed for a couple hours, and we can grab lunch or something afterwards. Sound like a plan?"

"Sounds great. I will see you soon," Lumen said smiling. He felt like he hadn't seen his mom much lately and was excited for the day.

Alice went to bed, and Lumen went to the living room to watch TV. Wrigley was next to the couch, chewing on another ice block. Lumen looked down at him very confused.

"Where are you getting these?" Lumen asked in an apprehensive tone.

Lumen picked up the ice and went to his mom's room.

"Mom, are you giving Wrigley ice? I keep finding him chewing on ice, and it's making the floor wet in the living room."

"What? No, I heard ice is bad for a dog's teeth. I wouldn't do that."

"Where is he getting it then?"

"I'm not sure, hun. Maybe one of the neighbors is giving it to him over the fence," She seemed too exhausted to be concerned.

Lumen went out to the backyard and scavenged around for the source of the ice. He soon realized it was ridiculous to search for blocks of ice outside in the middle of the day with the sun out. He started to see more and more of the lights around him. More colors than he saw last night. He figured it was a good time to start another puzzle and forget about the ice. Lumen concluded that there was nothing to worry about, it was just ice and Wrigley is probably getting it from a neighbor. His mom was right.

He grabbed the Starry Night puzzle his mom had got him, opened the box, dumped out the pieces, took a deep breath, and got to work.

He put the pieces together with his usual ease, but not as fast as usual. He felt distracted. The ice and lights lingered in the back of his mind. Three hours passed, and he hadn't finished. His mom came out yawning in her robe.

"How's it going? I see you finished the Paris puzzle already."

"Huh . . . Oh, right. Yeah, I finished it last night. This one is taking me a bit longer."

"Oooooo, I found a challenging one! I will have to go back to the store I got these from!" Alice said smiling.

"I can finish it later. Should we get going?" Lumen walked over and poured his mom a cup of coffee. He realized it was cold and put it in the microwave. This was the first time Lumen had not completed a puzzle in one sitting.

"Yes. Let me take a quick shower and get changed, and we can head out."

"Okay, where should we go for lunch?"

"Anywhere you want." Lumen handed her the cup of coffee, and she headed to her room to get ready.

Lumen took Wrigley out to go to the bathroom and then went back to his room. Wrigley bounced around, clearly wanting to play. They both jumped up on the bed and began to wrestle. After a couple minutes of wrestling on the bed, Alice came in. She noticed the drawing on the desk and picked it up.

"Wow, Lumen, this is. . . um. . . interesting. When did you start drawing?"

Lumen jumped off his bed and grabbed the drawing.

"I didn't. I found that on my desk last night. I must have accidentally taken it from a classmate."

"Well, it's interesting. It is good, but . . . odd. This is a very odd looking man. And the cat is much too big. Is this man from a movie or something? He is dressed very odd."

"Hmmm, don't know, I don't recognize him. Probably from an *odd* movie . . ."

Alice put down the drawing and smiled at Lumen.

"Where to?"

They walked across the street to Lumen's favorite restaurant. Lumen could eat there for every meal, and Alice didn't mind coming here often; she liked to see her son happy. They walked in and didn't wait for anyone to greet them. They sat down at an open booth. Shari walked over with two waters, one with lemon for Lumen.

"Back so soon! Well, is it the usual again, Lumen? Shake before or after?"

"After!"

"And for you, Alice?

"I will have the club sandwich with a side salad-- Oh, and a soda, please!"

"You got it! I will be back with your orders soon." Shari walked away smiling.

"Always so happy," Alice said as Shari walked away. "So how was your night, Lu?"

"Um, pretty normal, watched some TV, did a puzzle, folded the laundry." He thought he shouldn't tell her about running. It would worry her, and he didn't want to get lectured right now. He also remembered how Alec showed up unannounced to the house. He decided not to tell her about that either as Alec was his only friend and Lumen didn't want his mom to dislike him.

"Good, good. Any plans with Alec this weekend?"

"Nothing planned right now."

"Well, I'm sure you two will do something. Maybe we can all catch a movie later or something? How does that sound?"

"Yeah, sure. That sounds like fun."

Shari came back with their food. She set down Alice's sandwich and Lumen's chicken pot pie. Lumen immediately dove in, feeling a sudden burst of hunger. It was still a bit too hot to eat, and he burned his tongue. It didn't stop him, though. They both gobbled down their food for a few minutes. Alice decided to break the silence and put down her sandwich.

"Sooo, have you asked anyone yet?" Alice asked, inquisitively.

Lumen swallowed his food as he looked up confused.

"Asked anyone for what? Is something missing from the table? I'll tell Shari." Lumen looked around for Shari.

"No, silly. Have you asked a girl to the homecoming dance yet?"

Lumen responded as if he had been insulted.

"What? No. No way. I'm not going to that."

"You can't miss homecoming, Lu! It will be so much fun! It will be good for you to get out a little bit. It's next weekend. We can get you nice little rental suit by then."

"Mom, I don't think any girl would want to go with me. I'm the crazy kid, remember? I'm sure girls would laugh in my face." Lumen thought of the one girl that was always nice to him at school, Sofia. She always said "hi" to Lumen when they passed each other, and she once helped Lumen pick up his books after Blake knocked them out of his hands. She had pretty green eyes, like Lumen, and always wore a green headband to match, which kept her long black hair out of her face.

"With or without a date, I think you should go. It could be a lot of fun, and you don't want to miss out. You and Alec can go solo-dolo together. If it's boring, I can pick you two up and bring you home," Alice said with a huge smile.

Lumen thought about it for a moment. He was worried about Blake and his buddies at the dance, but if he had Alec there, it should be okay.

"I'll talk to Alec about it," Lumen said reluctantly. But in the back of his mind, he was thinking about an opportunity to dance with Sofia.

Alice smiled. "I'll start looking for a suit. We only have a week to get you one!"

They finished up their meals. Lumen got his shake and sucked it down, barely breathing. Alice paid, and they walked out of the restaurant. Lumen always enjoyed spending time with his mom. They didn't get to hang out often. They crossed Inventa Way and were almost to their house when Lumen realized Alec was at their front door, knocking and looking through the window.

"Hey there, Alec!" Alice shouted.

"Oh, hi Miss Haaken. I thought you were working today?"

"I took the day off to spend it with Lumen," she said, smiling.

"That's nice. I'll head back home then. I can come back later."

Alec started to walk away when Alice stopped him.

"Oh, don't be ridiculous, Alec. We are going to go to the movies. Join us. On me!" Lumen stayed silent throughout the conversation. He stared at Alec, who seemed paranoid. He usually didn't come over without calling first.

"Uh, yeah, why not?" Alec asked.

"Great! Let me grab a coat first, it's always so cold in the theatre."

As his mother walked away, Lumen began to notice more lights. He decided to focus his attention back on Alec.

"What's your deal man? You show up late last night without telling me, and now you're standing at my front door, again without calling, pounding on the door. Are you okay?"

"I tried calling dude, no one picked up. I thought your mom was working today, so I figured I would just head over."

"You still haven't really explained yourself for last night. You seemed worked up about something," Lumen said.

"I thought something had happened, but I was wrong, I told you not to worry about it."

"What do you mean?"

"Nothing." Alec shrugged off the conversation.

"Okay, boys, you ready?" Alice said as she locked the front door.

They all hopped in Alice's pale-green station wagon.

"So, Alec, did Lumen talk about the dance with you yet?" said Alice, breaking the silence.

"What dance?"

"Oh my goodness. Homecoming! It's next weekend."

"Oh right, uh. . . I'm not sure. I don't have a date."

"Well, I was telling Lumen you guys could go together, solo-dolo, and check it out. I think it would be great for you two to get out there." Lumen's mom was very excited about it. Lumen turned red.

"Are you going, Lumen?" Alec asked.

Lumen hesitated to answer.

"I'll go if you go . . ."

"Well looks like we are going. We'll have to buy some tickets on Monday."

"Do you have a suit, Alec?" Alice asked.

"Uh, no. Where can I get one?"

"I have a friend who works at a rental shop. I can pick up one for you as well if you'd like?"

"Yeah, that would be great. Thanks, Miss Haaken."

"I'm so excited for you boys!" Alice was beaming. She loved when Lumen could be a normal high-schooler. She just wanted him to be involved.

They pulled up to the theatre.

"I figured we would just pick a random movie."

They all walked up to the kiosk.

"How about that one?" Alec pointed to a board with the movie *Aurora* on it.

"I heard it's pretty good. It's about some weird sci-fi alien under the Northern Lights in the Arctic that is taking people down. He only attacks when the Northern lights are out," Alec explained.

"Sounds scary. But Halloween did just pass, so let's do it!" Alice said excitedly.

"Three tickets for *Aurora* please." Alice handed them their tickets, and they all walked in. Alec walked to the bathroom while Lumen, and Alice ordered some snacks.

"Do you think Alec wants anything, hun?"

"Uh. Just get him a drink. He can get his own snack if he wants anything else."

They ordered and walked into the theatre. They found seats toward the middle. Alec walked in after them and sat next to Lumen.

"We just got you a drink. We tried to wait, but you took too long in the bathroom."

"Thanks, sorry, was just taking care of something."

"I don't need to know what you were doing in the bathroom, thanks," Lumen laughed, and Alec chuckled nervously as he wiped sweat from his forehead. The lights dimmed, and the previews began.

Chapter 3 -

Homecoming

"**W**ell, that was . . . good, right boys?" Alice remarked after the movie was over.

"Yeah, it was pretty exciting, like the one part where the alien snatched up those two guards." Alec tried to convince Alice he liked the movie. Lumen didn't hide his feelings.

"It was awful. The CGI wasn't great, and the acting was stupid. Why didn't we check the reviews? Last time we randomly see a movie, Mom."

Alice seemed taken back a bit by Lumen's harshness. He wasn't normally this forward.

"It wasn't that bad, Miss Haaken. I liked it. Thanks for taking us."

"Yeah, thanks so much," Lumen said sarcastically.

"You are very welcome, Alec, and you better watch your tone, young man. I don't remember the last time you paid for a movie." Lumen didn't make any more comments about the movie. They all got into the car and headed back home. Lumen was silent all the way home while Alice and Alec talked about their favorite parts of the movie. Lumen noticed Alec sweating more than usual today. It was like he was trying really hard to be kind to his mom. Lumen laughed to himself at the thought of that.

"Well, I am going to rest for a bit, Lu," said Alice as they got out of the car. "I will make dinner in a couple of hours. Can you take Wrigley out before you and Alec do anything else?"

"Yeah, okay."

Lumen went into the house and called for Wrigley, who didn't respond. Lumen knew where he was this time.

He walked into his room and found Wrigley chewing on some ice again on his bed. His sheets were wet.

"Wrigley! Get up!" Lumen was angry about his sheets being wet and not understanding where the ice came from. He yelled at Wrigley to get out. His mom and Alec came to the room almost immediately. Lumen began to notice the blue lights again.

"What's wrong, hun?"

"My sheets are wet."

"Did Wrigley pee on them? He hasn't done that for a long time now."

"No." Lumen began to stare at the lights around his room, hardly paying attention to his mom. The lights bunched toward the center of his room again, almost pulsating. Lumen tried to look away but couldn't think of anything else to distract him. Alec was silent.

"No? What is it then?"

"Ice. . . More ice. . . He keeps getting ice from. . . somewhere," Lumen said slowly.

"That's strange. I will have someone come check out the freezer this week. You seem a bit out of it, hun. Why don't you take your medicine?"

"Okay." Lumen stared at the lights in the center of his room. He had never seen them like this before. *What is going on? They look incredible right now*, Lumen said to himself.

Alice went to the kitchen to grab the medicine.

"Dude, are you alright? What do you see?" Alec asked curiously.

"The lights; they're everywhere," he said, pointing to the center of the room.

"Like everywhere you've been today?"

"No, just in my room right now."

"What color?"

"Mostly blue."

"Oh, I see." Alec rubbed his chin.

Alice returned from the kitchen with medicine and a glass of water.

"Here, Lu, drink some water."

Lumen washed down the pill, unaware of what he was doing. He felt out of body, as if he were on another world. They were oddly calming as much as they were overwhelming to him. H had never felt their presence as he did that day. His body tingled as he laid in his bed.

"Alec, you can go if you'd like. Lu usually gets pretty tired when he takes his medicine."

"No, it's okay. I'll take out Wrigley for you and hang with Lumen. I don't have much of anything else going on today."

Lumen looked away from the lights as he begun to reconnect with the room around him. For once, he noticed Alec wasn't sweating.

Lumen awoke from a deep sleep. It took him a minute to realize what had happened and where he was. He remembered feeling overwhelmed by the lights and looked around, wondering if they were still there. The lights were not pulsating as they were before, but they were still there. He got up, stretched, and walked to the living room. Alec was still there watching TV. Lumen walked over and sat on the couch beside him.

"Hey there, sleepy head. How you feeling?" Alice asked from the kitchen.

"I'm good, thanks. Can you get me a glass of water, please?"

"Sure."

Alec looked at him. He seemed antsy. He had been squirming in his seat since Lumen sat down.

"Are you alright?" Lumen asked, put off by Alec's restlessness. "You want one of my pills? You haven't stopped moving since I came in here."

Alec chuckled.

"No, it's just been a little while since you fell asleep. I was starting to get bored."

"How long was I out?"

"Almost two hours. You feel alright?" asked Alex.

"Yeah, the lights got a bit mind-boggling. Maybe I should take my medicine more often."

"No," Alec said curtly.

"No?" Lumen asked, slightly alarmed by the abrupted answer. "Why?"

Alice walked in and handed Lumen a glass of water.

"Would you like anything, Alec? You've been waiting so patiently. You're such a good friend."

"No thank you, Miss Haaken."

"Please, call me Alice. How many times do I have to tell you?" Alice walked away and murmured to herself about how nice Alec had been.

Lumen drank all of his water, took a deep breath, and looked intently at Alec.

"So, why shouldn't I take my medicine?"

Alec took a couple seconds to answer.

"Well . . . uh, we wouldn't be able to hang out as much."

"We wouldn't be able to hang out as much if I can't function. If I take the medicine more often, I probably wouldn't be so tired every time I took it."

"I don't think it is a good idea," Alec fidgeted in his seat again and tried drying his hands on the couch.

"Let's face it, my sickness is only going to get worse. Doctor said the lights were only the beginning. I should just face the fact that I need to take my medicine or I could become a danger to myself or someone else." Lumen didn't like to talk about his sickness most of the time. He never felt like he was a sick person, just different. But he had never become overwhelmed by the lights as he did earlier.

"A danger? You were just staring off into space, dude. I wouldn't say that's dangerous."

"Well, what if I stop in the middle of the street one day and get hit by a car? Or walk onto a frozen lake because I'm following the lights, or---" Alec cut him off.

"I don't think it will get that bad. You just need to learn how to use the lights--"

"How to use them?"

"--I mean how to cope with them," Alec said quickly.

"I guess."

"I would hold off on dumping a bunch of medicine into your body, man. I don't think you need it."

"Yes, *doctor*. Whatever you say, *doctor*," Lumen said sarcastically.

Alec tittered forcibly and leaned back into the couch as he wiped the sweat from his forehead.

Lumen and Alec both turned toward the TV to watch. Lumen surfed through some channels before deciding to ask Alec if he just wanted to play some video games. As he turned to ask, Lumen noticed Alec was as sweaty as ever, momentarily remembering how dry he was before the pill lulled him to sleep.

They agreed on what game to play and turned on the console. They played for an hour or so before Alice asked if they just wanted to order a pizza. Lumen and Alec agreed, and Alice called in an order.

They waited around until the pizza lady came. They chowed down a few slices each at the dinner table as they talked about the upcoming school week. Lumen and Alec agreed to go to the rental shop on Tuesday to try on some suits for the dance next weekend. Once they were done eating, Lumen and Alec helped clean up and then headed to Lumen's room.

"Are we sure we want to go to this dance, dude? It could be super lame. We could just play some games or something instead," Lumen said anxiously.

Alec shook his head.

"What if Sofia is there? You could totally dance with her."

Lumen blushed at the thought slow dancing with Sofia. He thought about how it would go and played out a few scenarios in his head. He'd never had a girlfriend. Did he hold her hips with both hands, or would he need to hold her hip with his right hand, and his left hand in her hand? Or the other way around? He snapped out of that thought, realizing he'd never told Alec about Sofia before.

"What? Why Sofia? Why would you even say that?" Lumen laughed awkwardly and continued to blush.

"I see how you look at her, man. You think she's cute. You always stare at her when she walks by or when you see her across the hall; it's like you're looking at your lights. You always stare at her in math class too and never pay attention. Yet somehow you have a better grade than me . . ." Alec trailed off into thought.

"You think I would have a chance?" Lumen asked excitedly, feeling embarrassed for asking.

"I'm not sure. Only one way to find out, though. You have to try and talk to her. The dance is the perfect place. "

The idea of talking with Sofia made Lumen's heart race. The idea of dancing with her made Lumen feel as if his heart was going to pop out of his chest.

"I don't know man. She's not that cute. I mostly look at her because her hair is so long. She should get a haircut, don't you think?" Lumen laughed awkwardly again. He didn't want to seem desperate to Alec for liking a girl he'd never actually talked to.

Alec smiled. "We'll practice what you should say throughout the week."

Lumen thought that was a good idea. He forgot about being embarrassed in front of Alec and immediately got to thinking about what he would say. He was on edge just thinking about it. He ran through a couple of scenarios in his head, and all of them ended in disaster.

Alec sat down in the desk chair and picked up the papers on the desk.

"We didn't have homework this week, did we?"

"Huh?" Lumen barely heard Alec, he was still thinking about what he would say to Sofia.

"Homework? Did we have any this weekend?" Alec repeated.

"Oh, right. No. No homework this weekend."

"Phew, I was worried for a second there."

Alec looked down and noticed a drawing of a man in a green trench coat with a large cat.

"Where'd you get this drawing?" Alec said, his tone abrasive.

"Uh, I'm not sure. I think I took it from someone in one of my classes. Do you know anyone who can draw? It's pretty good. Weird, but very good. Also, whoever made it clearly doesn't know that cats aren't that big. I mean sheesh, the cat's head is halfway up the weird man's thigh. Right?" Lumen said in a joking manner.

"It's just a large cat. Probably just a breed of cat we've never seen," Alec said matter-of-factly.

Lumen stared at the picture for a moment.

"Hmmm, maybe you're right. What's with the vest and goggles on the cat? It's like a cartoon character or something. It's a great drawing, but the cat looks kind of stupid if you ask me." Lumen said.

"Yeah, maybe," Alec laughed.

"Well, who do you think drew it? I'm sure they want this back. Seems like they took a lot of time to make this." Lumen grabbed the paper from Alec and took a closer look. He looked at the back of the drawing and noticed a small signature.

A.A

Lumen read aloud, "A-A." He hadn't noticed the signature when he looked at the drawing before. Alec remained silent.

"Hm, A.A. . ." Lumen said again, this time more slowly. "Do we know anybody that has a first and last name that starts with an A?"

Alec stayed silent for another moment. He was thinking hard about it as he peered up at the ceiling.

"Hmmmm, yeah I think this girl in my first-period class does. I think I have seen her drawing in class before. I'll take it to her on Monday," Alec stated.

"Really, who?" Alec seemed caught off guard by the question.

"Uhhhh, Ash . . . ley. Ashley Amber is her name, I believe," Alec claimed.

"She has two first names? I've never heard of an Ashley Amber before."

"You wouldn't know her, she is . . . uh . . . a new girl. Just moved here," Alec said nervously. Lumen took notice.

"Why are you being so weird about it? Do you like this girl or something?"

Alec stayed silent again and stared at Lumen as if he was trying to think of something to say.

"You do like her, don't you? Well, perfect. We both have girls we can ask to dance. You can practice this week, too. Don't worry dude. It'll be easy. I see girls looking at you all the time. We'll just have to get some extra deodorant or cologne or something to get you to stop sweating and smelling," Lumen stopped himself and realized he may have hurt Alec's feelings.

"Sorry, I didn't mean that. You don't smell," Lumen lied.

"Oh, don't worry. We both know I sweat a lot," Alec said, still seemingly distracted. "I should go home now." Alec folded up the drawing and put it in his pocket.

Lumen thought Alec was mad at him; but, before he could say anything, Alec walked out of the house, clearly headed home. Lumen felt a bit confused by what had just happened. He followed Alec as he walked out the front door without another word.

"Did Alec head home?" Alice said as the front door closed.

"Yeah, I guess so," Lumen said bluely.

"He left without saying goodbye. Is he okay?" Alice amiably said.

"Yeah, I think so. I accidentally made a comment about his sweating thing. We don't really talk about it. I guess he's sensitive about it."

"Oh no. . .Make sure you apologize when you see him again! You know how that feels."

"Yeah, I know. I'm sure it's okay. I'll see him at school."

Lumen walked off to the bathroom to ready himself for bed. He got into his pajamas, took Wrigley out one last time, and headed to bed. He didn't want to seem tired at school in case he ran into Sofia.

The weekend moved along quickly for Lumen. On Monday, Lumen went to school to find homecoming posters hanging everywhere.

"BROMIDE HIGH HOMECOMING DANCE THIS SATURDAY. COME ROOT FOR YOUR COYOTES AT THE GAME FRIDAY NIGHT. GET YOUR DANCE TICKETS AT THE ASB OFFICE BEFORE THURSDAY."

Lumen thought they should have made two different posters. He was absolutely not going to go to the football game. He didn't care for football, and his only friend had to babysit on Friday nights. He didn't want Sofia to see him alone at a school event and think he was a loner.

Lumen and Alec bought their tickets for the dance at lunch. Sofia was a few spots behind him in line. He looked behind and could see her green headband holding back her long black hair. She wore a black, long sleeve dress with a green scarf. Lumen caught her green eyes peered up in his direction. His heart nearly skipped a beat. He wondered if she noticed he was there, or if she was worried about the crazy kid going to the dance, or if she even remembered who he was. She smiled at him as he walked out of the ticket office. Lumen panicked and put his head down and walked out quickly. Alec smiled at him but didn't say a word.

Lumen hadn't apologized for what he said the other night. Because Alec wasn't acting weird and never brought it up, Lumen thought it was best to leave it be. He did notice that Alec seemed distracted by something still, but not like he was over the weekend.

Lumen asked about Ashley Amber. He still thought it was amusing that this person had two first names. Alec seemed confused when he was asked about it.

"So, did the picture belong to that Ashley girl in your first period class?"

Alec looked at Lumen puzzled.

"You know, Ashley Amber? The one you got all weird about the other night?" Lumen said.

"Oh right,--yeah, it was hers," Alec said as he looked the other way.

"Did you talk about anything else? Like the dance?"

"What? No. She isn't going, I don't think."

"Oh bummer. You'll have to show me this girl sometime. I've never seen you get so weird about a girl. You must really like her."

Alec smiled but didn't answer.

When Tuesday came, Lumen and Alec went to the suit rental shop after school with Alice. They both stood on a stand in front of a mirror while Alice's friend did the measurements. Lumen felt embarrassed because his mom kept making comments about how handsome he was going to look. She said the same when Alec tried on his suit, but Alec thanked her instead of acting embarrassed. Alice's friend said they would be ready by Saturday morning.

The rest of the week dragged on but continued without trouble for Lumen. He had a test on Thursday morning that he aced, and he had to run a mile on Friday in physical education. There was even a very noticeable absence of altercations with Blake and his crew of bullies. Lumen thought it was strange but did not complain.

Friday night came, and it brought with it an unending trail of thoughts, all of which pertained to the dance the following day. What would he say to Sofia? How would he approach her? How long should he wait to ask her to dance? Until the slow song or sooner? He had no idea what to do. He didn't want to overthink anything, but he couldn't help but question everything. What if she says no? What if she slaps him? What if she laughs in his face? Lumen began to question his decision to go. He didn't know what he was thinking. Why would a nice girl like Sofia want to dance with him, the supposed crazy kid that doesn't even stick up for himself when he gets picked on?

Lumen began feeling stressed and dismayed. He realized he walked a block past his house. When he got home, he called for Wrigley, who came running up to him right away. Lumen put on his leash and took him for a short walk.

Curiously enough, Lumen had noticed there hadn't been many lights around that day and decided to check his room to see if he could see any. He peeked inside and hardly saw any. He was relieved to not have to worry about those the night before the dance. He had enough to think about.

Lumen got into his pajamas and headed into the living room. He looked on the side of the couch and saw Wrigley chewing on something. Lumen looked closer and noticed it was just one of his toys.

"Hopefully mom got the freezer fixed . . ." he said to himself.

Lumen folded the clothes, sat back down, and melted into the couch. He oddly felt very relaxed. No one bothered him at school today. He didn't have to worry about anyone on his run. He had a great dinner at his favorite diner. Wrigley wasn't acting strange, and best of all, the lights weren't bothering him. The only thing he had to worry about was the dance tomorrow and what to say to Sofia. Lumen thought for a moment these things were almost harder to deal with than anything else, then realized this was what *normal* people worry about, and it made him happy. He wished most days were like this. He smiled to himself and continued watching some cartoons. He almost fell asleep on the couch when he decided to head to his room. He looked out his window and noticed more stars than usual. He slept like a rock that night.

Lumen awoke Saturday morning to the smell of bacon. *Mom must be off today*, he thought. He got up and hurried to the kitchen.

"Hey, sweetheart. How'd you sleep? I was home pretty early last night, and you were already knocked out," Alice said.

Lumen stretched as he walked into the kitchen.

"Yeah, I was tired I guess. I slept pretty well."

Lumen felt very refreshed.

"Good, well I have the day off. I made some eggs, bacon and pancakes. Dig in before it gets cold."

Lumen served himself and chowed down the breakfast. He loved his mom's breakfast. Alice sat down with a cup of coffee across from Lumen.

"So, we can pick up your suit around noon today. You should call Alec to see if he wants to come with us."

At that moment, the doorbell rang. Wrigley barked at the door as Alice went to answer it. It was Alec.

"Oh hiya, hun! We were just talking about you. Come in, come in. I just made breakfast, you are welcome to have some!"

"Hi Miss Haaken. And thank you, that sounds great."

They went into the kitchen. Alec grabbed a plate and dug in.

"So, do you need to come with us to get your suit for tonight?" Alice asked.

Alec swallowed his mouthful of food before answering. "Oh right, yes please."

"I am so excited for you boys. I borrowed one of the other nurse's cameras so we can take some pictures before I drop you off."

"Oh c'mon, Mom. Is that necessary?" Lumen asked with a mouth full of pancake.

"Yes, yes it is, Lu." Lumen turned red as he dove back into his food, and Alec smiled as he ate his. When they finished eating, they helped clean up the kitchen. Lumen and Alec went to the living room afterwards to play some video games until they had to leave to get their suits.

Alice called for them to get going, and they all got into the station wagon. They drove across town to Alice's friend's rental shop. Lumen's suit was a dark blue, and Alec's was black so it would be harder to see any sweat coming through. They both decided to go with bow ties to match. Alice's friend asked if they had dates.

"No, we don't," Lumen answered, embarrassed.

"Well, that's okay! No pressure to impress a girl then. Those school dances are more fun to go to single anyway!"

Lumen thought otherwise. He had to impress Sofia, and the dance was the perfect way to do it. He felt it was his big chance to make an impression on her.

They thanked Alice's friend and headed back home. They stopped to get some fast food on the way home for lunch, but Lumen could barely eat any of it. They hung around the house for the rest of the day. They took Wrigley out to play fetch, played some video games, and watched some TV to pass the time. Finally, it was time to get ready.

Lumen got dressed quickly and started pacing around the house, practicing what he would say to Sofia. Alec took his time getting ready. When he finally emerged from the bedroom, Lumen was still pacing around.

"Dude, relax. Whatever happens, happens. No need to overthink it." Alec said as he adjusted his bow tie.

"How can I relax? There is so much that could go wrong. What if I trip walking over to her or I accidentally spit on her face when I am talking to her or . . . wait how are you not nervous? Aren't you worried about seeing Ashley? Or Amber? Whatever her name is . . ."

"She isn't going, remember?"

"Oh, right . . ." Lumen went back to pacing.

Alice came out with the camera.

"Oh my goodness! You boys look so handsome! I can't believe my Lu is going to the dance!"

Alice appeared to get teary eyed and used her hands to wipe under her eyelids.

"Mom, stop it." Lumen was embarrassed again. "Just take the pictures."

Lumen and Alec put their arms around each other and smiled for the camera. Alice took a few pictures, and then they were off to Bromide High.

It was a short five minute car ride but, to Lumen, it felt like an eternity. The scenarios kept running through his mind. Lumen put his hand over his mouth to smell his own breath six different times. He checked his appearance in the sun visor mirror as they rolled up to the school. Lumen took two deep breaths before opening his door.

"Lu, remember I will pick you up out here at 10:30 sharp. Call me anytime to pick you up if you need to leave. You have your medicine right?"

"Yes, Mom. It's in my pocket," Lumen lied.

"Okay, well have fun boys!"

Lumen and Alec walked to the auditorium. They handed their tickets to the teacher at the door and walked in. The bleachers were all pushed in so there was more room for the students to mingle and dance. There was a DJ in the back with tables scattered around the sides. In the center of all the tables were shiny, purple letters that said "HOMECOMING".

There were blue and purple streamers above them that twinkled when the lights hit them. A sign posted in the front that said "WELCOME TO BROMIDE HIGH HOMECOMING!"

Lumen noticed signs posted on the wall that listed the rules for the dance. *How weird,* Lumen thought One of the rules stated that you had to stand at least 3 inches apart when dancing. Lumen scoffed when he read that. He looked around and noticed that no one else was wearing suit coats; he felt overdressed. He and Alec looked at each other and took off their jackets, setting them on a chair.

They both sat down and instantly felt out of place. Lumen looked at Alec and noticed he was starting to sweat through his shirt already.

An hour had passed, and they hadn't left their chairs. Lumen hadn't seen Sofia walk in. He did, however, see Blake and his friends walk in as he looked around for Sofia. They all had dates. Blake and his crew immediately walked to the dance floor and started dancing. This was the only time Lumen had envied Blake.

Another 30 minutes passed, and still no Sofia. A girl that was a year older came over to ask Alec to dance. They headed out to the dance floor. Hating everything about the dance, Lumen wanted to leave. He felt stupid for thinking he could dance with Sofia. He got up to head outside to get some air when he saw her walk in... alone. She looked beautiful. She wore a long green dress that touched the floor with her hair up and in a nice bun and white heels. Lumen's jaw literally dropped. She looked like she might be taller than Lumen with the heels on, but he did not care.

His heart raced. *This is the moment*, he thought. He got up and walked toward her. She looked his way, and smiled. Lumen waved awkwardly and felt himself start to sweat a little bit. He was almost there. He thought about what to say. He decided he would start with "You look nice" and ask her how she was doing. After they chat for a little bit, Lumen would ask her to dance. Lumen had it figured out. He was almost there when some other boy passed from right behind him and went up to Sofia. They hugged and walked the other way.

Lumen stopped dead in his tracks. Sofia looked back at Lumen for a moment. He couldn't believe what had just happened. He lost his chance. Lumen felt defeated and didn't know what to do. He looked back at the dance floor and saw everyone having a good time. Blake and his friends were all smiling and looked to be having the best time. Even Alec was dancing with some older girl. Lumen put his head down and walked outside to get some air. He wanted to leave but didn't want to ruin Alec's night. At least one of them was having fun.

Lumen went and sat on a bench outside the auditorium. Nobody else was there except for the lone teacher checking tickets. Even he was on the phone, laughing obnoxiously about something with someone.

Lumen tried to ignore the teacher talking. He looked up to the sky and saw that there was no moon. There were a lot of stars out, though. Lumen laid on the bench and stared at them for a while. He wondered if he would be alone forever. He thought that Alec would probably get a girlfriend soon so he wouldn't have him to hang with anymore. Wrigley and his mom would be all he had, but even his mom had friends..

He stopped himself and tried to not think about that stuff. At least the lights weren't bothering him. He decided to go back inside to go to the bathroom to pass some time. As he walked past the teacher into the auditorium, he noticed it was only nine o'clock. Lumen groaned at the idea that he had to wait another hour and a half for this to be over. He sighed and walked over to the bathroom. He could hear the DJ say something about slowing it down. Lumen knew that meant it was time for the slow dances. He thought about what it would have been like to be with Sofia. She would have her hands on his shoulders, and he would have his hands on her hips. He would make a comment about how pretty her eyes were, and she would make a comment about his green eyes. They would stare at each other for a moment, and then they would both go in for a kiss.

Lumen snapped himself out of it. He knew there was no chance for that anymore.

Stop sulking you baby, Lumen said to himself. He thought he never had a chance anyway, so there was no reason to be upset about a fantasy.

He walked into the bathroom and went into the stall at the end and locked the door. He figured he could just hang in there for a little bit. He sat down on the toilet until he heard someone come in. It sounded like a few people actually. They came in, and Lumen heard the door lock.

"Lulu, where are you? You think we forgot about you?"

It was Blake and another three or four guys. Lumen looked under the stall, and saw five pairs of legs. One of them set down a fire extinguisher and another set down what appeared to be a bag of feathers. They were going to make Lumen's night even worse.

"We took it easy on you this week for a reason, skitzo. We didn't want you to see this coming. We got a big surprise for you. Why don't you come out and make this easier on yourself?"

Lumen froze on the seat the moment he heard Blake speak. He covered his mouth to cover up any noise his breaths would make. He looked up and around the stall for anything to help himself.

"You don't got anything to say freak? Wouldn't have made a difference anyway," Blake sneered.

Lumen wished Alec could help him. He was out on the dance floor having the time of his life, while Lumen was in the bathroom, about to have the worst night of his life. The door was locked, so there was no hope of anyone coming in to save him.

"Which stall are you in, skitzy?" They picked up the extinguisher and feathers and walked to the first stall. Lumen got up on the toilet so they couldn't see his legs. He looked around for something to help him. All that was there was an empty roll of toilet paper and a bunch of blue lights.

Great, they're back, Lumen thought.

Blake kicked open the first stall. Lumen began to panic. There were only two more stalls to go before they were at his. He couldn't think clearly with the lights bothering him.

Blake kicked open the second stall. Lumen thought about trying to slide under to the stall next to his as they kicked open his stall.

Blake kicked open the stall next to him. Lumen had to act fast. Suddenly he felt frozen, paralyzed by the lights around him. They were all bunched up in front of him, just like in his bedroom. They were pulsating. He didn't know what to do. He heard Blake making his way to the front of his stall.

"You ready freak? I hope you are, this isn't gonna be fun. Well, not for you at least." All of Blake's friends were laughing.

Blake raised his leg to kick the door. At the very same moment, Lumen saw a hand coming through the pulsating blue lights. It looked like it belonged to an older person with a large black ring on the pinky. The hand grabbed Lumen by his bow tie and pulled him through the lights.

Blake kicked open the stall, and no one was there.

Chapter 4 - A.A.

Everything was white for a moment. Lumen didn't know what was happening. Was he dead? Everything was white and calm until suddenly, it wasn't. The room was only lit by candle-light. Lumen looked for a light switch but didn't see one on any of the walls. He found himself on a wooden floor. He rubbed his eyes to make sure he could see correctly and got up to look around. There were drawings on the wall, which hung above some older couches and chairs set up around an old oak coffee table with a chess board on top. It looked as if a game had just ended. The dark king piece had been cornered by the lighter queen piece.

Lumen took a deep breath through his nose and smelled something cooking.

"What is that?" Lumen said aloud, piqued.

Lumen stood up and saw a desk behind the couches. There were a lot of papers in a messy pile on the top and sides of it. Lumen walked over and saw what appeared to be maps. The top of one of the maps read "BONUMALUS". He looked at the other words on the map and hardly recognized any of them. Lumen put the map down and noticed there were drawings on the desk as well. He picked up one of a large black cat, wearing a vest, standing on his hind legs. The cat had goggles on top of his head and almost appeared to be smiling. Lumen thought it looked familiar for some reason.

He put the drawing down and continued looking around. He decided the room smelled of burning wood and chicken pot pie. He looked back toward the couch and saw a fire burning in the fireplace.

"Where am I . . ." Lumen said aloud to himself.

Lumen looked around and noticed a window. The edges of the window were frosted with wooden mullions.

He walked over and took a look outside. It looked like it had just started to snow as it was perfectly white and there were no footprints or tire marks anywhere. Seeing the snow, Lumen realized he was cold. He turned back to the room and walked over to the fire. He sat in front of it and warmed his hands as it was beginning to smolder and go out. He tried to remember what had just happened.

Blake came into the bathroom with his friends, they had a fire extinguisher and feathers, they were opening all the stalls to find me, they reached my stall, and . . .

Lumen was having a hard time remembering what happened after that.

"Did I die? Is this like the waiting room for heaven, or hell? You can tell me, I think I get it . . ." Nobody answered him. Lumen pinched himself to make sure he wasn't dreaming.

"Ow. . .Well, I'm not dreaming. I think. . .Maybe a coma. . ."

He looked up at the walls and noticed some more drawings, many of which included the large black cat. There was a painting of what appeared to be just fire. There was a painting of a forest, one of what seemed to be an island floating in midair, and one of an old man with a green trench coat on. He also had goggles on his head.

"Wait a minute, I've seen this guy before . . ."

Lumen remembered the drawing that he had found on his desk. It was the same man and cat.

He then remembered a hand had grabbed him right before Blake had kicked open the door. It came from the lights.

"Oh no, have I completely gone insane . . ."

47

At that moment, Lumen noticed that there were lights all over this place, realizing they had been present all over the cabin.

"Yep, I lost it." Lumen didn't know how to snap himself out of it. He thought to himself how he should have taken his medicine. He would have much rather gotten beat up by Blake than go insane. If he ever came back to reality, he decided he would never lie again about taking his pills.

Suddenly, a small bunch of blue lights appeared over by the coffee table. The lights came together and pulsated, just as they were in his room a few nights ago.

A taller man stepped through the lights. He had long grayish hair, a large nose, goggles on top of his head and wore a trench coat. Lumen recognized him from the drawings.

The man carried a pile of wood. Upon entering the room, he immediately went over to the fire and threw in a few logs. He blew firmly, yet effortlessly, on the flames to try and get them going, and the fire kicked back up almost immediately. The man turned toward Lumen.

"Sorry about that, Lumen. I wanted to give you a few moments; I went to get some firewood. Fire is always better when it is made naturally. Those Liros always give me a hard time about taking wood. I understand where they are coming from but sheesh, it's just some wood; they can make some more if they really wanted. Great people but can be real sticklers for their stuff. I guess everyone is simply watching out for themselves. I can't blame them. We all need our resources. Anywho . . ." the man trailed off as he poked the fire.

The man clapped his hands together and looked at Lumen, who sat there dumbfounded. His mouth was stuck slightly open. He didn't say anything.

"Oh right, where are my manners? I am Allister Alvetande. You can call me Al, A-A, or simply Allister. They all work for me. Good thing we got you out of there, right? It looked like Blake and his buddies had quite the plan for you. I wanted you to figure this out on your own, but I couldn't bear to watch any more of the bullying. There are more important things you should be worried about. Quite honestly, I am surprised you didn't figure it out earlier. You're a smart young man. I've seen those puzzles you do and your ability to ace your classes with ease. It is quite impressive what you have accomplished all while believing you were sick. Quite impressive indeed," Allister said in a seemingly friendly manner.

Lumen still didn't know what to say. He and Allister stared at each other for another moment.

Lumen cleared his throat and finally spoke.

"Did you say we?" Lumen asked. It was the only question he could think to ask at the moment.

"Yes, yes. My partner and I were arguing on what was best for you. He finally convinced me it was time to stop the nonsense. You should thank him when he gets here. You would be covered in feathers at this very moment if it weren't for him," Allister stated.

Suddenly, another cluster of lights appeared and oscillated for a moment when a black cat stepped through the lights. He wore a red vest with goggles on top of his head as well. He was walking on his two hind legs. Lumen noticed he was wearing fingerless gloves and carried what appeared to be a loaf of bread and a slab of meat. The little gloves fit perfectly around the cats claws and looked natural. He had never seen a cat walk on its hind legs like this one was. He was confused as to why Allister dressed the cat up.

"Ah, I was just talking about you, Janis. I was telling Lumen how you convinced me to get him out of there. Right, Lu?" Allister looked at Lumen for confirmation.

Lumen looked at the cat, and the cat looked back at him. Lumen responded slowly.

"Thanks. . ."

"Oy, no problem mate. We should watch each other backs, especially in these times. No time for crock. We pulled ya out of there. She'll be right, you know what I mean, mate?"

The cat seemed to be talking in an Australian accent. Lumen deduced that he must be in Australia. Lumen said nothing.

"Excuse my friend, Lu. Since his transformation, he feels the need to speak in different accents. Where are my manners? Lumen, this is Janis," Allister said as he pointed at the cat.

Janis looked at Allister angrily for a moment before turning toward Lumen. Janis walked over to Lumen and stuck out his paw.

"Nice to finally meet ya, mate." Janis smiled at Lumen.

Lumen thought it was very odd to see a cat smile. He slowly shook the cat's paw with just his two fingers and a thumb. Janis was strangely able to grip Lumen's hand.

"Transformation?" Lumen asked.

"I wasn't always a cat you see. That is a story for another time, another place. How are you feeling? We have been waiting for this moment for a long time," Janis said with a grin.

Lumen had a hard time understanding the accent, let alone take in everything that was happening.

"Will you stop with the accent, Janis? The boy has been through enough tonight, don't make it even more difficult by talking in your accents," Allister said calmly but sternly. Janis just looked at Lumen smiling. Lumen had a hard time keeping eye contact with the cat.

"Well then, are you hungry Lumen? We have some food prepared. It is on the coffee table. We have some wetchop meat, some bread and some pockets," Allister said as he set down a wooden plate of food. There was cooked meat sliced thinly, along with a muffin like bread that was steaming.

Lumen didn't dare ask what wetchop was.

"What is a pocket?" Lumen said with a shaky voice.

"Oh, I think you'll like those," Allister claimed.

Lumen sat down at the table. He was strangely hungry. He thought he had already lost touch with reality so he might as well not starve.

Lumen took a bite. He was amazed at how great it tasted. Everything on the plate was cooked to perfection. There was chicken-like meat, creamy sauce, and vegetables inside the muffin-like bread .

"This tastes like chicken pot pie! Only mini bite-size pies!" Lumen was ecstatic and grabbed a few more.

Allister smiled at Lumen and grabbed some wetchop and bread.

"We thought you would like it. Can I offer you anything to drink?"

Lumen's mouth was full but managed to spit out, "water."

Allister grabbed a few glasses, held them by the table, waved his hand, and ice cubes seemed to just fall from the air into the glasses. He waved his hand again, and all the glasses filled up with water. Allister set them down. Lumen stopped chewing and stared at Allister. He gulped all the food in his mouth.

"Okay, I have officially lost it, right? How do I get back to reality? Am I still in the bathroom, or did I lose it before that? Was there even a dance? I thought I was getting worse but I didn't think it was this bad. My mom is probably so worried . . ." Lumen trailed off and just stared off into space.

Janis cut him off.

"Relax, mate. You're not crazy. This is all real."

Lumen began to laugh.

"Yeah, says the talking cat wearing goggles and some gloves," Lumen sat back and started laughing even more.

Allister got up and looked at Lumen with a very stern face. Lumen looked at him and noticed the wrinkles on his forehead and cheeks.

"He is right, Lumen; this isn't an illusion or a hallucination. You're not crazy, you never were. You are an extraordinary human. Very few humans have the power you have. There are some with the power you contain that have gone crazy because they didn't know what they were seeing and it became too hard to handle. Others used their powers for the wrong reasons. You on the other hand, you are different. You are a brilliant young man. We have been watching you since you were just a boy and can see your potential. We have been waiting for the right time to introduce you to this world. We wanted you to get here on your own, but enough was enough."

Lumen looked at Allister very confused and began to laugh again. He laughed for a few moments and caught his breath to speak.

"Right, right. I'm special, yeah, yeah. Are you my doctor, and is this my nurse?" he pointed at Janis.

"Why would I be the nurse?" Janis responded.

"Look, I am aware that I am losing it, okay? I have accepted what my sickness can do to me. You two need to get out of my head so I can get help. I guess I have to try and get myself out of this hallucination or whatever this is." Lumen closed his eyes shut really tight and seemed to be trying to do something challenging without actually moving.

He opened his eyes and nothing had changed. Allister and Janis stared back at him. Allister grabbed his glass and refilled the cup with ice and water, again he seemed to pull the ice and water out of midair. Lumen took notice of the ice. The blocks looked familiar.

"That ice-- I have seen those cubes before. Wrigley has been chewing on ice in our house that looks just like that," Lumen said concerned.

"Right, most dogs love ice. I was just checking in on a couple of things and calmed him down with a treat. Ice is always a good one to give dogs. They won't get an upset stomach from some frozen water, and they think it's a treat," Allister said with a smirk.

Lumen was very confused now.

"Oh my gosh," Lumen was thinking very hard.

"See, we told you it was real, mate? Nothing to worry about," Janis replied, back to his Australian accent.

"No, I have been hallucinating for so much longer than I thought. Have I even been in school? What was the last thing that happened that was real? Am I going in and out of hallucinations?"

Janis sighed dramatically. Allister looked at him and put his hand out to signal patience.

"Lumen, I cannot express the utmost importance of this. We need you. Humans on Earth need you," Allister stated.

Lumen got serious for a moment.

"Okay, I'll go along with this for a little. I know I shouldn't, but I am fascinated that my mind can create all of this. First off, what is Wetchop?"

"It would be like a . . ." Allister looked at Janis for help.

"Uh, it's like a rabbit, only bigger, and faster . . ." Janis shrugged at Allister.

"Fine, how did you get water and ice from the air? You just waved and there appeared some ice and water?"

"Well, this is where things get a bit complicated. I can conjure water from the air. If there is moisture, I can manipulate it to do what I want it to do. It takes a lot of practice and concentration; people like us, you included, can do it. There is much more to learn, but we can delve into that another time," Allister snapped his fingers, and more ice fell into each of their glasses.

Lumen looked at Allister; he wasn't sure if he was amazed or scared.

"Right, what were you doing in my house, and how did you get there? How did nobody see you? You would stick out like a sore thumb. And the cat? You would be a worldwide sensation." Lumen's eyes were open as wide as they could be. He was hardly blinking.

"We aren't seen unless we need to be," Janis said.

Lumen felt relieved.

"That makes me feel better. How did you give Wrigley ice then?"

"Dogs can see the lights. He always knew when we were coming. We didn't want him to bark at us, so some treats always helped. We have had some bad experiences with dogs," Janis seemed to be thinking about one of those experiences and he rubbed his paws together feverishly and stared off into space.

"My mom says ice is bad for a dog's teeth," Lumen said.

"Oh, I wouldn't worry about a few ice cubes now and again," Allister replied.

Lumen was quiet for a moment and realized Allister said dogs can see the lights as well.

"So you're telling me the lights are actually there? Why doesn't Wrigley speak like you?" Lumen looked at Janis. Janis and Allister chuckled.

"Don't be ridiculous; dogs can't talk, mate. They can just see the other side," Janis said.

"What's that mean?" Lumen asked quickly.

Allister held his hand up to signal to Janis to allow him to answer. He adjusted the goggles on top of his head and ran his hands through his tangled salt and pepper beard.

"The lights you see, they are portals between your world and this one. When you put the lights together, you can move between the worlds. Become skilled enough, and you can manipulate the lights to take you anywhere you want. Why do you think dogs can sometimes sense when something is going to happen like an earthquake, or a twister? They can see it coming."

Lumen only felt more befuddled at this point.

"What does that mean? Earthquakes and tornadoes come from here?"

"Indeed, yes. In a way, most of the natural disasters present on Earth come from here. Luckily, for most of the time, there has been more good here to stop the evil trying to enter your world." Lumen found it very hard to not listen and nod at everything Allister was saying. Allister was stolid when he spoke.

"How does an earthquake come from here?" Lumen asked curiously.

"It is complicated, Lumen. We can speak of that another time," Allister said, smiling.

Janis cut in.

"Just tell the boy; it could help convince him." Allister hesitated for a moment while he and Janis looked at one another. It was as if they were speaking telepathically.

"All right. You have your four main elements," Allister continued.

Lumen was focused more than ever on him.

"You have water," Allister again waved and water fell from midair into the cups.

"You have fire," He then waved at the fire and made the flames rise and rise until the room was so bright Lumen could barely see. Allister waved again, and the flames subdued.

"You have air." He then began swirling his index finger over the chessboard, and a very tiny tornado appeared, knocking over some of the pieces. Allister stopped moving his fingers and, the twister disappeared.

"And you have Earth." He stomped his foot down lightly a couple of times, and some yellow flowers appeared from underneath the floorboards.

"These are all controlled by the figures of this world. The people of Bonumalus control and manipulate the weather patterns on Earth to make it a sustainable environment for you all to thrive in."

Lumen's eyes widened. He was in disbelief that his mind could make this up. *Is this real?*

After a few moments of silence, Lumen spoke again.

"What do I have to do with this?"

Allister and Janis stared at each other again. Allister looked back at Lumen to respond.

"Well, beings from this world are always able to travel between the two worlds. We can all see the lights. Your people, on the other hand, hardly any of them can. Even less have what it takes to handle what they see after they learn of this world. Many, like you are now, question if what they are seeing is real. They end up leaving and never returning, only to hide away from their truly remarkable abilities." Allister sounded as if anything he said was fact.

Lumen couldn't help but finding himself believing everything the man said. Allister seemed to be trustworthy, someone who was a straight-shooter. His mind wanted to question the validity of all of this, but his gut told him otherwise.

Lumen did not know what to think at this point. He still debated if what he saw was real. There was no way. Or could it be? He couldn't believe that his mind could create this, but what Allister was saying was absurd. People from here are the ones creating fires, hurricanes, and earthquakes on Earth. That doesn't make sense. But the ice, he remembered talking with his mom about the ice. She saw it too. Alec saw it too. That had to have been real.

"So you're telling me that all the great disasters on Earth came from here?"

"Yes," Allister and Janis replied.

"And you can control things like water and fire just by waving your arms?"

"It's a bit more complicated than that, but yes," Allister responded with a little smile.

Lumen felt comforted the more Allister spoke.

"And cats can talk in this world?"

"Ah, Janis was like me before. Magic is existent here as well. Or I should say *was*. It is very rare nowadays to see and hear about, and not many can practice it. Janis is a victim of an angry ex-girlfriend that happened to be from a long line of Operres. I don't want to bore you with that story; Janis can tell it another time."

Janis stayed quiet. He seemed to turn away when Lumen looked at him.

"Op-whats?" Lumen asked.

"Operres. People that practice magic. She transformed Janis into a cat. Rough breakup, I'm afraid," Allister said as he shook his head.

Janis looked at his feet. He seemed saddened.

"So he used to be like you? He can move the air and water and all of that like you? Why don't you just change him back?"

Janis spoke up.

"Don't be silly. Mastering one of the elements is extremely difficult, let alone all of them. I have mastered the element of air. Allister isn't like most of us. He has mastered them all, and has mastered each one better than most of us. There are very few people like him. We call people like him Omnis. Very few left in this world, very rare," Janis stated with a defeated tone.

Lumen looked at Allister and then back to Janis.

"Why don't you just change back to a human?"

"Magic is a rare and lost art, not many practice it anymore. We can talk about that more later."

Janis spoke with an accent that Lumen was more familiar with.

"There is much to learn, Lu. We can go over more at another time once the others arrive. Now, enjoy your pockets. Try the wetchop, very tender and tasty."

Lumen suddenly felt his blood boil. He was angry, confused.

"How can I relax? This doesn't make any sense. How can this be real? I'm supposed to be crazy. The doctors diagnosed me as a skitzo." Lumen's face turned red.

"We have seen that before. Doctors and others in the world aren't sure how to diagnose people like you. They need to label everyone to explain why they are different from themselves."

Lumen got even angrier and was almost yelling.

"Why wouldn't you tell me earlier, then? I have been bullied and called crazy for a long time now! Why not tell me earlier to prevent all of that? I've been down my whole life when none of it was true." Lumen was even redder now. The room seemed to get colder. Lumen looked around to see if a door was open.

"It is not that simple. The time had to be right. We wanted you to figure it out on your own. Times are different now. You have been close to figuring it out, only to stop yourself from finishing what you started. Very unlike you to not complete something, but we understood why," Allister said.

Lumen was fuming.

"No. No. I don't believe it. I have just lost it. I must have. I need to get out of here. I need to see my mom. I need to take my medicine. I'll never lie again about taking a pill. Please let me out of here. Get me out of my head."

Lumen was on the verge of tears. He looked around to find a way out. A door was near and he scurried to it, opened it, and found snow all about. He started to run. The snow was really coming down, and Lumen had difficulty running. He saw some lights get bright for a moment, and Janis stepped through. Things began to get dark. Lumen suddenly felt the energy drain from his body, and he fell into the snow. His eyes began closing shut when he saw Allister and Janis standing over him. They were saying something to each other but he couldn't hear it. He closed his eyes fully. Lumen passed out.

Lumen opened his eyes to find himself in his bedroom, still wearing his clothes from the dance. He looked outside and saw the sun high in the sky. He must have slept in much later than usual. He had a dull headache. He rubbed his temples with his index fingers and suddenly remembered what had happened last night.

"How did I get here?" he said aloud to himself.

He thought he must have been out all night and about how worried his mom must have been.

Lumen threw his blanket off and hurried into the kitchen. His mom was sitting at the table, Wrigley lying next to her, chewing on a toy.

"Hi, honey! How was the dance last night? I heard you had a good time!"

Lumen thought she seemed overly chipper for him not coming home when he was supposed to.

"Uh, yeah it was fun I guess . . ."

Lumen was very confused. He thought this might be some sort of trick.

"It looked like you must have danced your butt off! You could hardly walk when you got home! Good thing Alec was here. He helped you to your bed. Such a good friend he is! He told me all about Sofia and how you and she danced the night away. Why didn't you tell me you liked this girl?" Alice exclaimed.

Lumen was even more confused now.

"Alec told you what? Who drove us home?"

"Alec said the dance was going to go past 10:30. He told me you two rode with one of his friends. Why don't you remember? Did you drink last night? Not only are you underage but you are sick, young man! And the medication, it probably doesn't mix well, oh my goodness . . ."

Lumen didn't really pay attention to the question. He tried desperately to remember what happened last night.

"Was I dreaming last night?" Lumen muttered to himself.

"That explains why you could hardly walk last night!"

Lumen sighed.

"Mom! I didn't do anything illegal last night, I promise. Just a long night, I guess."

Alice opened her mouth to say something else, but relaxed in her seat after a moment.

"I need to talk to Alec. I'll be back later."

Lumen ran to the door, still wearing his dress clothes and all.

"Lumen. I was talking to you. Get back here," Alice said sternly.

"Sorry, mom, something came up. I need to talk to Alec. Bye."

"LUMEN!" Alice yelled this time.

Lumen stopped just short of closing the door and walked back in.

"What?"

"Alec is here. He is sleeping on the couch. Now come tell me about your night until he wakes up, and we can all grab some breakfast."

Lumen wasn't paying attention to his mom, distracted by the previous night's activities and an unusual amount of lights in his house.

"Alec, wake up."

"Lumen, let the boy sleep. He is probably tired from carrying you around."

Lumen didn't listen. He went over to Alec and shoved him a little. Alec woke up immediately.

"What, dude? Can you shut the blinds, so bright . . ." Alec grunted.

"Wake up, I need to talk to you."

Alice chimed in from the kitchen.

"Lumen, leave him alone. It can wait."

"Alec, c'mon."

Alec rolled over slowly and rubbed his eyes for what seemed like an eternity to Lumen. He finally sat up.

"Can I get some water please?" Alec asked.

"Oh, of course dear!" Alice hurried into the kitchen to grab a glass of water.

Lumen looked at Alec intently. He sat down on the edge of the couch, on the armrest.

"Hey, listen to me. What happened last night? How did I get here?" Lumen snapped his fingers a few times.

"What are you talking about? We took a car, and I helped you walk in."

Alice handed Alec the glass of water.

"I'll let you boys talk about last night!" Alice seemed happy again.

Lumen was still staring at Alec, waiting for answers.

"What? Can you stop staring at me? You're creeping me out," Alec said as he squinted back at Lumen.

"Tell me what happened. Where did you find me after the dance?"

"Well, I couldn't find you at the dance."

"What do you mean?" Lumen asked abrasively.

"I was dancing with that girl, pretty awesome might I add, and I looked around and didn't see you. Then I saw that Blake and all of his buddies were also gone. I figured that meant they were looking for you. Or already had you. I walked out of the dance and into the bathroom and found Blake and his friends standing around. They had a bag of some feathers, or something like that, and a fire extinguisher. I thought they already caught you, but they said they hadn't seen you."

Lumen was confused again.

"They hadn't seen me? I was in the last stall."

"That's what they thought also. They said they got to your stall, and no one was in there. Blake said he swore he saw you walk in there. Didn't know how you got out without anyone seeing."

"Blake was awfully generous telling you all of this."

"Oh, I had to nudge him a little bit to get answers," Alec said, smiling.

"Okay, so where'd you find me?"

"Well I figured Allister or Janis got you. They didn't tell me last night was the night, so I had no idea."

Lumen fell off the couch.

Chapter 5 - Bonumalus

"**W**hoa there, dude, you okay?"

Lumen popped up off of the ground the second he hit it.

"What did you just say?"

Lumen grabbed Alec by the shoulders until his face was just an inch away from Alec's face. Alec put his hand on Lumen's chest and gently pushed him away. He picked up his water and drank the whole glass.

"I said I had no idea last night was the night. Allister and Janis didn't keep me in the loop."

Lumen tried to find the words but couldn't think of anything to say. Lumen looked at Alec, his eyes narrowed with skepticism.

"Sorry, it was really hard to keep this all a secret, but Al and Janis thought it was best for you to find this all out on your own. Which didn't end up happening. So close though, can't believe it's taken this long," Alec said with a surprised tone.

Lumen felt offended.

"I thought you were my friend."

Alec's face went long.

"We are friends, Lu. I was in your position not too long ago. Very confused. Didn't know what was going on. Then one day, it all made sense. Now I am on my way to being an

Eauge, and I have been lucky enough to protect you as well as make a new friend. I wish I had someone like me before I found out everything."

This didn't make Lumen feel any better.

"To protect me? From what? And what was that you said, an Oosh?" Lumen asked angrily.

"An Eauge, someone who masters the element of water. Allister said he briefly went over the elements. I am still learning. I have trouble controlling water in this world, hence the sweating."

Alec chuckled. Lumen didn't find it funny.

"Okay, welp, looks like I'm lost in my head. I can't believe this all happened so fast. My mom, I hope she's okay and can find me . . ." Lumen whispered quietly to himself.

"Hey!" Alec yelled at Lumen.

"You need to cut that out. The sooner, the better. You're not crazy. This is all real. I know it is hard to accept, but your brain couldn't make this up. You're smart, Lu, but you're not that creative."

Lumen just looked at Alec, thinking.

"What can I do to prove that this is real?"

Lumen sat thinking again.

"Uh, I don't know . . ." Lumen laughed nervously.

"Here, I got an idea." Alec went to the kitchen and filled a glass up with some water. He walked back to the living room and sat down. "Wrigley!"

Wrigley came running over to Alec.

"Good boy, now sit down."

Wrigley sat down. Alec picked up the glass of water and poured it in front of Wrigley. As the water fell to the ground, Alec quickly snapped his fingers twice, and the water instantly froze into two pieces. Wrigley picked one up and trotted to the other side of the room to lick and chew on it.

"Allister just taught me that one, only he can do it without the glass of water on this side. I don't get how he does it." Alec seemed enthralled thinking about the trick. He looked at Lumen who was staring in disbelief at Alec, then at the ice, then back at Alec.

"Oh, right. Alice!" Alec called Lumen's mother into the room.

"Yes, dear?"

"Hey, I think the freezer is still broken. Looks like Wrigley has some more ice."

"Oh my goodness, I can't believe that repairman didn't fix it! I will call them back right now to get back out here." Alice walked out immediately to call the repairman.

Alec looked at Lumen, nodding his head at him for approval.

"What? That doesn't prove anything, Alec. It just means I have been crazier for longer than I realized," Lumen said fiercely.

"No way! That proves everything, dude! It is impossible for you to have been hallucinating all those times! You even took the medication at one point, and you saw the ice afterwards!"

Lumen sat thinking and did remember when that had happened.

"I guess that's right, I still don't know if I can believe this . . ." Lumen seemed nervous. He began to bite his nails.

"Lu, look, for a long time you have been pushed down, bullied, looked at funny . . ."

"Making me feel a lot better, Alec."

"My point is that you're not just some weird crazy kid. You're more powerful than anyone you have ever met before last night; you just didn't know it."

Lumen turned an ear to the sound of that. He thought about what he could do with powers like Allister's to Blake. Maybe he could drop some water on his head whenever he was talking to a girl, or set his hair on fire, or make him trip on a tree root whenever he walked by him. Lumen was warming up to the idea.

"Okay, well what now?" Lumen appeared more confident. He was sitting up more straight than usual.

"Well, we'll need to get you back to Bonumalus and start some classes. Most the others are ready to start also," Alec said.

"The others? There are others like me?" Lumen said with a disappointed tone.

"Well yeah, and you are all going to start classes soon. You'll be learning to be an Eauge. Hopefully."

Lumen felt a bit deflated by this.

"Oh, so I'm not the only one who can see the lights?" Lumen asked.

"Don't be ridiculous; though we are very rare, there are others who can see the lights too. Like I said, I was like you a couple years ago. Now here I am."

Lumen was quiet for a moment. He didn't know how he would like learning with others.

"Do we all learn together, or is it more of a one-on-one thing with Allister and Janis?" Lumen asked curiously.

"Janis won't be teaching you to be an Eauge, though he will teach you about the Aeris people and what it means to be one."

Lumen put his hands up to signal for Alec to stop.

"Slow down, a what?"

"An Aeris is someone who mastered the element of Air. I know they have weird names, but it becomes more normal the more you are in Bonumalus."

Alice walked into the room, and both Lumen and Alec quieted down.

"I am just checking on you, boys, you have been talking for a while! I think it is my turn to hear about your night!"

Alec did most of the talking as he lied about Sofia and Lumen dancing most of the night. Alec explained what Sofia looked like and what she was wearing to Alice.

"When do I get to meet this young lady, Lu?" Alice exclaimed.

Lumen quietly said he wasn't sure. "We never really talked before last night, so I am not sure you will." Lumen was cherry red.

"Well, by the sound of it, this Sofia seems to be interested in you! You should invite her over for dinner next week!" Alice stared at Lumen until he answered.

"Um, I'll see if she can. Can you order us some pizza right now? We are pretty hungry."

Lumen looked at Alec for assistance.

"Right, yes pizza would be great Miss Haaken. We are starving from last night."

Alice stood up with a big smile on her face.

"Of course, I will call it in and go pick it up now." Alice walked out of the room, called the pizza parlor down the road, and took off a few minutes later. Alice yelled that she would be right back and closed the door. Lumen immediately turned to Alec. His face was still red.

"Why would you lie to my mom?" Lumen asked bitterly.

"Would you rather have me told her how you traveled through your lights and met two men, one of which is a talking cat, and they live in this place called Bonumalus?" Alec asked sarcastically.

Lumen calmed down after hearing that.

"Well no, but did you have to tell her I danced with Sofia? How am I supposed to get her over for dinner? My mom will never let it go!"

Alec laughed at Lumen.

"Guess you'll have to step out of your shell and talk to her."

Lumen turned bright red again at the thought of talking to Sofia.

"She won't come over; she was with some boy last night. I'm sure that was her boyfriend or something."

Alec scoffed at Lumen.

"Are you stupid? That was not her boyfriend, just some kid that she is friends with, trust me. They talked for a few minutes, but she mostly sat by herself for the rest of the night. I went and talked to her. She asked about you."

Lumen almost fell off the couch again.

"Wha- what di-. . . did she say to you?" Lumen couldn't find the words.

"She just asked where you were. She hadn't seen you since she arrived and wondered where you went. I told her I didn't know where you were either. She seemed disappointed."

Lumen felt as if his heart dropped to the floor. Sofia thought about him. He couldn't believe it. If only he had stayed on the dance floor, he could have avoided this whole predicament. Who knows? They could have talked, danced, and had a great time. Lumen got lost in his thoughts for a moment.

"Wait a minute, what do I tell my mom, and the school? I can't just drop everything and leave to learn to be an Oosh or whatever."

"An Eauge, say it right, sheesh. They don't take kindly to the ignorant. And you won't have to drop anything. You might have less time for homework and going on your little runs, but you'll have plenty of time to go to both. You'll go to Bonum after school and on weekends for classes. I know you hardly have to try in school here, so you should have no problem keeping up." Alec said.

"This is a lot to take in. . . Do I have the option to not?" Lumen asked.

"To not what?"

"To not go and learn to be an Eauge. Wait, Eauges master water, correct?"

"Correct, and of course you have a choice. This isn't for everyone. You're right, this is a lot to take in. I know you though, you want to learn, you want to do more than what you're doing now. This is your opportunity Lu! You may not be saving lives as a doctor but you will be saving lives. Lots of them, I might add," Alec said.

Lumen put his head down, lost in deep thought.

"Seems like a lot of responsibility, I need to think about this, Alec," Lumen said concernedly.

Alec smiled and nodded his head.

"I understand. I have a meeting with Al and Janis in a little while. I'll get out of here. I think you have some new puzzles over there." Alec pointed to the kitchen table.

Alec waved his left hand and opened up a window with the lights. He winked at Lumen and walked through. The window closed, and the lights dispersed. Lumen stared at the spot Alec left from for a moment before walking over to the kitchen table. He looked down and saw two new puzzles. One was of a baseball stadium filled with fans who all looked the same. He thought that would make it difficult.

He picked up the other puzzle. This one was called "Savannah: The city of New Beginnings." This one was of the city of Savannah's skyline. It looked a bit less challenging. Lumen chose the Savannah puzzle. He ripped off the plastic, took the lid off the box, and dumped the pieces out. His mind began to race, just as it always did when he opened a new puzzle. He felt like he knew what he had to do. He was about to begin when his mother walked in with the pizza.

"Hi, boys! I got some breadsticks as well. They didn't have the marinara sauce, so I just have the garlic sauce and some ranch."

Alice paused for a second when she saw Lumen working on a new puzzle.

"Oh! You found the puzzles. Is everything all right?" Alice had a concerned tone suddenly.

"Yes, mom. I just needed a break to think."

"Where did Alec go?"

Lumen thought of a lie as quickly as he could.

"Uh, his mom called. Said he had to watch his siblings for the day."

Lumen thought about how he would have to lie to his mom all the time if he left to the other side for class to become an Eauge. He still didn't know what that meant entirely.

"Well that's too bad, more pizza for me and you, I guess. I'll get you a plate and leave you to the puzzle. Don't forget about your medicine, young man."

Lumen rolled his eyes but told Alice he would take the medicine. *Another lie*, he thought.

Alice set down a plate with a couple slices of pizza and a breadstick with some ranch. She also brought him some water. Lumen thanked her and almost immediately zoned into his puzzle. He had a method for completing them as fast as possible. He turned all the pieces over so they faced upwards. He separated all of the edge pieces into one pile, the pieces with the skyline in another pile, and the sky behind the city in another pile. Next, he sorted those piles into smaller piles according to color. After he had all the pieces separated, he began to assemble the border. The border took him almost no time at all. He chose the first piece at random and built off of

67

it. The piece he needed always stuck out to him like a sore thumb. He finished the border and transitioned to the upper left-hand corner as he worked his way across and down. The sky was almost all one color but Lumen had no problem finding the next piece to fit. Once he had that part finished, he moved on to the city. This part was even easier as there was more color differentiation. Two hours, three minutes, and two thousand pieces later, Lumen was finished. He realized he only ate a bite of his pizza. He sat in his chair, finished his food, and drank all of his water. He continued to sit and think for a few moments. He had decided.

Lumen was going to do it. He decided he would at least try out a couple of the classes, and if it seemed too crazy, he would tell them he wasn't interested any longer. He wanted to tell Alec but didn't know how to reach him.

He walked into his room to think about what to do next. He decided he would just talk out loud. These people were listening and watching for a while now apparently, maybe they are now, he thought.

"Okay, I'll do it. I'll become an Oosh or whatever."

Nobody answered him.

"Hello?"

He sat silent for a moment, but no one answered. Wrigley walked in and sat in front of Lumen.

"Can you see them, Wrig? Where are they?"

Wrigley barked at Lumen and then turned to the middle of the room. Lumen looked up and noticed several of the lights.

"Oh right, I guess I can do this myself."

Alice walked into the room.

"Hey Lu, I'm taking off to work. I left some money on the counter if you want to grab some food for dinner. There's leftover pizza in the fridge. Please pick up your mess in the kitchen," Alice said hurriedly.

"Sure, Mom. Have a good night."

Alice smiled and walked out quickly. Lumen waited until he heard the front door close. He realized he would have to be very cautious with when and where he would do this. He had the night to himself now though, he could plan it out another time. He went back to the middle of the room.

"Okay, okay, where to start . . ."

Wrigley sat in the middle of the room. Lumen started to focus more on the lights. He put his hands out and pushed one of the lights aside. He didn't have to touch them to move them. If he focused on one of them, he could just use his arm to indicate where he wanted the light to go. He started to use both of his hands to move the lights around. He separated them into three bunches. One was what he thought were the outer pieces of the window, one was the inner window, and the others were pieces that didn't seem to fit in with the others. He worked with the outer pieces first and quickly made a border. He then filled in the window with the pieces that went inside. He put in the last piece, and instantly the window beamed.

Lumen was nervous. He looked at Wrigley. Wrigley looked back at Lumen, barked and jumped through the window.

Lumen was stunned.

"Wrigley! Wrig! Come back!"

Lumen stood in front of the window, yelling for Wrigley to come back. He couldn't hear anything or see anything, just the colors of the window.

Lumen shook his hands out, preparing himself to jump through the window. He took a step back and ran.

He stopped just in front of the window, taking a deep breath and sticking his hand inside. He looked on the other side of the lights, where his desk was, but could not see his hand. Just then he felt that his hand was getting wet.

Lumen took a deep breath, put his other hand over his nose, closed his eyes, and stepped through.

Everything went white for a moment, and suddenly he was standing in what appeared to be a forest. He looked up, and the trees were bigger than anything he had ever seen before. They seemed to go up a mile. The bark was grooved and aged. Branches grew from all different spots along the trunk, all of which were covered with buzzing life.

He looked back down and around and noticed how almost everything here was unfamiliar to him. The plants, the trees, even the dirt on the ground, it was all different.

He was mesmerized by the vibrant scenery. He took notice of a vibrant purple flower and reached down to pluck it. After he picked it up, the petals unfolded one by one to reveal a neon green center. The color was so bright that it hurt Lumen's eyes to look at it directly. He tossed it aside and continued to look around at his surroundings. He noticed a plant with leaves that were bigger than his entire body. Through the crowded tree branches, the sky seemed more blue than any sky he had seen. It was as if he were looking up at a sky blanketed by a bucket of royal blue paint. He decided this had to be real; it didn't seem plausible to him for his mind to create what was before him. Lumen took a deep breath and the crisp air energized his body and mind. Lumen felt awakened.

He felt some raindrops hit his face and suddenly realized he hadn't seen Wrigley.

"Wrig! Where are ya, boy?"

Lumen looked in all directions through some speckled flowers and thorny trees before he heard a bark coming through the crowded trees. He took off, running towards it. He jumped and ducked through all sorts of shrubs and bushes, stepping over the tree roots jutted from the ground, sometimes as high as Lumen's hips. The forest, or whatever this place was, wasn't dark but wasn't the most well-lit place either. It was as if it were lit by a few candles. The trees covered most of the sky above. Lumen could see some brighter light in the distance. He heard Wrigley bark again, but still couldn't quite make out where it was coming from. The bark sounded closer; he was going the right way. He continued to run when an unfamiliar creature darted in front of him from one bush to another. The black blur moved very quickly and seemed to be moving on all fours. Lumen paused for a moment, scared of what kind of creature crossed his path, before running even faster.

Lumen continued to run out of the forest until the land seemed to come to an end. He slowed down just in time. The dirt stopped to reveal a razor-sharp edge to a steep cliff. He stopped and slid to the edge, doing everything he could to keep his balance. He peeked over the edge without getting to close, but couldn't see anything below except for some tree roots and vines dangling from the ledge. He leaned over some more and couldn't see anything at all except for a few clouds. Wrigley barked again. Lumen looked left and saw Wrigley sitting a few feet from him.

"There you are. I need to get you home."

Wrigley sat wagging his tail. He barked again, not at Lumen, but at something or someone to Lumen's right.

Lumen looked to his right where a familiar tall and peculiar-looking man had just appeared seemingly from thin air. It was Allister.

"Hi, Lumen. Welcome to Mighty Falls Island."

"Oh, thank goodness someone is here. I thought I was lost. I swear when we were at your cabin it was snowing, and there weren't any of these trees." Lumen scratched his head.

"Good observation, Lumen."

Allister smiled at Lumen.

"Right, thanks. Uh. . . can I get my dog home? I don't think he should be here."

"First things first."

Allister stepped toward Lumen, and put his hand on Lumen's back.

"Remember to focus."

Before he could open his mouth to say "what", Allister pushed him off the side of the cliff.

Lumen felt the ground ripped from under him as his stomach dropped. He desperately reached for the tree roots and vines hanging off the side as he fell but couldn't get a grip on anything. He was too scared to yell. He fell through the clouds in silence as they soaked him. He came out the other end of the clouds and could see more of the cliff. He was falling quickly as his surroundings became a blur. The cliff stopped, and Lumen continued to fall. Lumen looked up to see that the forest, or whatever that place was, was floating in midair. Lumen couldn't think about that now. He was going to fall to his demise; he thought his life should be flashing before his eyes. He looked down and could not see much. The ground looked to be miles below. Lumen closed his eyes so that he couldn't see when he would hit the ground. As he closed his eyes, he saw a light in front of him that seemed to be falling with him. He turned himself around in midair and saw more of them. He quickly pulled them all into one spot and worked frantically to put them together into a window. When he put the last piece in, the window beamed. Lumen swam toward it and, with all his might, thrusted himself through.

He landed flat on his chest in some sand, still wet from the clouds. He had some sand in his mouth, but he didn't care. He was alive. His body ached from the landing.

"Great job, Lumen."

Lumen turned around to find Allister standing beside Wrigley.

"Are you insane?! You could have killed me! I thought I was going to die!" Lumen was breathing heavily from what just had happened. He had never felt so alive and scared at the same time in his life.

"Oh, don't be ridiculous. It was a long fall; I knew you would get it. It was a test. Plus, Janis was down there just in case," Allister said nonchalantly.

"Oh, just in case, huh? That was the most insane thing that has ever happened to me. I don't even know how I knew to make a window, I just did."

"In life or death situations, there are two types of people. Those who survive, and those who don't."

Lumen thought that was an obvious statement. He shrugged that off and looked around. There was sand everywhere. As far as the eye could see, it was a dry and deserted environment.

"Where are we now? What was that last place? I could have sworn that last place was an island floating in the sky," Lumen said.

"That would be an accurate statement. Follow me."

Allister and Wrigley took off. Lumen didn't see anything in that direction but didn't know how else he would get out of there. He took a few steps forward before realizing his feet were stuck. He looked down to see his feet sinking. He tried pulling one of his legs out of the sand, but they wouldn't budge. He kept sinking.

"Hey, wait up. I'm stuck, Allister. What the . . . could you help me out?"

"That you are . . ." Allister remarked.

Allister waved his hand, and a window opened up. He whistled for Wrigley to follow him, and they both stepped through the window. Lumen was alone.

"Are you kidding me?!" Lumen yelled.

At this point, Lumen's hands were in the quicksand. He didn't know what to do at that point. He didn't have his hands to move any lights.

He was sinking quickly.

"Who knew quicksand was so quick," Lumen said aloud.

The sand was at his neck. He took a deep breath before he became fully submerged. The sand seeped into his nose and ears. Lumen thought that this was it. He would die of suffocation. Lumen gasped for air only to inhale more sand. He couldn't breathe. He couldn't move. He thought of his mom for a moment and how devastated she would be.

Everything went black, and he couldn't see a thing.

As Lumen was just about out of breath, he saw the lights. He wished he could move them. He visualized where he would maneuver each light. He pictured each piece coming together before realizing that he could move them with his mind! The lights began to form a window. *How do I get to it now?*

Can I just try to move the window towards me?

He focused on the window, and it moved toward him in the depths of the sand, in the pitch black.

Just then, his head and arms popped out in a field of snow. Lumen spit some sand out of his mouth into the snow, still able to feel the rest of his body stuck back in the sand. He took a few deep breaths of air before he realized Allister and Wrigley were standing nearby.

"Ah, there you are. Give me your hand," Allister said.

Allister grabbed Lumen's hand and pulled him through the window entirely onto the snow.

"Okay, that time I was for sure going to die. There was no backup plan there! Again, are you insane? Are you just trying to kill me?"

Allister chuckled.

"Most of the students don't have this many questions and comments on the first day. You are a funny one, Lu."

Lumen was about to say something back to Allister when he saw Wrigley run by him after what appeared to be an extremely burly critter. It was small but very muscular with long ears, just like a rabbit. It was a dark gray and its short fur was mangled and dirty. Lumen could see the animal's veins running through its legs and its teeth sticking out of its mouth.

"Wrigley? Get back here! What is he after? Is that thing going to kill him? Wrig, wrig!"

"Oh no, don't worry. Wrigley won't be able to catch that. If you recall, your first night here we had some wetchop meat. Well . . ."

"Right, wetchop . . ."

Wrigley came trotting back, empty-mouthed.

"Here ya go, boy," Allister waved his hand again, and an ice cube fell to the snow. Wrigley jumped on top of it.

"My mom says ice is bad for dog's teeth. You shouldn't give him so much."

"My apologies, Lu; I just want the dog to like me," Allister said.

"Yeah, well, I think he is starting to like you more than me. I need to take him home. My mom would be furious if I lost him," Lumen retorted.

"Don't worry, my boy. Dogs are very loyal. I just want him to know we are the good guys."

Lumen nodded his head slowly.

"Right . . . Anyway, where are we now? This looks more like the first place I came to," Lumen said.

"Right again. Alec did say you have a good memory."

"Okay, great," Lumen answered sarcastically.

They were both silent for a moment.

Lumen cleared his throat and spoke again.

"Okay, so what now?"

"Oh, right! One last thing," Allister said quickly.

Allister waved his hand again. Lumen tried to move towards Allister but couldn't. He was frozen inside of some giant ice block that encompassed his entire body. He couldn't move, he couldn't breathe, and felt unbearably cold. Lumen didn't panic this time though; he knew what to do. He could see the lights in front of him and pieced them together to create a window and moved it toward him. The window moved over Lumen's frozen body. Lumen, still frozen in the block of ice, plopped down on the floor of Allister's cabin.

"Croaky! He took the whole block of ice with him!" Janis yelled.

"Well, at least he reacted quickly," Allister said.

Janis and Allister conversed casually while Allister held his hand above the block and snapped his fingers. It all turned to water instantly. Lumen hit the floor with a thud.

"Okay, I have had enough!"

Allister and Janis laughed loudly, each of them doubled over, trying to catch their breaths. Wrigley howled once. Lumen gave him an angry look, and Wrigley sat down with his ears back.

"I'm sorry, what is so funny?" Lumen demanded.

Janis took a few seconds to stop laughing. He wiped the tears away from his face and whiskers.

"Everyone reacts differently to this little test. This is the first time we have seen someone so angry. It's hilarious, mate."

Allister chimed in. He was serious again.

"Most of our students aren't angry after those dangerous endeavors. Most are scared, confused, panicked . . . you get the point."

Lumen responded more loudly than he intended, his adrenaline still pumping through his body.

"Well, that is a normal reaction for someone WHEN THEY ARE ABOUT TO DIE!"

"That is correct. But you, you were, for the most part, calm and collected. You were able to quickly escape all three predicaments. Every single person before you has had to be rescued at some point or another. I will say, we did have to get

75

you out of the ice, but most don't get this far without failing. You should be proud of yourself, Lumen," Allister said.

Lumen smirked. He liked hearing that he did something well. He didn't get much praise from anyone other than his mother and Alec.

"Well, thanks . . ." Lumen tried to keep an angry look but was failing miserably.

It fell silent in the cabin. Lumen realized he was soaking wet, and he was beginning to get cold. He walked over to the fire to warm up.

"Hey, could I get a towel or something to dry off?"

"Oh, my apologies, my boy . . ." Allister looked at Lumen and snapped his fingers. Lumen felt the water being pulled off of his body and clothes. He looked up and saw it accumulating in a ball above him. Allister moved the ball of water over to a plant in the corner of the cabin and let it drop. Both Lumen and his clothes were now dry.

"That was amazing! When can I learn to do something like that?"

Allister and Janis looked at one another, as if they were speaking to one another, then looked back at Lumen.

"In time. Performing something like that is a bit tricky. You don't want to accidentally pull water from within the body. It can get messy," Allister said casually.

Lumen thought about what awful things could have happened to him if Allister had performed the magic, or whatever that was, the wrong way. He decided it was best not to think about it.

"Okay . . . well, what's next?" Lumen asked.

"You will begin classes in a week. We like to do this little charade to see what our students are capable of. Once the students have all experienced what you have, we will begin classes," Allister said.

"Classes?"

"Right. You will begin learning about the world and the power of Eauges. I pick the students I want to learn to be an Eauge. You will learn about the culture and history of the Eauge people as well as how to wield the power of water responsibly," Allister stated matter-of-factly.

"So I am going to be an Eauge?" Lumen asked the question very slowly.

"That is correct. I hand select my peers as do the other heads."

Lumen was confused. He hadn't even realized other people lived in this bizarre world.

"Other heads? What do you mean?"

"Well, there are the Aeris people who are led by our good friend Janis here. He wanted you to be his student as well, but I have convinced him you would be better suited in the Eauge caste."

Lumen looked over at Janis laying on the couch. The catman was keeping a feather floating above his mouth by blowing air out of his mouth.

"There is the Liros tribe, which is led by our good friend, Sasha. You will meet her soon," Allister continued.

"Liros? What is that?"Lumen asked.

"They are the people of the element earth. That forest in the sky was their land. You will be back there again."

"Okay, so that leaves the fire people. What are they called?"

"The Ignous. You will be learning from Aidan," Allister said.

Lumen said the tribe names in his head to try and remember them.

"Oh, I will learn from all these people you mentioned? I thought I was going to be an Oosh."

"You are. But it is important to know of all the elements, Lumen. You will need to understand how they all work together, and the power of each," Allister said.

Janis sat up.

"Oy mate, vr'y import'. We all work t'gether. When we don't, thas when thangs git a bit messy."

"Right . . ." Allister shot Janis a look as if to say don't confuse the boy anymore than we already have. Janis caught the look and he laid back down. The feather was still floating there.

"What Janis meant to say is it's important for us all to work together. Like we told you, there is a constant war. It is important that we all cooperate to manage it."

"What war? Are we going to be fighting someone?" Lumen asked.

"Not quite, Lu. It is not that kind of war," Allister said with a smile.

"Oh okay . . ." Lumen brushed off the statement, thinking instead about what he was going to learn. He was eager to get started.

"So, can we start now?"

Allister laughed again.

"Not yet. We will wait for the other students to begin next week."

"Right, you already said that. Well, I have two questions for you then," Lumen said.

"Let's hear them."

"I thought you said you were a master of all the elements?"

Janis jumped into the conversation again.

"Righto he is, mate! Better than n'one 'round!" Janis said, loudly.

Allister looked at him again and Janis laid back down.

"I wouldn't say master, Lumen, but I do practice all four."

"Why do you teach Eauges then? Are you like the leader of this world or something?"

"No, no, don't be ridiculous. The Imperiums are the ones in charge here," Allister said.

"Imperiums? What's that?" Allister looked over at Janis for help. "Oy, now ya want me help? Fine . . . The Imperiums are like a group of governors. They are like a council that decides what goes on here. They try and keep balance here as well as in your world," Janis said without an accent.

"Wow, I could understand you this time."

Janis rolled his dark eyes and laid back down. Lumen realized how crazy this would seem to the normal human. He was talking to a cat.

"Thank you, Janis. The Imperiums try to keep order. You do not need to worry about that right now. You will learn more about Bonumalus the more you are here," Allister added.

Lumen nodded.

"Okay, well what were all those places you tried to kill me in before? Is that all part of Bonumalus?" Lumen asked.

"I have to say, this is starting to seem like more than two questions," Allister said with a smile.

"These are all a part of the first question."

Allister smiled at Lumen. Lumen couldn't help but feel at peace and secure around Allister. There was something about the way Allister carried himself. Lumen thought back to one of the few conversations he had with his mom about his dad.

"What was he like?" Lumen asked his mother on a random Sunday afternoon.

"Well honey, he was a great man. He cared for others, and others cared for him. A lot of people looked up to him. He was very charismatic. There was just something about him that everyone liked. He was a good man, at least I thought he was until he left abruptly," Alice said.

"What's charismatic mean again?"

"Hmmm. . . someone you look up to. A person that is appealing," Alice said.

Lumen thought Allister was charismatic.

"Well, Lu, Bonumalus is really segregated into four separate areas, each of which corresponds with the caste of people that live there. The floating forest is where the Liros live, the desert is where the Ignous reside, and the Eauge people live in this area."

"What about the Aeris people? Where are they?" Lumen asked curiously.

"Oh, they live in the clouds, of course," Allister said.

Lumen thought that was crazy, but he didn't question it. Allister and Janis didn't even bat an eye at the comment. People just live in the clouds-- that was normal here.

79

"Right, the clouds. Dumb question. Okay, and my second question . . ." Lumen stammered to find the words for a moment.

Lumen turned and looked at the walls of the cabin.

"What's up with all the drawings of you and Janis?"

Allister peered back at the drawings with a smile before answering Lumen.

"I like drawing. I have always felt drawing myself and the ones closest to me to be a great challenge. I find we are always more critical of oneself. Trying to perfect myself and others I care for through art is a great test for me. Plus, it is fun drawing Janis now that he is a cat."

The feather fell onto Janis' face, and he got up to give Allister a foul look.

"Well, I think it is time for you to get going. Rest up for the week. I will have Alec go with you to get some supplies you will need to get started. See ya soon."

Before Lumen could say anything, Allister waved his hand, and a window opened. He moved the window right through Lumen, and suddenly Lumen found himself sitting on his bed. About a second later Wrigley came jumping through the window as well, then it disappeared.

"Supplies? What could I possibly need for Oosh class?" Lumen looked at Wrigley.

Wrigley turned his head sideways, trying to understand Lumen.

Chapter 6 - Lumen's Luxem

Lumen had a hard time focusing on Monday morning. He was lost in thought multiple times throughout his morning classes. He decided to accept that Bonumalus was real. Not one person treated him differently that week; his mom was worried as usual, and the other students at school treated him the same. His teachers were still boring. Lumen had a lot to think about this morning. Not only did he have to prepare for classes in this exotic new world, but he had to muster up the courage to speak to Sofia. Not only that, but he had to ask her to come to dinner.

Lumen looked around for Sofia as we walked from second-period. He always saw Sofia on his way; she had a class next to his. He decided to catch her before she walked into her class. He would just approach her, ask her how the dance was, and ask her to come over. It was that easy. Lumen felt confident for a moment and then felt sick immediately after as he began to think of every way this could go wrong; the possibilities were endless. Lumen thought he might puke.

He was almost to his next class when he saw Sofia walking by herself from in the opposite direction. *This is it. Do or die,* Lumen thought as he took a deep breath. He cupped his hands and put them over his mouth to make sure his breath was okay. He asked a random student walking by if there were any signs on his back. There weren't. Lumen straightened his posture and made his way toward Sofia, feeling confident. *She asked about me at the dance,* he thought as he walked her way. She had to like him.

Lumen was a few steps away and about to call her name when Alec ran up behind him.

"Hey man, how you feeling? Big week, we got to get you ready. I was thinking every night this week we should discuss what you can expect in these classes, where to meet every day . . ."

Alec was standing between him and Sofia. Lumen tried to sidestep him, but Alec followed his moves.

"Dude, what are you doing? I'm talking to you."

Lumen moved Alec aside, and Sofia was already walking into her class. He was too late.

"Will you shut up, Alec? Thanks a lot. I was going to talk to Sofia . . . it's your fault I have to do this anyway."

"Next time, just say that and I will get out of her way. Much better than staring at her like a creeper. And my fault? I did you a favor by telling your mom what I told her. Now you are forced to speak to someone other than me, big deal. Also, that someone is a girl you're madly in love with."

Lumen turned red.

"I'm not in love! I just think she's cool. I mean look at her, her big, green eyes and long, dark hair."

Alec rolled his eyes.

"Oh jeez, stop now before I puke. Just be ready to meet up after school. Don't pansy out of talking to her either. I'll see you later."

Alec took off for class as the bell rang. Lumen walked into his class.

"Great, now I have to wait until lunch."

Lumen had two more periods until lunch. They went by slower than ever. He wished he could use the lights to travel in time. He could jump to the future and just talk to her already. He was getting tired of feeling like his heart was going to pound right out of his chest.

Period three ended, and he walked to fourth. He took a test that he completely forgot about. He finished faster than anyone else and just sat at his desk, staring up into space. He rubbed his eraser down to the nub. The student next to him gave him a dirty look when the metal end of the pencil began to screech on the desk. Lumen deferred to twiddling his thumbs.

Fourth period finally ended after an eternity. It was lunchtime but Lumen didn't have much of an appetite. He had to find Sofia. Lunch lasted about 30 minutes. Plenty of time.

He walked around the courtyard where most students ate their lunches and socialized with one another. Lumen usually ate near the principal's office. He figured most people wouldn't bother to go over there. Not today though.

He wandered out and about the courtyard.

Where would she eat, and who would she eat with? he thought to himself.

He walked around for 15 minutes and couldn't find her.

Is she here today?

He remembered he had seen her before third period, when Alec ruined it.

Time was running out. He thought about waiting until tomorrow to talk to her but thought he might die from stress if he did that. He had to today.

He walked into the library to think about where she could be. He walked in and sat at a table to think.

After getting frustrated and deciding that she must have had left school early, he got up ready to face the disappointment when he looked up and realized she was sitting on the other end of the library. By herself. This was perfect. It was quiet, and nobody hung out there during lunch. She looked up, saw him, smiled, then waved. Lumen looked behind him to make sure nobody was there, then awkwardly waved back. He started to head over when Blake and his buddies walked into the library.

"There ya are, skitzo! We missed you on Saturday! You been practicing magic? You did a great disappearing act on us . . . You owe me now, though."

Not now, that is all Lumen could think. Lumen would take a swirly any other time if he could just talk to Sofia now.

He looked back at Sofia and saw her gathering her things. She looked at Lumen and seemed sad. She mouthed something to Lumen, but he wasn't good at reading lips. She walked out of the back of the library.

"Looks like it is just us buddy. Make this easier for all of us and come into the bathroom."

Lumen was still staring where Sofia had just been. He couldn't believe his luck.

Lumen turned toward Blake and walked toward the bathroom in the library.

"I'll handle this one on my own boys. Keep watch for his friend Alec. Don't let anyone in here. The locks on these bathroom doors aren't very reliable either."

Blake and Lumen walked in.

"Let's see which toilet we will use today."

There were three stalls in this bathroom. It wasn't as clean as the other bathrooms.

"Stall number one . . ."

Blake kicked the door open.

"Looks to be clogged with toilet paper. Can't use this one."

Blake walked to the second one and kicked the door open.

"Behind door number two, we have a toilet seat covered in old pee and an unflushed toilet. I think we have a winner!"

Lumen thought Blake was talking like some sort of sick game show host. He wasn't amused.

"Contestant number one, walk on down. You are our lucky winner tonight."

Lumen walked over slowly.

He thought there was no way he could talk to Sofia today. He would be wet and probably smell for the rest of the day. Who was he kidding? He may never be able to talk to her. She probably thought Lumen was lame and weak. He couldn't even stand up for himself.

"Hurry up, crazy!"

Blake shoved him into the stall and down to the ground.

"Take a deep breath, you ain't coming up for a while. I'd keep your eyes closed; you'll probably get pink eye from the pee."

Lumen decided he would never be able to talk to Sofia.

He took a deep breath. He closed his eyes. The sooner this was over the better he thought.

Blake cracked his fingers and did some stretches as if this was an exercise.

"No Alec to save---"

Before he could finish his sentence, everything went white until Lumen found himself standing behind Blake. Alec was next to him.

"What the . . . how'd you do that? Alec? How'd you get in here?"

"Your buddies aren't the best look outs I guess. You hear that, Blake?"

"Hear what?"

"I think that toilet's broken."

Blake looked behind him and at the same time Alec moved his hand up. The water in the toilet began to gurgle and the pipes trembled. The water from the toilet came flying out all over Blake. He was covered in pee water.

Blake turned around with his hair and shirt soaked and walked out of the bathroom.

"Oh my. . . oh. . . I think I'm gonna puke. . ." Blake shook his hands to try and rid them of the pee water.

"You two better watch yourselves. I'm coming for you too now, Alec. You're dead."

Blake walked out of the bathroom, followed by a trail of pee water. Lumen and Alec could hear him yelling at his friends about letting Alec in.

"We didn't see him, we swear! He must have slipped by!"

"Shut up! One of you idiots get me some clothes! Oh m . . . this smells so bad . . . Hurry up idiots! This is all of your faults!"

Lumen and Alec listened to them walk out of the back of the library. They heard him gagging outside from the smell. Blake must not have wanted the rest of the school to see him.

"Thanks dude. How'd you know I was here?"

"Sofia found me. She told me you were in trouble. I jumped here as quick as I could."

"That was awesome what you did with the water. Oh man, Blake is so mad. That was great."

They both laughed.

"So, you talked to Sofia then? How'd it go?" Alec asked.

"No, Blake got me before I had the chance to talk to her."

Lumen shrugged.

"Bummer. Well you'll have to talk to her tomorrow I guess."

"I guess so. Or after school . . ."

"No rush man, you'll see her again."

There was a rush though, Lumen thought. He was going to stress himself out if he had to wait until tomorrow.

"Yeah, right. I got to get to my next class. Thanks for your help. I'll see you tonight."

They both walked out and headed to their next classes. The lunch bell had just rung.

Lumen thought about when he would see Sofia again. He knew that she always walked to the stoplight after school. She must cross the street to get home. Lumen decided he would try and catch her there.

He felt confident this time would work out but also couldn't believe she helped him out. She must care at least a little about him; enough to find Alec to help him out. He couldn't stop smiling and was as ready as ever to talk to her. He just needed to get through these last two classes.

Fifth period came and went at a turtle's pace, and sixth period, history, was no different.. He walked into class, and Ms. Preston took attendance. She told the class what they were doing today.

"We will be splitting into groups today. You will work together to answer the questions on this sheet. We are working from chapter six, so I hope you all did the assigned reading."

Ms. Preston split the class into groups the same way she always did. The groups were almost always the same. Lumen was always put into a group with one of Blake's friends, Cody, a quiet kid that was also picked on, and Terri. But today there was a new girl in their group, Francine. The three moved their single desks toward Lumen, and all looked at him as Ms. Preston dropped the assignment in front of him. Lumen looked at the clock. He was sweating a little bit.

"Hey, skitzo, pay attention, we need you to answer these questions." Cody never did the reading.

Terri did the reading but hardly had any input in these group assignments. Lumen didn't know about Francine.

Lumen didn't fully hear his classmate; he just took the assignment and started to fill it out blindly and handed it back to his group after a few minutes. Cody and Francine grabbed it and whispered to each other.

"What the, you see what crazy wrote?"

Francine took the paper and read over the answers.

"Oh my gosh, I thought you guys said he was really smart?"

The three of them glanced at one another and back at Lumen.

"Yeah, he normally gets all the questions right. Even I can tell some of these are wrong. He must really be losing it," Cody said.

Ms. Preston spoke up.

"Two minutes folks. We will be going over the answers afterwards."

Cody and Francine frantically scribbled and scratched out some of the answers and put in what they thought was correct.

Lumen didn't hear any of this. He kept looking up at the clock. Every time he looked at the clock, it felt as if only seconds had passed.

The teacher collected all of the groups' assignments and had everyone move their desks back.

Ms. Preston went over the questions while looking at each group's answers.

"Let's see here, interesting . . . Cody, your group wrote all the correct answers initially, it looks like, but scratched them out. Looks like you should have listened to whoever wrote these first."

Ms. Preston glanced at Lumen.

Lumen heard Ms. Preston and looked at Cody and Francine. Lumen rarely got things wrong in his classes. He was angry for a moment as he thought he should have insisted on keeping his answers, but it passed when he looked back at the clock and noticed there were only 3 minutes left.

Cody and Francine looked at each other, embarrassed and red in the face.

Ms. Preston was almost finished going over the last question when the bell rang. Lumen already had his bag packed up and was the first out the door. He knew where Sofia would walk by and didn't want to miss her.

He quickly walked out of the school to the streetlight.

He waited. He looked back at the school to make sure she wasn't coming towards him as he needed to mentally prepare to speak to her first. He took notice of the dull gray color of the office building with the bland blue letters that spelled "Bromide High School". He thought that they could really update the colors or maybe repaint. Maybe people would enjoy coming to school more.

At that moment, he saw Sofia walk out of the school. She walked right where Lumen thought she would, to the streetlight.

Lumen got really nervous and started to sweat again. He thought it might be weird if he was just standing there, staring at her. He wasn't sure what to do. She was getting closer. Lumen leaned up against the light pole and put one foot up.

He whispered, "What the heck am I doing?"

Sofia walked up next to Lumen and stopped. Lumen pushed himself off of the pole. He froze; he couldn't think of anything to say. All he had to do was say something, but his mouth wouldn't move.

"Hi Lumen," Sofia said. "You don't normally come this way. I thought you lived toward Inventa Way?"

Lumen took a moment to answer as he couldn't believe she spoke to him first.

"Uhhh, ye . . . yeah. I do."

"Oh, what are you doing here then?"

Lumen thought of lie quickly.

"Oh I'm just waiting for Alec; he's taking forever. Class ended like 10 minutes ago."

Lumen awkwardly laughed loudly and immediately turned red when he realized how loudly he laughed.

Sofia smiled. "Class ended 3 minutes ago Lumen. I was just going to ask how you got out here so fast. I'm usually one of the first at the crosswalk."

Lumen just laughed and turned even redder. He thought his cheeks might burn right off of his face.

They were both quiet, just waiting for the crosswalk to allow them to walk across.

They both opened their mouths to speak at the same time, and both interrupted one another to let the other speak. The crosswalk turned to allow them to walk.

Sofia looked at Lumen and then turned to walk across.

This is it, Lumen thought. How could he let it slip?

No, he thought, he had the ask her. He turned to go after her and she had already turned back toward him.

"Hey, look, would you want to hang out sometime?" Sofia said to Lumen.

"Yes, definitely, for sure . . . This might be weird, but would you wanna to come for dinner at my house?"

Sofia smiled. Lumen stared right into her big green eyes. He couldn't believe how green they were.

"Yes. That sounds nice. What day?"

Lumen had to think for a few seconds about what day his mom had off.

"How about, uh . . . Wednesday?"

"Okay. Meet here on Wednesday after school again? We can walk back to your house."

"Great...Sounds great, yeah." Lumen said. He wiped the sweat off his forehead.

Sofia smiled again and waved goodbye to Lumen.

Lumen turned to head back in the direction of his house. He pinched himself several times on the way home. He wasn't dreaming.

89

Lumen walked into his house feeling like a million bucks. He walked into the kitchen, though he felt he was walking on clouds. He saw money on the counter, with a note that read "Love you, take your medicine!" and knew what that meant. He turned back and went to his room. Wrigley was laying on his bed. Lumen fell onto the bed and stared up at the ceiling. Wrigley jumped on top of him to say hello and licked Lumen's face a few times. Once Wrigley calmed down they both just laid there for a few moments.

"What a day . . ."

Lumen decided that this was probably the best day of his life. He was going to hang with Sofia in a couple of days. He never thought this would happen to him.

"I guess being the crazy kid isn't the worst. You think she's into me? Maybe she's just being nice because I'm the crazy kid. What do you think?"

Wrigley just turned his head, trying to understand him.

"Oh, no answer until you go to the bathroom? Fair enough."

Lumen took Wrigley outside for a walk to go to the bathroom.

They went back inside and Lumen threw Wrigley's toy around for him to fetch a few times. He got bored of it and decided to watch some TV. He had some homework but figured he could finish it in almost no time later.

A few reruns of his favorite cartoon passed and he decided he was hungry.

"Time for some La Derniere Piece. I'll be back in a little, Wrig. Don't do anything crazy."

Lumen grabbed a jacket and headed across Inventa Way. It was getting colder now. He realized he should have layered up some more. His mother would be upset if she saw him out with just one jacket.

He walked across the road and into his favorite diner. He waved to Shari when he walked in and sat at an open booth.

Lumen even said hello to the busboy, Henri. Henri seemed caught off guard and didn't say anything back as he walked by.

Shari walked up to the table and placed a water with lemon down.

"Well you look awfully chipper today, Lu! What can I do ya for?"

"The usual. And I will have the shake with my meal today."

"You got it, hun." Shari winked at Lumen and walked off to the kitchen.

Lumen thought about how much he liked Shari. She was always nice to him. He really appreciated that.

Shari came back a few minutes later with Lumen's chicken pot pie and a chocolate shake. Lumen switched between the two, a few bites of the pie and a big gulp of shake until both were gone. He made sure to finish both at the same time; one last bite and one last gulp. He put the money down on the table, waved goodbye to Shari, and headed back toward his house. It was even colder now. Lumen did wish he brought another jacket, but his house was so close it wasn't that big of a deal. He breathed out heavily a few times to see his breath. He remembered a couple years ago when he saw Blake and his friends standing outside in the cold in middle school. They all put their index and middle fingers to their mouths as if they were smoking. Lumen always thought that was stupid.

The thought quickly left him, and he got back to thinking about how great of day he'd had. The girl of his dreams would be here on Wednesday.

He walked up his cracked driveway and back into his house. Wrigley was right where he left him, only now sleeping.

Lumen tried to be quiet to not wake him and headed to his room. He took off his jacket and figured he should start to get ready for bed. He untied his shoes and started to take off his shirt. The shirt got stuck above his head and he couldn't really see when there was a sudden flash of white light. Lumen struggled even more with his shirt and fell down, wrestling with the shirt in a panic. He finally ripped it off in a fright and stood up with his fists raised.

"Dang man, you should really hit the weights. And maybe work on that tan. You're almost transparent."

"Shut up, Alec. You scared me half to death. Can you stop showing up unexpectedly all the time now? I would like to think I have some privacy."

Alec was chuckling about Lumen falling down earlier.

"Sorry dude, can you please find some sunlight before you blind me?"

"Ha-ha, you're so funny. At least I don't look like I just ran a marathon when walking down the street."

"Touché. To be fair, however, that is only here. I am as dry as ever in Bonumalus." Alec wiped his forehead and flicked the sweat at Lumen as he spoke.

Lumen almost forgot about that place. His day had been so stressful he barely had any time to think about what had transpired over the weekend. He needed to start getting ready for classes, or training, or whatever it was that started next week. Lumen still wasn't sure what he had gotten into.

"Right, Bonumalus . . ."

"That is right. Did you forget about us already? This life is so great down here that you already forgot?"

Lumen shook his head.

"No, it's just been . . . it's been a long day." Lumen smirked as he said this.

"I saw that little smile. Looks like you finally talked to Sofia. I told you she was into you, man."

"Yeah, I guess so . . . wait a minute. How do you know? Do you guys spy on me all day?" Lumen's voice raised as he said this.

"Well no. But we check in on you. I just happened to take a peek when school ended. Smooth moves out there, man."

Lumen turned red instantly.

"You can't be spying on me all the time. I don't like that at all. How am I supposed to get any privacy? What if I am going to the bathroom? Or in the shower? Are you guys watching then?"

Alec took a few seconds to respond to Lumen.

"Well no, that'd be weird. I just do what the boss man says. We keep an eye to make sure you're okay. You're one of us. We're just looking out for you."

Lumen thought about all the times Alec showed up out of nowhere to protect him from Blake and others.

"Okay, how about a warning next time? At least let me get tidy and decent before you come barging in."

Alec thought about it for a moment.

"Deal. Okay, now that we have that all figured out, we should head out. We have just a couple of things to pick up."

"Now? I was about to shower though. I had a few things I wanted to do for my mom, and I need to take Wrigley . . ."

Before Lumen could finish Alec grabbed his hand and pulled him through a window of lights.

They were suddenly standing in a very cold and snowy area filled with hundreds, maybe even thousands, of people. There were small wooden huts and cabins all around covered in fresh powdery snow. The town smelled like Lumen's town smelled after the first rain of the season. People of all sizes and colors walked in every direction--most of the people seemed to be in a hurry to get somewhere. Lumen saw people talking and bargaining for things Lumen had never heard of.

"Oi! Don't toush tha mate! Theyrya fiften smoots eash! Tha ursa meat is twantey smoots! Pay up or scram!"

About ten feet from Luman in a small wooden hut, a larger bald man and what appeared to be a young boy were having some sort of argument. Lumen could hardly understand the bald man. It looked like he lost most of his teeth. He didn't know what ursa was, but he assumed it was some kind of meat, as all around the hut was hanging meat. The hut was covered in snow and had icicles hanging from the roof all around it.

The bald man looked at Lumen.

"Oi, boy! Yu wan some ursa? twantey smoots norm', but I'll give i' to ya fo eighteen!" The man smiled and Lumen saw he only had 3 teeth.

Lumen wasn't sure what to say.

"No thank you, mister. We will be on our way," Alec said to the man.

The man waved his hand at Alec as if he was telling him to go away.

"What did he say?"

"Don't worry about. He is always yelling at people to buy the meat he caught. So aggressive. He should really try a different sales tactic."

Alec shook his head.

"Well, anyway, welcome to Entropolis! This is where a good amount of the Eauges live. This is the market. It's pretty hectic around here, but once you get out of here it mellows out. Don't worry."

"That is awesome, Alec. You know what would be even better though--if I had at least a shirt on in this frozen metropolis."

"Entropolis."

Alec looked at Lumen and laughed.

"Sorry dude, stay here."

Alec flashed opened a window and jumped through, leaving Lumen alone to observe this new world. He stood hunched over with his arms crossed trying to stay warm. He could see his breath. He noticed how most people here dressed in ragged clothing that looked like pieces of gray and brown cloth sewn together with a single large thread. Both men and women wore big boots made from some sort of animal hide. There were little huts and cabins all over the place decorated with different signs and flags -- one of the flags was present on most of the buildings. It had four stripes, two gray and two blue, alternating. In the top left corner was the same symbol, a blue circle with three wavy lines in the middle.

An enormous, snow-covered mountain loomed behind the city, mostly covered in clouds.

"Why would so many people want to live here?" Lumen said under his breath. A man bumped into him from behind and Lumen almost fell over.

Lumen noticed that others here used the windows of light to travel as well. After watching a few people arrive and leave, he realized he had been standing there for a few minutes now.

"Where are you Alec . . . ?"

A window opened up next to Lumen. Wrigley came jumping through, and Alec followed.

"When I said Wrigley needed to be taken out, I didn't mean to bring him to this foreign world with no leash."

"I thought he would have fun. Plus, I grabbed a leash just in case. Took a few minutes to find it, sorry."

Alec threw a shirt and jacket at Lumen, and Lumen quickly put on the shirt and zipped the jacket all the way up with the hood on so just his face was showing.

"Why are we here? I feel like we don't fit in. Almost everyone is wearing those weird clothes and boots."

"Oh don't worry; nobody will judge you for what you're wearing. They know some of us come from the other side. Fashion isn't a big deal here, as you can see. There is just one store that sells clothes; same boring stuff for everyone. Random pieces of cloth sewn together and some boots made from ursa hide. It's all really warm, which is what's most important here."

"Yeah, why would anyone live here?"

"It's not that bad here. The people are all like us. There are a lot of different people here that you will meet, all with different stories."

"No, I mean why would the Eauge people choose to live here?"

"Look around, there is water all around us. We thrive here. We are more protected here. Yeah, it's really cold, and is a bit rugged looking, but we are all protected and at full strength here."

"You mean you aren't able to do your water tricks outside of this town?" Lumen asked.

"You saw me do something in the school bathroom, remember?"

"Oh right . . . thanks again for that."

"Anyways, there are just some places we are less powerful, more vulnerable. For example, if we were in Incendious we would have a harder time as opposed to here."

"Incendious? Where's that?"

"You remember almost dying in the quicksand? The desert? That's where the Ignous people live. They flourish in dry environments, and, conversely, would have a difficult time here in Entropolis..."

Lumen squinted his eyes and nodded his head as if he were starting to understand this new world.

"So, are the Oosh people and Ignous, like, enemies? Fire vs. Water? Is that who you fight or battle?"

At that moment, a man walking barefoot in what appeared to be a thin, tan loincloth passed by them. Lumen looked at the man's feet and noticed a small puddle of steaming water where a footprint should've been.

"No, Lumen. We are at peace with the other three tribes. We all trade with one another and work together to limit the rebels who cause chaos on Earth."

"There was a time when we were at war though," Alec continued, "The Ignous once had a leader come to power that led the people to rally against the rest of us. They believed that we all deserved to reign over Earth and were determined to, well, destroy the people of Earth. As you can see, he was defeated and removed from power, and we have been at peace since."

"What happened? Did you guys go to war? Did he die?" Lumen asked curiously.

All of the sudden, a window opened up beside them. Slightly taken aback, Lumen tried to make out the two figures stepping through the white light. It was Allister and Janis, of course.

"Hello boys! We need to pick up some materials for classes starting next week. Thought we would say hello."

Lumen waved.

"Hey, Al. I was just telling Lumen a little bit about the Eauge history," Alec was giddy.

"Oh, no need to go over anymore now! Let the boy take in this new world. Show him around a little bit! There will be plenty of learning next week."

"Oi Alec, don't overwhelm the boy. You talking about war and the bloody battles of the past? Don't worry Lumen, we have been at peace for some time now. Alec has never experienced those things first hand. Just what he has heard." Janis shook his head at Alec. Lumen forgot that there was a talking cat named Janis who wore a little red vest and goggles on top of his head. Of all things in this new world, this is what made Lumen question his sanity.

"I think I have experienced enough to talk about it, Janis . . ."

Allister spoke up before Janis could say anything else.

"Give the boy a break, Janis, you know very well he has every right to talk about the past. Just don't overwhelm Lumen. We will be on our way now. Good day boys, see you soon."

Allister turned the other way, followed by Janis. Allister looked down at Janis, saying something as they walked away. Lumen couldn't hear what he said to the cat but caught that Allister was speaking about Alec. Janis put his paw over his heart and put his head down momentarily, seemingly apologizing.

Lumen thought they looked weird together. Allister was well over six feet tall, had long grayish/white hair with goggles holding his hair back, wearing a long green trench coat. Janis only went up to Allister's knees when standing on his hind two paws.

"Why do they wear goggles?" Lumen asked.

Alec seemed a little flustered about the conversation with Janis. His face was red and he muttered something under his breath.

"Oh, the goggles? I'm not really sure. Allister is a master of all, so maybe he is always testing stuff. Nobody knows really. We think Janis tries to be like Allister sometimes. Just a poser. Probably why he wears the goggles," Alec said bitterly.

Lumen figured out then that Alec and Janis don't necessarily get along. He was curious as to why.

"Well alright, what now?"

"Right, well let's take a look around for a little while and pick up what we came for," Alec replied.

Lumen scratched his head as he tried to remember what they came for.

"Right, and we are here for . . ."

"Your luxem, you know, so you can hold lights . . ."

"Duh, my luxem . . ."

"I thought we talked about this?"

"Maybe. . .I doubt it."

"Your personal luxem will hold lights. So wherever you are, you can open a window. Most people use it to save lights that take them home, or a safe place. My luxem takes me to Allister's cabin."

"Where is your luxem?"

Alec held his wrist out.

"This bracelet is my luxem."

Lumen looked at the bracelet and saw "Mom, Dad, and Marty."

"Marty? I thought you had multiple siblings?"

Alec pulled his wrist back quickly and covered it with his other hand. He kept his head down while answering.

"No, just the one. It's a gift from Al when I first got here . . . Let's go."

Why would you lie about your siblings? Why haven't I have ever met them? What are you hiding? Lumen immediately thought to himself

He decided not to push him for any more.

"So will I be getting a bracelet as well? How does that even work? I didn't see any buttons or anything on it. How does it hold light?"

"It just does, not really sure how it works either. The person who invented them was a genius apparently. . . Anyway, when you need the lights, they are there."

Lumen didn't understand but decided not to question it.

They continued walking through the village. Lumen was very observant, and the two didn't say much to each other while walking. Lumen was distracted by the new world, and Alec seemed to have a lot on his mind. Wrigley stayed close to Lumen.

Lumen noticed that almost everyone from here looked similar. Most of the men and women had long hair. He figured it was to help them stay warm. There was a plethora of shops and markets selling all sorts of things. One shop, with a hanging wooden sign that read "Cibus Mart", seemed to be filled with people. He looked in and saw rows of shelves filled with what appeared to be fruits and vegetables. He figured it was like a grocery store. They walked by another shop called "Licor", and inside were some men and women sitting at a bar with large mugs. Lumen guessed that this was where the adults hung out.

Most of the buildings were hard to tell apart as they were all covered in snow and icicles. They were all made of wood, and almost all of them were without doors as he could see right into each shop. He noticed there weren't any street lights or stop lights. *They must not have electricity here*, he thought.

They walked by people playing music, which sounded much like that on Earth. A girl sang, a man strummed a makeshift guitar, and another played the drums. The instruments looked like they had been put together on the spot; the drummer used what appeared to be trash cans and the guitar was composed of some wood nailed together and had only three strings. Nonetheless, Lumen thought they sounded nice. The girl had a good voice. It was soothing. She winked at Lumen as they walked by. Lumen blushed.

They passed another lady that appeared to be preaching to people while standing on top of a wooden box. Her clothes were more ragged than the rest of the people there, and her hair seemed to have not been combed in quite some time. She wasn't wearing shoes either. Nobody was around her. She was yelling things to people as they passed, and her voice sounded hoarse, as if she had been there for hours. She pointed at Lumen and yelled, "You, come here!"

Lumen hesitated but walked over to the lady.

"Yes?"

"I can see you are new here."

She placed her hand on Lumen's shoulder. Her eyes rolled back until only the whites were showing.

"Oh my, oh no . . . " she opened her eyes and looked wide-eyed at Lumen, her grip tightening. "Leave now while you can. No. . .no this can't be right. Leave now, child."

Lumen was confused. The woman's grip started to hurt Lumen's shoulder and he tried to step away. The woman wouldn't let go.

"Your future is short if you stay. All of us have limited time, but yours is particularly short. Stay away from him!" She warned while glaring wide-eyed at Lumen.

She pulled her hand away and held it with the other as if Lumen's shoulder had hurt it. She appeared to be shaken and stepped off of the box and walked away quickly. Wrigley barked at her as she left.

"Oh, don't listen to that nonsense, Lu. She says that stuff all the time," Alec said.

"What's wrong with her?"

"She still practices magic. The Opperes have kind of disappeared and are now frowned upon. That's why no one listens to her. She has been spewing that stuff ever since I've been here, and who knows for how long before that. She used to be respected until the war. Everything changed after that. I think she lost her mind when everyone lost respect for her kind. She couldn't handle it . . . At least that's what I heard."

"Is that the war you mentioned before?" Lumen wanted to hear more.

"Yeah. The Opperes sided with the wrong team. Let's just say most were exiled...most."

Lumen wanted to know more about the "guy" who led the charge.

"Is that who the lady was talking about when she told me to stay away from 'him'?"

"Who knows man; he is dead anyway. Nothing to worry about if it was."

Lumen wasn't sure why but that news brought him some relief.

"How'd it end?"

"Well apparently the Ignous leader and Allister got into an intense battle. It was huge, like really big. Obviously Al came out on top. Best there is around."

"What about--" Alec cut him off.

"Look, I don't know everything that happened. You can ask questions when you have class or are with Allister, though he is pretty hush hush about the past. Now that I think about it... I don't know anything about his past..." Alec trailed off again as if he were in deep thought.

Lumen had a lot of questions but they would have to wait.

They continued walking and finally approached a shop with a lot of younger people inside. Some of the people were dressed like him, bringing him a bit of comfort.

"What is this place?"

"This, my friend, is where you get your luxem. This is where all Eauge come to get their luxem. Nemo will help you get what you need. He is right up there." Alec pointed toward the back of the store where an older man stood with several people surrounding him, all asking him questions. The man wore a top hat, made of the same material as the Eauge's clothing. He had a very thick, white mustache that matched his enormous eyebrows and wore glasses on the tip of his nose. His coat was almost like a dress as it went all the way down to his boots. The man was hunched over just a bit. Lumen wondered how old he was.

The store was filled with random items from bracelets, like the one Alec owned, shoes, necklaces, hats, gloves, and much more. The items laid somewhat scattered throughout the store. There were people all over looking through the shelves and racks. Lumen wasn't sure if these were all supposed to be luxems.

Lumen walked over to the man who was surrounded by young people. Nemo turned as he approached and took his glasses off.

"Well hello, Lumen. I see you have finally made it. I've been waiting to give this to you for a long time."

Lumen didn't have any time to say anything before Nemo reached behind a counter with shelves loaded with random boxes. He grabbed one particular box that had Lumen's name written over the front. Nemo set the box down on the counter and opened it.

There, in the box, was what appeared to be a long, black ring. Engraved on it were four small symbols. Lumen only recognized one of them. It was the same symbol on all of the flags he had seen in Entropolis: a circle with three wavy lines in the middle. The other three symbols were unfamiliar but they looked sort of similar to him.

Nemo took the item out of the box and held it out to Lumen.

"This belongs to you."

Lumen took the item from Nemo and held it out himself, hesitant. He looked up. "Uh, do I just put it on?"

"Yes of course, my boy. Here."

Nemo took the ring and grabbed Lumen's hand. Before he placed it on one of his fingers he observed Lumen's hand, wiggling each finger.

"Ah, this one will do."

Nemo grabbed Lumen's index finger on his left hand and slid the black ring over it. It went all the way down and covered the entire area between his knuckle and where his finger first bent. It fit perfectly and felt cold on his skin.

"Perfect. I knew it would be perfect for you."

Lumen held his hand out. He thought it looked cool. He had never worn any accessories before. He touched it with his other hand, and the ring felt matte. The two edges were ridged all the way around, and the four engravings were on the top of his finger.

Lumen held his hand out to look at it and saw Nemo smiling at him.

"How'd you know who I was? And how'd you know this would work for me?"

"Oh, we have been waiting for you for some time, Lumen. I always know what will work for the Eauges." Nemo smiled at Lumen. He put back on his glasses, patted Lumen on the back and went back to talking with the others there, helping them figure out what luxem to use.

Lumen walked out of the store, feeling the luxem with his other hand on the way out. He walked up to Alec and Wrigley, who were talking to a woman selling pockets. Alec handed her something and she handed him three steaming pockets.

"Wow, that was fast. Let's see whatcha got . . ."

Lumen held out a fist so that Alec could see the black ring.

"Whoa, I've never seen anything like this. Did you pick this? I've never seen this in there."

"Uh no . . . he pulled it out of some box. Behind the counter. He said he has been waiting to give this to me."

"Lucky. Everyone usually gets a bracelet or necklace. This, you got here, is unique."

Alec's smile faded.

"How does it work?"

Alec reluctantly handed him a pocket and bit into his own. Alec held the third pocket behind his back for Wrigley to take. Wrigley grabbed the whole pocket and swallowed it all in a couple of bites.

"I saw that, Alec."

"Huh, what are you talking about?" Alec smirked at Lumen as Wrigley licked his lips.

"Anyway, when you know where you want your safe place to be, we will open a window. The ring will know it's your safe place and will save the window."

Lumen scratched his head in confusion.

"Wait, what? It just knows? That doesn't make sense. Where do the lights go?"

Alec rolled his eyes and took a bite out of the pocket. He spoke with his mouth full.

"Du, it just wors tha way. You'll see. To man questins Lu. Your curiosity kils me sumtims."

Lumen could hardly understand Alec but picked up that he may have asked one too many questions. He decided to drop it.

"Thanks for the pocket. What did you hand the lady for them?"

Alec swallowed his food before speaking this time.

"Another question? Sheesh, I gave her five smoots. It's basically money here."

"Oh okay . . . how do I get smoots?"

"Last one I'm answering for at least five minutes, Lu. There are people here who value American money. You can exchange dollars for smoots. I'll show you next time we are here."

Lumen nodded to say okay.

Alec took off back in the direction they came from.

Lumen yelled after him.

"Hey, where are we going now?"

"What did I say, Lumen? Five minutes." Alec held up his hand to show the number five.

Lumen looked at Wrigley and rolled his eyes. They both started walking behind Alec, back into the heart of Entropolis.

Lumen looked down at Wrigley.

"You know I saw you eat that pocket. You're lucky we are in a new world. You'd be in timeout if we were at home."

Wrigley put his ears back as if he were ashamed and knew what "timeout" meant.

"I'll let that one slide," Lumen smiled at Wrigley and his ears perked back up. They looked ahead and kept walking.

Chapter 7 – Hot Date

Lumen, Alec, and Wrigley walked for a few minutes to look around the village. After asking a few more questions, Alec became more and more agitated, and Lumen thought he should get back home.

"Alright, well I'll bring you back here the day before you start to pick up a few more things. Like I said, we'll work on some things this week. Oh, and we'll set up your ring. Think about where you want your safe place to be. Don't lose that thing."

"I won't." Lumen looked at the ring on his finger. He liked the look of it.

"Okay, well off you go." Alec moved his hands together as if he were putting something together, and a window popped open.

Lumen realized he hadn't seen the lights as often. He worried he may be losing his capabilities to jump between worlds.

"Hey, how come I'm not seeing the lights as often? Does it mean I'm unable to . . ."

"Had to get one more question in, didn't you? Let me stop you there before you really start thinking crazy. Now that you know what they are for, they will only be present when you need them. . . Don't worry, they are always there when you need them. See ya later!"

Alec gently pushed Lumen and waved goodbye. Lumen stepped through the window with Wrigley close behind.

They were back in his bedroom. Lumen looked at the clock on his desk, it read *12:08 am*. He didn't care that it was so late; the past day had been the most incredible he had ever experienced. He laid on his bed and peered up at the ceiling. He held his hand out in front of him again to look at the ring.

"My own luxem. I didn't even know what that was a few hours ago." He sat up and looked for Wrigley. He was asleep already at the foot of the bed.

"Guess you don't care."

Lumen rubbed his fingers over the four symbols. He recognized the Eauge symbol and concluded the other three must be the other castes.

The second symbol was a circle with three jagged lines, sort of like a mountain range. The third symbol was another circle with three straight lines. The last was another circle with three wavy lines, sort of like the Eauge symbol, but vertical.

Lumen put his hand down and figured he should get to sleep. He laid back down.

"Nope."

Lumen couldn't stand not brushing his teeth. He got up and went to his bathroom to brush and clean up.

"Some things will never change."

Lumen awoke the next morning, as he always did, at 6:40 am. He had a pounding headache as he wasn't used to not getting a full eight hours. He took Wrigley out to go to the bathroom, fed him, went back to the bathroom to clean up, got dressed, brushed his teeth, and ate a bowl of cereal.

On his way out, he cracked open his mom's bedroom door. She was sound asleep. He decided not to wake her; school was only a ten-minute walk. Lumen grabbed his things and headed out.

It was a typical day at school, although classes were less stimulating and more boring than ever for Lumen. He found it easier to pay attention to his teachers now that the lights weren't everywhere he looked, which made classes even more dreary.

The first four periods passed at a snail's pace until lunch. Lumen thought he should find Sofia to talk about dinner tomorrow--or maybe he shouldn't. She had already told him to meet her at the crosswalk tomorrow after school. He wasn't sure if approaching her again would seem too eager, but he wanted her to know he was looking forward to dinner. Or was that weird? Lumen couldn't decide and thought he should talk to Alec. At that moment, he noticed he hadn't seen Alec yet and wasn't sure where he was.

As soon as he realized Alec's strange absence, Lumen noticed lights dotting the room around him.

Heart racing, Lumen sped off for the bathroom and went into a stall. He put his backpack on the toilet and put his hands together, just like he had seen Alec do. More lights appeared, and he moved them around in an attempt to create a window. After a few moments of moving the pieces around the lights beamed. He wasn't sure where this would lead to but decided to jump through anyway.

Lumen landed in Allister's cabin. The fire crackled with a tea kettle whistling above it. Allister walked over and grabbed the pot and poured it into a giant copper mug.

"Hey Allister . . ."

Allister turned around, startled, as if he didn't expect anyone to be there.

"Ah Lumen, my boy, good to see you back so soon. What can I do ya for?"

"I'm, uh, looking for Alec. Is he here?"

"As a matter of fact he is, he should be right out. I see you are getting the hang of the lights."

Allister smiled at Lumen.

"Uh, yeah, I think I'm getting it. How do you guys create the windows so fast? I see you just wave your hand and a window opens up."

Allister kept smiling at Lumen as he answered.

107

"Practice, my boy, practice."

Alec came through a door on the other side of the cabin.

"Still asking questions, huh? Your mind never rests, does it Lumen?"

Lumen wasn't sure how to answer. Luckily Allister spoke before he could.

"Curiosity never hurt anyone, Alec; he can ask whatever questions he likes."

"I heard curiosity killed the cat. . . Anyway, what are you doing here? School is in session."

Lumen looked at Allister nervously; he didn't want Allister to hear his dilemma with Sofia because he was embarrassed.

"I'll let you boys talk; I need to get more firewood anyway." Allister winked at Lumen, waved his hand, and walked through a window. Lumen felt more comfortable speaking now.

"Do you think I should talk to Sofia about tomorrow? We already planned where to meet, but I don't want her to forget . . ."

Alec chuckled.

"Dude, relax. She isn't going to forget. If you ask me, she is just as interested in you as you are in her. Play it cool. You'll see her tomorrow. Don't go looking for her. If you see her before, you can talk."

Lumen scratched his head.

"Um okay. I'm not sure that helped. Talk to her if I see her but don't go looking for her? Are you sure?"

"Yes, Lumen. You hungry?"

Lumen realized he hadn't grabbed lunch money from his mom before leaving. She usually handed it to him when she dropped him off at school.

"Um, yeah, I am actually."

Alec walked over to the kitchen area of the cabin and grabbed some pockets. They looked freshly cooked.

"These things are so good. They might be my new favorite."

Lumen grabbed a couple of them from Alec and started eating.

"Alright man, you should get back before someone finds your stuff in the stall."

"Yeah, wait . . . Why aren't you in school?"

"Oh, I'm thinking I might not go back. Now that you're aware of what's going on, you don't need me."

"No, you can't do that. It's good to be there so you can live a normal life if it doesn't work out here. What about your family? Won't they be mad?"

"Don't worry about that stuff dude; I haven't decided for sure yet. I am at least taking a couple of days off. I'm tired. It's been a long school year."

Lumen didn't like that his only friend may not be back at school.

"I think you should stay . . ."

"I'll think about it. Get going now."

Alec waved his hand, and a window opened.

"Wait a minute, how'd you know my stuff was in the st-- "

Before Lumen could finish, Alec pushed him through the window. Lumen landed on the floor.

"He's good at that."

Lumen stood up and walked out of the stall. He saw Blake on his way out of the bathroom.

"What're you doing in there weirdo? That where you eat your lunch now?"

Lumen ignored him and walked out as fast as he could. The bell rang right as he walked out, just in time. He finished his pockets on the way to class.

The rest of the school day went by just like the first half. He passed Sofia on the way to his last class, and she waved at him. Lumen remembered his conversation with Alec but was having difficulty saying anything at all.

Before Lumen could manage to utter a word, Sofia said, "Hi, Lumen."

Lumen awkwardly waved back and walked by without saying a word. *That definitely was not cool*, he decided.

School finished, and he walked home with thoughts of his first date.

When he walked onto Inventa Way, Lumen noticed that the street was blocked off by an ambulance and a firetruck. He immediately forgot about his date plans and became worried about his mother. He rushed up his street when he caught a

109

glimpse of his mom standing in their driveway with her arms crossed. He hurried up the street and called for her. He walked up to her and gave her a hug, feeling nervous about the news he was about to hear.

"What happened?"

"I think the old man that lived in the house across the street had a heart attack. . . So sad. . . Let's go inside. We don't need to see this," Alice said as though she was trying not to cry.

"Well, it's nice to see you. How was your day?" she asked Lumen.

He thought about his day. He traveled to Allister's cabin in Bonumalus, through the lights he had seen all his life, to speak with Alec, who also can travel through these lights, about Sofia, who he asked to come over for dinner tomorrow.

"School was good."

"That is good to hear! How is the thing?"

Alice didn't like to address Lumen's "hallucinations" directly sometimes. She thought it would make it worse.

"It's been really good the last couple of days. Haven't bothered me at all."

Alice smiled at Lumen.

"Good. Well I got you a couple more puzzles. They are on the dining room table."

"Thanks, Mom."

"Well, what should we have for dinner? Should we order in? I have the next two nights off so we can eat together!"

Alice seemed really happy. Lumen hadn't brought up Sofia yet. He thought maybe he should just take her to the diner tomorrow night. He didn't want to overwhelm Sofia on their first date with his mom's eagerness to know everything about his life.

"About tomorrow night, Mom. . . I think I'm going to not eat dinner here. I have plans."

"Plans? Are you and Alec going somewhere?"

"Um no, I have a . . . uh . . . date."

Alice screamed, "OH MY GOSH!"

Lumen covered his ears quickly. He firmly decided this was why he couldn't bring Sofia here right away.

"My Lulu has a date? I cannot believe it! You're growing up so fast. We need to get you a new outfit and a haircut. I'll grab my things!"

Alice hurried off to grab her purse, and they both scurried out the door.

Alice asked Lumen at least a hundred questions on the way to the store.

"Is this the same girl from the dance?"

"Is she your girlfriend?"

"Sofia is such a beautiful name! How did you ask her?"

"Where is she from?"

"What does she look like?"

Lumen could hardly answer any of the questions.

They got to the local clothing store called *Seamstrip*. It was a small business ran by a neighbor, Otto. Lumen said hello to Otto.

Alice said, "Hi there, my boy has a date tomorrow. Where should we look for clothes?"

Lumen blushed and whispered, "Mom, stop it . . . please".

The man smiled and pointed toward the end of the store, and they headed that way. It was all polo and button-up shirts. Alice began grabbing some and holding them up in front of Lumen.

"This might work; it's a little big, but green is your color."

Lumen didn't want to dress fancy. He wanted to be himself.

"How about just a new shirt and maybe some new shoes . . ."

Alice smiled at Lumen.

"Keeping it casual for the first date. Good idea, hun. Over here, c'mon."

They walked to the other end of the store and found a nice black and green long sleeve shirt and some new black sneakers. They checked out and headed to the barber. Lumen did need a haircut; it had been a while. They walked into the only barber shop in town.

"The usual?"

"Yeah, please."

Alice waited in a chair, reading a magazine that was dated from two years back. Regardless, she still loved reading about all of the celebrities.

Lumen's haircut only took about ten minutes to complete. Alice paid and left a couple dollars for tip, and they left.

"What should we eat?"

Lumen thought about the diner but remembered he was going there tomorrow night. He didn't want to overdo it.

"How about some Italian?"

Alice's thick black eyebrows rose, surprised as she too expected Lumen to say *La Dernier Piece*.

"That sounds wonderful, honey. I haven't had Italian in a while."

They drove a couple minutes down the road to the local Italian restaurant, *Classico Italiano*.

Lumen always thought they could have come up with a better name.

They went in, found an open booth, and began perusing the menu. The table had a fake plastic candle in the middle. It was a rounded booth with plush Brunswick green seats. They both decided and put in their order with the waiter as he set down some waters. Lumen ordered a plate of spaghetti with meat sauce and requested some lemon for his water. The two sat and talked about Lumen's date, how school was going, how Alec was doing, and so on. Lumen batted off the first few questions about Sofia and steered the conversation to something else.

"Is she pretty?"

"Uh. . . yeah, I think so. Anyway, did you hear what had happened to the old guy across the street?"

"I heard he had a heart attack. He might make it, which is great news. His wife must be so worried right now. Speaking of wives, do you think Sofia is the one?"

Lumen rolled his eyes each time this happened but eventually gave in and told Alice everything. After getting over the embarrassment, he started to really enjoy his time out with his mom.

Lumen always loved hanging out with his mom when she wasn't nagging him about his medicine. He appreciated how hard she worked and how much she cared about him. He wished he could hang out with her more often. He almost felt bad about going on a date with Sofia on a night she was off. But he knew she would want Lumen to go out. *Is this what growing up feels like?* Lumen thought.

They both ate slowly as they talked some more and ordered a chocolate cake dessert that they split. Once they were finished, Alice paid the bill.

"Thanks, Mom. For everything. The shoes, dinner . . . Thank you."

Lumen felt himself choke up a little bit. He didn't think too often about how much she did on her own for him.

"Oh no problem, hun; you're a good date. You can take me out anytime!"

They laughed as they walked out with arms around one another.

They drove onto Inventa Way, and all of the firetrucks and ambulances were gone. Lumen couldn't imagine if anything happened to his mother. He didn't want to think about it.

They went inside, and Lumen followed his typical routine. Cartoons for some time, and then he walked Wrigley. He hadn't been running lately and considered going for a second, but he knew his mother wouldn't let him go this late. He went to her room to say goodnight, and she was fast asleep. Lumen figured he could just go for a run around the block and slip back inside without his mom noticing.

He threw on some shorts and running shoes and crept out the front door as quietly as he could. He put his finger to his lips, telling Wrigley to keep quiet, and did some quick stretches on the driveway before taking off.

It was freezing. Winter was right around the corner. Lumen should have dressed a bit warmer, but the cold just made him run harder. He passed by Blake's house. It looked like the family was already asleep as the house was completely dark.

He kept running, and he reached the hill. He ran to the top where there weren't any houses and stopped to gaze at the sky. It was a clear night. Clear nights were usually colder. Lumen could see his breath as he huffed and puffed, trying to catch his breath. There were more stars than usual, and a crescent moon hung in the sky. Without the lights distracting him, he was able to appreciate this a bit more.

A few lights started to pop up. Lumen almost missed having them around all of the time. He looked down at his ring and thought about where his safe place should be. *Maybe the house is the best place, I'll set it up to take me to my room.* He looked back up, and there were a lot of lights now, bringing his attention back to getting home quickly. He ran down the other side of the hill. When he arrived Wrigley tackled him, attacking his face with his hot, slobbery tongue.

"Alright, alright, I was gone for 20 minutes! Relax, relax!" Lumen aggressively whispered.

He pushed Wrigley to the side.

"Sheesh, man! I love you and all, but that was a little ridiculous."

Wrigley turned his head to try and understand, as he normally did when Lumen spoke to him. Lumen headed for the bathroom to brush his teeth and take a shower. Wrigley insisted on being in the bathroom with Lumen, and simply stood looking at the shower curtain.

"You want to get in here with me? Weirdo."

Wrigley wagged his tail and stepped toward the shower.

"I'm joking, I'm joking. Get back. Give me a few minutes of privacy. It's hard to come by these days."

Lumen finished up, got dressed, and decided to go to bed. He had a big day planned for tomorrow.

He turned off his lights, crawled into bed, and plopped his head   down   on   a   pillow. He noticed Wrigley at the foot of the bed with his ears perked up, alert.

"Go to sleep, you weirdo. What's wrong with you?" Lumen asked as he pushed him with his foot. Wrigley didn't budge. Lumen sighed and plopped his head down on the pillow. His eyelids quickly got heavier and heavier. Suddenly, there was a flash of white light in the middle of his room, springing his eyelids wide-open.

"In bed already? Get up. You shouldn't have gone on a date with your mother if you were going to sleep so early. I told you needed to go over some stuff."

Lumen rubbed his eyes.

"Alec?"

"No, it's your fairy godmother. Get up. We'll just do a quick session."

Alec turned on the lights, and Lumen could see he was already sweating.

"What are we doing?" Lumen yawned.

"Well, I want you to be a step ahead of the other new Eauges. We are going to practice some things."

Alec left the room and returned a minute later with a glass. He snapped his fingers, and the glass filled with water.

"You want me to do that?" Lumen asked.

"No, no, but you'll be able to do that in due time. Allister just taught me that one. Cool, huh? Anyway, all I want you to do is to get the water to move. Here, sit."

Alec placed the glass down on the desk and pulled the chair out for Lumen to sit in.

"Okay, now what?"

"Focus on the water. You really have to dig within yourself to control it. Focus everything in your being to move that water. Imagine where you want it and how you want it to look, where you want it to go. Just focus on everything about *this* water. Here in *this* glass."

Lumen bent down in his chair to get eye level with the glass. He stared at the glass, trying to focus on just the water. Lumen wanted the water to rise from the glass into a ball. The water began moving back and forth in the glass. Lumen looked up at Alec, surprised at what he had just done. Alec rolled his eyes and pointed to Wrigley itching his back, using the desk as a scratcher. Lumen frowned.

"Dangit. I thought I had it."

"I mean, it was a good try. It's not that easy, dude. Anyways, I'm gonna go. Don't go to sleep until you get that water to move--and without Wrigley's help this time. Good luck."

"Wait, I don't know---"

Before Lumen could finish, Alec had already opened a window and left.

"Great, what the heck am I supposed to do?" He looked at Wrigley, and he just tilted his head again.

"You're not much help either. Go to bed."

Wrigley jumped up into bed and laid down. He was asleep in minutes.

Lumen stared at the glass for a while, with no progress.

He tried closing his eyes to focus more. Nothing.

He put his hands together and crossed his legs, as if he were meditating. Nothing.

He stood across the room and yelled for the water to move. Nothing.

He moved his hands up and down as if he were able to control the water that way. Nothing.

He put his fingers on his temples and stared at the water. Nothing.

"This is useless. I have no idea what I'm doing."

Lumen decided to give up for the night. He turned off his lights and crawled back into bed. He kept his eyes closed for what felt like five minutes before deciding he couldn't sleep. After all, he was never one to leave something incomplete.

"Stupid water. Just move!"

Lumen jumped back onto the desk chair and stared at the glass of water again.

He took a deep breath, closed his eyes for a moment, exhaled, and opened his eyes again. It was just him and the water. Lumen imagined how he wanted the water to look, to move, where to move, and when to move. Nothing could keep him from moving this water when suddenly, a small bump rippled through the water. Lumen gasped. He checked to make sure nothing was moving the desk.

"You see that?!" Lumen shouted at Wrigley. Wrigley didn't budge, he was snoring.

"Well I saw it. I moved it. Alec better believe me." Lumen wiped the sweat off his forehead and looked at the clock. Another night going to bed past midnight.

"That took an hour and a half to do?" Lumen whispered, slightly concerned.

He crawled back into bed and was out before his head hit the pillow.

The next day was the day. Even though Lumen went to sleep well past midnight, he was wide awake by six in the morning. He showered, brushed his teeth, combed his hair (and then decided it looked weird and tried to put it how it normally was), put on his new black and green striped shirt and shoes with jeans, checked that he was wearing deodorant three different times, flossed his teeth, picked out a jacket to go with his outfit (as it might snow for the first time this year), went to the mirror to check his hair again and thought about combing his hair, decided against it again. He was ready to go. Lumen looked at his desk clock.

"6:22, are you kidding me?" Lumen sighed and sat down. He had over an hour before he had to be at school.

He took Wrigley out to the bathroom, fed him, and decided to eat some breakfast himself. He poured himself a bowl of cereal and went back to sit at his desk. He started munching on his cereal when he saw the glass of water.

"Oh you again, I'm back for you," he said to the glass of water.

Lumen ate his cereal as quickly as he could and turned his focus to the glass of water.

"Let's make sure last night wasn't a fluke . . ."

Lumen took off his jacket, closed his eyes, took a deep breath, held it for a few seconds and exhaled slowly. He cleared all of his thoughts and tried to embody the glass of water. He wanted to drown his thoughts in the glass of water.

He opened his eyes and stared at the glass for a few moments when it suddenly rippled, as if a small pebble had been dropped inside the glass. Lumen jumped up and looked to make sure Wrigley hadn't moved the desk again.

"That's right! It's going to be a good day!" Lumen smiled as he paraded to the bathroom to wipe the sweat off of his face.

Lumen wasn't quite sure how he made the water do what it did, but he felt he was on the right track to start his training as an Eauge.

It was a few minutes past seven when Alice came out of her room in a black robe.

"You ready, hun?"

Lumen was sitting on the couch with a jacket and backpack by his side.

"Yeah, I'm ready."

"You look so cute. Oh my goodness, Sofia is one lucky girl!"

"Mom . . ." Lumen looked down embarrassed even though no one else was there.

"Okay, okay, sorry for being an excited mother."

They drove to school in silence. Lumen was deep in thought about how the day would go.

"Good luck today, hun! I'll try to keep to myself if you bring her over, don't worry." Alice pinched his cheek lightly and Lumen smirked just a little.

"Love you, Mom."

Lumen jumped out of the car and headed to first period with a smile on his face.

The day came and went faster than Lumen had anticipated. He passed Sofia as he normally did.

She waved and smiled, "See you after school."

All Lumen could manage to do was wave and say, "Yeah." Surprisingly, Lumen wanted the day to slow down a bit. It was already his last class of the day, and he felt he wasn't ready to embark on this date with the girl he has crushed on for as far back as he could remember. He went to the bathroom during class to check on his outfit one last time and decided he hated it.

"Real original Lumen, another shirt with green in it." Lumen sighed and went back to class. They had a pop quiz, and Lumen aced it, even being as distracted as he was.

Class ended, and he ambled to the crosswalk. He mulled over pretending to be sick and rescheduling. He would only be half lying as he did feel sick to his stomach. His hands were clammy, and he was sweating under his armpits even though it was nearly freezing out.

As he approached the crosswalk, he saw Sofia facing the street, waiting for him. Lumen thought she looked great with her dark green scarf and long, black duffle coat. This made Lumen even more nervous. He approached her and stood behind her for a moment. He thought about sneaking away before she saw him, but decided that was a stupid idea. Unsure how to get her attention, he was about to tap her on the shoulder when she turned around and smiled.

"Oh, hi! How long have you been there?"

Lumen stood wide-eyed for a few moments before stammering an answer out.

"I uh, I just-- I just got here. Hi."

Lumen gulped. He wasn't sure what to say next. Luckily Sofia did.

"Well, should we get going? Are we going to your house?"

"Yeah, um, is that okay with you?"

Sofia smiled at him, and Lumen turned bright pink.

"Of course. Which way?"

Lumen pointed down the sidewalk he often walked home, and they took off that way. Lumen wasn't good at starting conversations with Sofia, but he managed to answer her questions.

"Where do you live again?"

"Is it just you and your mom?"

"Oh I love dogs! What kind? How old?"

"I haven't seen Alec at school this week. Is he okay?"

Lumen lied and told her that he was sick.

"Have you always lived here?"

Lumen answered, and Sofia told him that she came from the west where it never got this cold. But she liked the snow, so she was glad she lived here. She had lived here most of her life.

The questions kept coming, and Lumen was glad. It made him more comfortable. He wasn't very good at returning any questions, but that was okay for now.

They reached Lumen's house, and he told her that Wrigley might jump on her and that it was okay for her to push him down.

They walked in, and of course, Wrigley tackled Lumen per usual; he turned bright pink again when Sofia laughed. Wrigley introduced himself to Sofia by licking her hand.

"Such a gentleman Wrigley is." Sofia laughed with Lumen and helped him off the ground. Lumen turned a brighter shade of pink as she grabbed his hand.

Lumen looked at the kitchen and could see his mom peeping around the corner.

"Hi, Mom."

Alice came right out of the kitchen to introduce herself.

"Oh! I didn't even hear you come in. You must be Sofia."

Alice came over and gave her a big hug.

"Nice to meet you, Mrs. Haaken. Very lovely home."

"It's just *miss*. Very sweet she is! Lumen, I think you found a keeper!"

Lumen just looked at his mom with angry eyes and signaled for her to leave.

"Oh right, well I need to work on a couple of things in my room. Just knock if you need anything. Feel free to help yourself to anything you want, you two."

Alice mouthed, 'so cute, Lu' as she walked by, and Lumen felt like he might explode from humiliation.

"Your mom is so nice. My dad is never that nice to people he first meets."

Lumen felt a little better after that but still felt very hot and red. He took off his jacket.

They stood there for a few seconds. Lumen hadn't planned what they would do before dinner. He was sure she would leave before dinner now.

"Oh, are those puzzles? I love puzzles."

Sofia walked over to the table to look at the new puzzles his mom had got him. Lumen hadn't felt the need to do one lately.

"Oh, yeah. Uh, me too."

"2,000 pieces? This must take you days to do. I wouldn't even know where to begin."

"Oh no, it would take a few hours max. It's pretty easy, you just need a method." Lumen felt comfortable talking about this.

"A few hours? That would be remarkable. Let's do one. I want to see you do one that fast. That's got to be some sort of record."

It was perfect. Lumen could work on this puzzle, something he was comfortable doing, and this would lead straight to dinner time.

"Okay, sure, which one do you want to do?"

Sofia chose the rainforest puzzle with a lot of greenery and trees. Lumen unwrapped it and dumped the pieces on the table.

"Oh my gosh, this is so much! Where do we even begin?"

Lumen never really explained his process to anyone and got excited that Sofia was so interested. He went over separating the pieces into different piles. After organizing the pieces, they started with the border pieces. With two people, finishing the border was even easier than usual. Sofia slowed Lumen down at some points, but it made him realize he wasn't doing this one for time. He needed to enjoy doing this one. Once they finished the border, they went through the rest of Lumen's process. They laughed together when Sofia put the wrong pieces down.

"How long have you been doing puzzles?" She asked, seeming genuinely interested.

"Really as long as I can remember. I've always been pretty good, but I got really good with them when I was diagnosed."

Lumen hadn't talked about that with anyone other than his mom and Alec. He became nervous.

"Oh, that's cool. It helps you focus?"

"Uh, yeah. Whenever it would get bad, I would just do a puzzle, and it would sort of snap me out it." Lumen surprised himself with how much detail he was giving.

"That's pretty cool. What's it like?"

Lumen hesitated to answer. He was nervous about scaring her away. This was who he was, though, he decided. Better she knew now.

"What? The stuff I see?" Lumen asked.

"Yeah."

"It's probably nothing like people at school say it is. All I see are lights."

"What do you mean? Like there are lights beaming all around right now?"

Lumen laughed a little.

"No, no, just like panels of light floating in the air. Like windows of light stopped in midair. All different colors."

Lumen realized he could see a few of them lingering around. They made him feel comfortable for some reason.

"Oh." Sofia seemed disappointed.

"What? Not crazy enough for you?"

They both laughed.

"No, the rumors are much different. It's really a shame how Blake and his friends portray you. They really must be insecure about themselves to attack you like they do."

"Oh, it's okay. I'm used to it."

Sofia placed her hand on Lumen's arm. Lumen looked at it and took a second to realize what was happening. His eyes widened, and he turned a bright shade of pink again. He felt as if a cat had his tongue. He literally couldn't speak. Sofia smiled.

"Well, what now? We have the border finished."

Lumen cleared his throat.

"Uh, right. We, uh, start here and work our way down."

It was silent for some time after that. Lumen wasn't sure how to react, and Sofia was bound to the puzzle.

They got about halfway through when Sofia said she was starting to get hungry.

"Hold on just a minute."

He ran to his mom's room to ask for money. He knocked on the door, and Alice told him to come in.

"How is it? She is so pretty, Lu. Oh my goodness. What are you guys doing? Should I come out there? Do you need anything?"

Lumen sighed. "Just some money please."

Alice gave Lumen a couple of bills.

"Make sure you get dessert!"

Lumen walked quickly back out to the living room. Sofia was sitting on the ground, rubbing Wrigley's belly. Wrigley's tongue was hanging out.

"Uh, should we get going?"

Sofia patted Wrigley's belly, and he rolled over and trotted away.

"Yes, where are we going?" She asked.

"My favorite place in town."

They both put on their coats and walked out down Inventa Way to *La Dernier Piece*. They didn't say much on the way over, which was good because it started to snow and Sofia put her arm around Lumen's arm. He wondered if it was possible to die from a heart attack at 15 years old. They reached the diner, and Lumen held the door open for Sofia. Shari was already at the front.

"Well, hi there, hun! Pick a place to sit as usual, Lu."

"Thanks, Shari."

They walked to Lumen's favorite booth. On the way to the booth, Lumen realized how run down this place was and how tacky it looked. *On no, this is not the ideal first date spot.*

"I've never been to a diner like this! I've always walked by here and wanted to go in. I'm excited!"

Lumen felt relieved.

Shari dropped off two glasses of waters, Lumen's had a lemon slice, and two menus. Lumen hadn't looked at a menu there in such a long time that he forgot what it looked like.

"I'll come back in a few minutes to see what y'all want." Shari smiled at Lumen, winked, and walked away.

Sofia was already browsing the menu.

"Oh wow, that sounds good. I love peanut butter shakes! Should we get shakes before our food?"

Lumen smirked and thought, *This is perfect.*

Shari came back, and they put in their orders. The usual for Lumen with a chocolate shake and Sofia ordered a club sandwich with a peanut butter shake.

Shari came back a couple of minutes later with their shakes.

"Ow, brain freeze!" Sofia put her head on the table and laughed.

"Put your tongue on the roof of your mouth, it should help."

Sofia listened and held her tongue on the roof of her mouth for a few moments.

"Whoa, that actually worked."

"Yeah, took a while to figure out something that worked. It's always annoying when that happens."

"Thanks." Sofia starting twirling her hair and looked out the window.

"Oh, look at that . . ."

She pointed at something outside.

"It looks like an ambulance and fire truck are turning onto your street."

Lumen looked out the window. There were a couple of fire trucks turning onto his street, and an ambulance followed.

"Oh, the old guy across the street was sick or something the other day. I'm sure they are back for him."

"Oh, that's too bad. Should we check it out?"

"No, no, let's eat. You don't want to see that anyway. It's sad."

Shari brought their food. Lumen chowed down his chicken pot pie as he usually did, and Sofia had no problem eating her whole club sandwich.

"Was that enough? We can get something else."

Sofia smiled with her mouth full and was able to spit out, "I'm OK," and gave a thumbs up. She covered her mouth and looked out the window as she turned red.

"Dessert?"

Sofia swallowed her food and looked back at Lumen.

"Only if you want something."

"I heard their chocolate cake is good. Should we split one?"

"That sounds great." Sofia smiled at him again. Lumen felt smooth. He felt this was going a lot better than he could have ever imagined.

The cake came with two new forks, and they both dove in. They hardly talked when they were eating as they were busy enjoying their cake. It wasn't awkward now. It felt normal and nice to have someone to spend time with.

"Oh, you have a little something on your cheek."

Lumen quickly tried to wipe it but kept missing.

"No, here silly." Sofia wiped the chocolate off with her thumb and wiped it on her napkin. Lumen thought about the heart attack again.

They decided it was time to go. Lumen left the money on the table, and they walked out. Sofia waved goodbye to Shari.

"Bye, you two! Stay warm out there; it's starting to snow!"

Lumen looked up to the sky and watched the snow come down, heavier than before. Lumen took a deep breath and managed to garner up enough courage to grab Sofia's hand. They walked hand-in-hand back toward Lumen's house. He thought the air smelled different than other nights. He took it as a sign that things were changing and smirked.

Lumen hadn't felt this happy in as long as he could remember. Somehow Sofia liked Lumen and could look past his "sickness." Lumen never thought about fate but thought that this was meant to be. He found 'the one' he decided.

He looked up and could see white smoke in the sky. The fire trucks were still on the street, only now there were at least four different trucks, as well as a few police cars and an ambulance.

Sofia put her hand over her mouth.

"Oh my goodness, I hope everyone is alright."

Lumen let go of Sofia's hand. He was trying to see at which house the trucks were. Suddenly he had a knot in the pit of his stomach.

His walk turned into a jog as he made his way up the street. He slowly realized all of the fire trucks were in front of *his* house. The air smelled acrid and pungent of smoke. The air in front of him was hazy and opaque. For a moment, Lumen couldn't hear anything except for a high pitched ringing. He could see a police officer taping off the area in front of his house and another was waving a car to turn back around off of Inventa Way.

"Mom!"

Lumen sprinted towards his house, leaving Sofia behind. The lights surrounded the street.

Chapter 8 - The Beginning

Lumen was stopped by a police officer taping off the area.

"Hold up there, kiddo! It's still dangerous over there."

"That's my house!" he exclaimed frantically, pushing the officer aside. He ran under the police tape and toward his house. The front door was taped off too. He made his way to what used to be the back gate and into the backyard. The lawn and garden were charred. The house was mostly intact, just the walls were blackened from the heat, but no burn damage. He went into the house through the back door. He immediately started coughing from all the smoke. Everything seemed okay in there. It was smoky, but nothing was burned.

"Mom! Wrigley!" Lumen took off toward his mom's room but ran into a firefighter.

"Slow down, kid; you shouldn't be in here. You're going to inhale too much of this stuff and get sick." The firefighter was wearing a gas mask. Lumen coughed.

"My mom, where is she?"

"Oh, uh, she's outside, I think. The ambulance might be taking her away now."

Lumen ran out the front door and coughed almost all the way to the ambulance. He reached the back of the ambulance and saw his mom sitting there with a blanket over her shoulders.

"Mom!" Lumen gave her a big hug.

"Hi, Lu. I'm okay, don't worry. Just a little burn on my arm. I was trying to put out the fire in the garden."

"Where's Wrigley?" Lumen's panic immediately returned.

Lumen glanced around the street frantically when a police officer came by with Wrigley on a leash. Wrigley jumped up on Lumen and licked his face. Lumen was relieved. He didn't know what he would have done if something had happened to either of them.

"What happened, Mom?"

A police officer came over with Sofia.

"Sorry about that, Sofia; I thought something happened to my mom."

"Don't worry, Lu, I'm just glad everyone is okay. Do we know what happened?" Sofia asked.

The police officer cut them off again.

"Ma'am, we'll need your statement before we go. Are you sure you don't need to go to the hospital?"

"Yes, it's just a little burn. No biggie."

The police officer smiled and walked away.

"So, what happened?"

Alice took a deep breath and coughed from the lingering smoke on the street.

"Well, after you two left, I went to the kitchen to do some dishes. Wrigley was acting odd. He was pacing by the back window and kept barking. I went to go let him out when I noticed someone back there."

Sofia and Lumen looked at one another and Sofia asked, "Who?"

"That's the thing, I don't know. I opened the door, and Wrigley ran towards the person. It looked like the person threw something down and took off."

127

"Did you see what they looked like?"

Alice shook her head.

"No, they were wearing a big grey hoodie that covered their face. The person was short. That was about all I could get. I was going to go after them, but the fire grew so quickly. I had to call 911 and I tried to throw some water on it. My garden is ruined." Alice's face went bleak.

"Well, at least you are okay, Miss Haaken. That's all that matters." Sofia gave Alice a hug.

"You're such a sweetheart. Thank you."

The police officer came over with a pen and notebook.

"So you said a gray hoodie, correct ma'am?"

Alice patted down her hair.

"Yes, officer. Gray hoodie. The man, or woman, was short. That's really all I saw. They were gone so quickly. Everything happened so fast."

The police officer wrote everything down.

"Not to worry, ma'am. It sounds like we have a neighborhood delinquent. Mr. Rogers across the street also recalled seeing a short person with a gray hoodie in his house the other day. The person startled him so much so that he had a minor heart attack. Are you sure there isn't anything else you can recall? Anything helps."

Alice put her hand on her chin to think.

"Hmmm, whoever it was had a high pitched voice. When Wrigley ran at them, they kind of shrieked. It may have been a girl, or a young boy. I'm not sure."

The officer took note and closed the notebook.

"Thank you, ma'am. You may want to open the windows tonight to let the house air out. Perhaps stay at a hotel for the night."

Lumen coughed.

"And you, see the medic, sounds like you inhaled too much smoke. You should really listen when the professionals tell you to do something. We know a thing or two."

"I'm fine. Sorry about that." Lumen's face turned red as he tried not to cough.

Lumen talked with his mom and Sofia for a few minutes, and they decided they should try and find a place to stay for the night. Lumen offered to walk Sofia home, but she insisted on having her parents come pick her up. She called them, and they walked to the end of Inventa Way where Sofia's dad picked her up.

They saw Shari leaving work.

"Everything okay over there, hun?"

"Yeah, thanks Shari," Lumen yelled. Shari waved from her car and drove away.

Lumen turned to Sofia.

"Hey, look, sorry about the way the night ended."

"Don't be sorry! I had a great time tonight, Lu. It's not your fault some lunatic decided to light your house on fire. I think it's great you care about your mom and dog so much. I don't really have that at home."

Lumen wasn't sure what she meant by that.

Sofia pulled Lumen in for a hug and kissed him on the cheek.

"We should do it again sometime soon, only without the fire next time," Sofia said with a smile as she stepped away and a car pulled up for her.

Lumen awkwardly waved goodbye and watched the car pull away. He held his cheek in disbelief. He turned back towards his house and saw his mom watching from a few houses down. She quickly turned away as if she wasn't looking.

"I saw that, Mom!"

Lumen and Alice went to Beverly's house for the night. She was a friend from work and came by on her break to let them into the house.

"Oh, don't worry! I'm working a double, so I won't be here until the morning anyway. Just please keep the dog off the couch. I hate dog hair."

Lumen looked at Wrigley looking at him. "You heard the lady, don't look at me."

Alice was exhausted from everything that transpired and went straight to bed. She took the guest bedroom, and Lumen and Wrigley took the living room, which had a nice, roomy couch with plush pillows. Lumen didn't mind sleeping there. Though, he didn't think he would be able to sleep much after what happened. The fire and Sofia. *What a night*, he thought.

He turned on the TV and started surfing the channels. He sunk into the couch and his eyes became heavy. Wrigley laid near Lumen and curled into a ball, trying to get comfortable on the rug. Lumen gave Wrigley a head scratch and rolled over to fall asleep. Suddenly, there was a flash of light and the room was illuminated for a moment. Alec was standing in the room.

"Dude, let's go. We need to meet with Allister."

Lumen sprung off the couch and whispered intently at Alec.

"Are you crazy? I can't leave my mom alone here after everything that happened. What if she was here when you made the jump?"

"I checked, relax. C'mon we need to go meet with Allister."

Lumen sighed and looked back at the bedroom. He was sure she wouldn't wake up but felt rotten leaving her all alone in this house.

"Fine. It has to be quick though."

Alec, Lumen, and Wrigley all jumped through a window Alec had opened and landed in Allister's cabin.

The fire crackled as usual, and Allister stood in front of it, arms crossed with a tobacco pipe in one hand and the other under his chin. Janis sat on the couch with his leg crossed over the other wearing his usual red vest and gloves. He also had a tobacco pipe in hand. Janis took a puff. Lumen never thought he'd see a talking cat smoking from an old wooden pipe a few weeks ago but was barely phased by the scene now. Alec took Wrigley to the other side of the cabin to give him a treat.

"Hello Lumen, good to see that you are okay. How is your mom?" Allister's voice was level and his face was stern. The wrinkles on his face seemed more pronounced than usual.

"Uh, she's good, just some minor burns. Nothing serious. She's more upset about her garden than anything."

Allister shook his head. He seemed to genuinely care.

"It really was a nice garden. I'm glad she is okay."

It fell quiet in the cabin. Lumen could hear the wood crackling in the fireplace. Janis took a puff from his pipe, and Lumen could hear the tobacco burn within.

"Well, you're probably wondering why I had Alec fetch you tonight. I know you want to be close to your mother so I'll be brief."

Lumen looked at Allister and Janis and back at Allister with a confused gaze.

"We believe the fire was started by someone from our realm. We aren't sure who. It has been a problem in the past; failed students, or ones who simply don't believe in our cause, try to scare off our new students. We want you to be aware so you can keep an eye out."

Lumen's face became hot.

"What do you mean? I have to worry about my mom and dog being burned alive? What will the person try next? Are they going to fill the house with water and try to drown them? Or is a tornado going to touch down on our house? You didn't warn me that any of this could happen."

Allister remained calm and kept his tone serene. He stayed facing the fire.

"It's not likely that the perpetrator will strike again. They know we will be watching. I just want you to be aware and keep an eye out for anything suspicious. If you do, report it to us immediately."

Lumen felt calm after listening to Allister's response. He almost felt idiotic for getting angry. For some reason, Lumen felt everything would be fine whenever he was in Allister's presence.

"It's a bloody shame what happened, laddy. Keep y'r trousers on though, don't worry." Janis winked at Lumen. Of all things Janis could do, winking was what weirded Lumen out the most.

Alec groaned from across the cabin.

"What is it now, Janis? Was that Irish? British?"

Janis stood up off the couch.

"Thou better watch what thou say next, laddy!"

Allister turned from the fire.

"That's enough. Alec, I happen to find it very entertaining. Let it be."

Alec huffed and puffed for a moment before letting it go. It looked like he had a response ready for Janis but decided not to go against Allister's command.

Allister turned to Lumen and smiled. Lumen felt warmth from Allister.

"Okay my boy, you can take Wrigley back. I don't want to keep you from your mother. She's still sleeping, so be quiet when you return."

"Will do, thanks."

They all stood there for a few moments before Lumen spoke up again.

"Uh, how to do I open a window to home? The one time I opened a window myself I landed in some weird jungle."

"Yeh need to visualize where yeh going before opening a window."

Lumen furrowed his eyebrows in confusion but figured he'd give it a shot. Lights appeared around him. Closing his eyes, he tried to picture Beverly's guest bedroom where his mom was sleeping. He needed to go where she was. He opened his eyes and felt he knew how to put the lights together. He moved them around and a few moments later, the window beamed.

Lumen looked at Allister.

"See ya soon, boy," Allister said with a smile, and Lumen got that warm feeling again. He whistled for Wrigley, and they both stepped through.

They landed in the guest room. Lumen didn't realize this would take him to exactly where he visualized. He figured he would land out front of the house or in the living room.

"Wha, what was that? Who's there?" Alice groaned.

Lumen's eyes widened in the dark.

"Hey, Mom. Sorry, just checking to make sure you were okay . . . Are you okay?"

"Yes, I'm fine," Alice said abruptly and turned away from Lumen.

Lumen let out a slow exhale of relief and left the room silently.

It had been a long day. Lumen and Wrigley headed to the couch in the living room. Lumen reminded Wrigley about not sleeping on the couch, and Wrigley somberly hopped off and laid on the ground. They fell asleep as soon as they laid their heads down.

The news got around quick in their small town, so it was no surprise that Bromide High's principal knew of the incident and called Alice first thing in the morning.

"Hi, Misses Haaken. I am very sorry to hear about your backyard. I must insist on Lumen taking the rest of the week off. It must have been a very traumatic experience."

"It's Miss Haaken. And thank you, Mr. Virtris. We appreciate the call. Have a nice day."

Lumen was standing in Beverly's kitchen.

"Well, looks like the school knows of the incident and you get the rest of the week off."

Lumen was unsure how he felt about that. On one hand, he would get to miss school for at least two days and help his mom with the house; but, on the other, he wouldn't be able to see Sofia.

"Cool, so, what do we do?"

"Well, breakfast first of course. We can head back to the house after we eat to assess the damage."

They cleaned up their blankets and made sure they didn't leave a mess. Lumen did his best to get Wrigley's fur off of the couch.

They headed to the local donut shop, ordered a half dozen donuts with a couple chocolate milks, and headed home.

They walked into the house and sat at the kitchen table to eat.

"It doesn't really smell in here. We won't have to stay at Beverly's house anymore, right?"

Alice sniffed the air a few times before agreeing.

"Yes, maybe we should open all the windows to air it out a bit more though."

They opened all the windows in the house and opted to keep the back windows closed as the air coming in smelled badly of burnt grass.

They went out back afterwards. Everything was burnt to a crisp.

"Well, I guess I'll have to start a new garden. We'll have to hire someone to put in some new grass. We'll need to paint the walls as well. We have a lot of work to do."

Lumen was taking a gander at all the damage when he saw an odd looking flower where the garden was near the house.

"Hey, Mom, looks like one flower made it. Looks pretty weird."

Alice came over and picked it up.

"Interesting, this is a thistle. It's a very pretty purple flower. I believe it is technically a weed though. They are very pointy and can hurt you if you're not careful. It's a misunderstood beauty." Alice said matter-of-factly.

"I've never seen it here before though. I have never planted one."

Alice looked at Lumen with a confused look.

"Yeah, me neither. Not sure how it got here," Lumen replied.

He remembered his conversation with Allister. He needed to bring this to him.

"Can I have it?"

"Sure." Alice handed it to him and went back to assessing the damage and talking to herself about what needed to be done.

Lumen found a few minutes of free time to drop the flower by Allister's cabin. He managed to open a window to the correct place again. The conversation was brief; Allister told him not to worry and thanked him for bringing the flower to his attention. He would have to do some research on whether it could mean anything. Lumen went back home. Alec canceled the rest of their meetings for the week so that Lumen could help his mom with the fire damage. Alice took the rest of the week off from work as everyone was understanding of the situation.

The next four days went by without incident. Lumen and Alice worked on the yard in the cold weather. Alec came by once to help throw out the burnt shrub from the backyard and headed back to Bonumalus afterwards. He told Lumen to try and practice with a glass of water if he could because classes would be starting in no time. Alice was able to get a landscaper to come to the house on a Saturday to put in new grass. The landscaper was happy to do it as she had heard what happened at the coffee shop the other day and was happy to help a fellow neighbor. Lumen wasn't sure why they got the grass as it would probably die in the winter anyway.

Sofia came by Saturday night. Her dad drove her there and waited out front while she checked to make sure Lumen was okay.

"Wow, you guys already fixed up a lot of it. I just wanted to make sure you and your mom were doing alright and to see if you needed anything."

Lumen could see Sofia's dad looking through the passenger window and waving as if to signal he was there to help if needed. Lumen got the sense he meant it.

"Oh, we are okay. Thanks, we appreciate it. Sorry again about everything."

"Don't be sorry! I had a lot of fun, I wasn't lying. How about you come over this week on Friday? I can take you somewhere."

Lumen felt himself turn pink, and he could feel his cheeks get warm. He wondered if that would ever stop happening.

"Yes," was all Lumen could manage to stammer out.

Sofia smiled, gave him a quick hug, and jogged back to the car through the light snow coming down.

Lumen could hear her dad say, "Are they okay? Do we need to bring them anything?" and Sofia telling him a couple times that it was okay and to go.

By Sunday, the backyard looked almost back to normal except for a few burn marks on the fence. Alice decided she would keep it for now as a reminder of how lucky they were to still have the house.

An officer came by on Sunday to ensure there wasn't any missed damage. It was the same one that did the questioning on the night of the fire. The officer assured them they were working as hard as they could to find the arsonist. They had a few suspects but nothing concrete, so they placed a patrol on the street in the meantime to keep watch at night. Lumen left the room and was pretty sure he heard the officer ask his mom out on a date. Lumen didn't hear his mom's answer but decided he didn't want to know.

Sunday night rolled by, and Alice ordered pizza because she was too tired to cook. It was a lazy Sunday night for them. Lumen decided to finish the puzzle he and Sofia had gotten halfway through. Doing so reminded him of his date on Friday coming up. It was going to be a busy week for Lumen.

After the puzzle, he decided to head to his room to practice with a glass of water. He was able to make it vibrate quicker than he had been able to before and it was taking less effort. Alec hadn't told him anything yet about where to go or what to bring. The ring on his finger was hardly noticeable. It felt like it belonged there. He wondered if he needed his "safe place" set up yet. After the fire, Lumen wasn't sure if his house was the best idea.

After some thought, Lumen decided to go to bed. He would rather be well rested for tomorrow than to stress about what he did and didn't need.

The day came and went as usual. Alec came back to school. Apparently, he had decided not to limit his options and would keep going to school for the time being. Lumen wasn't sure what he meant by that but agreed he should stay in school. *No bullies today*, Lumen thought to himself as he got to school. Lumen was pretty sure they were giving him a break on their parents' orders since his house almost burned down. He saw Sofia twice, and both times they hugged and asked each other how the day had been thus far. Lumen felt it was natural and liked how it had been going so far. Both times Alec asked when Lumen was going to ask her to be his girlfriend.

"You better ask her quick before I make a move."

"Shut up, Alec," Lumen replied quickly as Alec laughed.

Lumen had to plan that out. The thought of asking her to be his girlfriend made him nauseous. It was way too much pressure.

When he got home, he found money on the kitchen table, meaning Alice was back at work. Lumen was okay with it tonight; it was a perfect night to disappear for a few hours to Bonumalus.

He went to *La Dernier Piece*, of course, and had his favorite meal. He headed home and decided that he would dress extra warm because he figured he would be in Entropolis for his classes. Lumen looked at the time.

"7:33."

He figured now was a good time. He decided to head to Allister's cabin. Alec still hadn't told him where to go, and he forgot to ask.

He bundled up, opened a window, checked to make sure his ring was still on his index finger, told Wrigley he would be back and to "be a good dog"; he jumped through.

Lumen landed in Allister's cabin. No one was there.

"What the . . ."

The fire was smoldering. *Where was everybody?* He had no idea where to go and decided to wait it out. Lumen walked to Allister's study area. He looked down at his desk and saw what appeared to be his latest drawing. It was a remarkably realistic drawing of Allister sitting by the fire with a black cat wearing a red vest sitting by his feet. Lumen assumed it was Janis. He wasn't sure if the drawing was any good or just plain weird. He set the picture down and looked at all different sizes of frames filled Allister's pictures that lined the wall. There were a lot of him and Janis as well as him with some random people he had never seen before. One picture featured a lady with what appeared to be tree roots for clothing. She had brown skin and bright brown eyes that glowed in the sunlight. She had rosy cheeks and just a couple freckles on each of them. Her long black hair was held back by some sort of bandana. She had her right arm around Allister, and with a large wooden staff in her left hand. Lumen could see some sort of very intricate design carved into the staff. There was a bald man on the other side of Allister. He was wearing a darker shade of a saffron robe with a red sash across his chest to his stomach that had a black symbol on it near the shoulder. Lumen recognized the symbol from his ring. It was a black circle with three vertical wavy black lines in the middle. The robe went down to the man's ankles, and he was wearing worn, strapped sandals. It looked like he was missing a front tooth, but he had a friendly face. His skin was tan, and his left ear was pierced with a red gauge, while his right ear had a hole where a gauge may have been before. The three seemed friendly with one another. The detail in the drawing was meticulous and intricate. Allister really was a phenomenal drawer.

At that moment, Allister walked through the cabin door holding some logs.

Lumen jumped and tried to act like he wasn't just snooping around Allister's study.

"Well hello there, Lu. What are you doing here? You're going to miss the orientation."

"I'm not sure where to go. Alec never told me . . ." Lumen felt he had done something wrong and was pink again.

"Oh that, Alec. Great kid, can be very forgetful sometimes. Have to keep on that one," Allister chuckled as he tossed the logs into the fireplace, snapped his fingers, and a fire ignited. He turned and looked at Lumen with a soft smile. Lumen felt a familiar warmth and couldn't help but smile back.

"Oh right, here you go. I'll be down there soon to speak with you all. Excited to kick off the new year. I think we have a lot of bright students coming in," Allister said as he waved and opened a window. "Off you go."

Lumen waved awkwardly to Allister and stepped through.

He emerged into an area with a large group of boys and girls who were dressed like Lumen. They stood in a shallow quarry made of light-colored stone, surrounded by four pillars that held up a giant piece of circular stone. There was something completely different behind each pillar. Beyond one of the pillars was a heavily wooded area made up of more shrubbery and plants than Lumen had never seen, aside from his time on Mighty Falls Island. There were a few wooden cabins, covered in ivy, near the quarry but beyond that was heavy forestry. Behind another pillar was a vast desert. There was sand as far as Lumen could see, with only a few huts distributed in the landscape. The huts, Lumen guessed, were made of different colored sheets of metal. At another pillar contained an area that seemed to be covered entirely in clouds--Lumen couldn't see what was on that side. The fourth and last pillar stood at the forefront of an area that looked similar to Entropolis. It was a snowy environment with some pine-looking trees and a mountain far in the distance. Everything was covered in snow. There were a few cabins here as well, all of which had icicles hanging from the roofs.

Lumen found it odd that these areas were not separated by walls or barriers of any kind. It was like an imaginary line had been drawn between the four areas. The snow touched the sand of the desert, the sand of the desert bled into the clouds, and the clouds poured just slightly into the forest. The quarry appeared to be where all the lands met.

Alec approached Lumen.

"There you are. I was wondering when you'd show up."

Lumen scoffed at Alec.

"You didn't tell me anything, man. I went to Allister's cabin. Luckily he showed up to open a window to come here."

Alec gritted his teeth together.

"Oooooo, my bad. I forgot, had a lot going on the past few days. Well, follow me; come meet your fellow Eauges. Oh, and welcome to the Paxum."

Chapter 9 - Class Begins

L umen followed Alec through the crowd of people. Most looked like him: not from Bonumalus. There were a few that were dressed oddly, in Lumen's opinion. He noticed a couple of younger children dressed like the Eauge people of Entropolis, with the ragged maroon and wolf-gray scraps of cloth sewn together with large boots. Lumen thought they were overdressed; it wasn't even cold in there. He passed by a young girl that was dressed like the bald man from Allister's drawing. She said goodbye to her parents, who were bald and dressed like the man from the picture. Lumen wondered if all their people shaved their heads at some point as the little girl's head was not yet shaved. He passed an older man saying goodbye to a young boy, both of which had what appeared to be tree roots grown over their bodies, seemingly functioning like clothing. They looked similar to the woman Lumen saw in Allister's drawing. The boy started to cry, and his father walked away. He stood there with his outstretched hand, reaching for his father. A woman dressed like him came over to console him. The built, brown lady, covered in tree roots, picked him up and said something that made him laugh. She turned toward Lumen, and he recognized her from the drawing. She was just as beautiful in person. She held out her staff in front of the boy's face, and a small flower grew from it. The lady plucked it and handed it to the boy who laughed, appearing to have forgotten that his father left him there.

Lumen continued following Alec and got close enough to ask him a question.

"Hey, who is that lady? I've seen her in Allister's drawings before." He pointed to the lady holding the boy.

"Oh, that's Sasha. She is the head of the Liros at the Paxum. Allister is good friends with the three other leaders here."

Lumen looked at Sasha one more time, who was also looking back at him. She nodded in Lumen's direction. Lumen didn't know how to react, so he looked back toward Alec and continued following him.

They approached a group of four standing together. It looked like they either came here by themselves, as Lumen did, or their parents had already left them. They were all dressed *normal* in Lumen's eyes, which made him feel comfortable.

"Hey gang, this is Lumen. He will be training to be an Eauge as well. Let's not be shy; let's introduce ourselves."

Lumen turned towards a boy of Asian descent standing with his hand out.

"Hi, I am Yu Shi. You are . . .?"

Lumen grabbed Yu's hand and shook it.

"Lumen, I'm Lumen Haaken. Nice to meet you."

Lumen turned to the next person.

"Hi, I'm Till. Till Rief. Nice to meet you, Lumen."

Till had a very welcoming smile, and it made Lumen blush slightly. He couldn't help but think she was very pretty. She wore a sundress with sneakers and had wavy blonde hair. He wasn't able to say anything back to her, nodded, and moved to the next one. He felt his ring warm his index finger.

"Hi, I'm Lumen." Lumen held out his hand to another boy in the group.

This boy was slow to grab Lumen's hand back and shook it very briefly. Lumen looked at him, but the boy looked away. He seemed angry about something.

"That's Chester. He doesn't talk much. Don't worry about it," Alec told Lumen.

Lumen shrugged and turned towards the last person.

"Hi, I'm Lumen."

"Nice to meet ya. I'm Lucy." Lumen thought Lucy looked a bit quirky. She had a fanny pack on with a flannel tied around her waist. She wore a tee shirt with a band name he had never heard of, *The Horses*. On her shirt were three horses playing instruments, dressed in human clothing. She had the same shoes on as Lumen.

Alec stepped into the middle of the circle they had created.

"Great, now that we are all acquainted, let's check out where you will be training to start. Let me be clear, most of us will only learn here," Alec pointed to the pillar in the Paxum that led them to where the snowy expanse was.

"You will have a few classes in the other areas, but don't get used to it. Most of us here are only capable of mastering one skill. We can't all be the great Allister Allvetande. Trying to juggle more than one can be overwhelming and ultimately lead to you being unable to master anything."

Lumen was okay with that. Being able to move water like he had seen Allister and Alec do would be rewarding enough in itself.

They approached the pillar. Lumen noticed the intricate carvings on the pillar. He noticed the symbol he had seen on the flags in Entropolis. There were several people carved into the pillar, people Lumen had never seen before. They were all dressed similar to the people of Entropolis. Toward the bottom of the pillar were the words *Intuition & Compassion* engraved.

In that moment he felt a rush of the air around him move. It felt as if the air was continuously vibrating around him. He looked around. Nobody seemed to know what was going on. He looked behind to see Allister standing in between the clouds and the desert areas, a step above the quarry where most everyone else was. Janis stood on his hind two legs on Allister's right. And to the left were the two others from the drawing, Sasha and the bald, extremely tan man. Lumen was curious if the man had ever heard of sunscreen and if his skin had begun to turn to leather.

Allister held out his hands. Lumen was pretty sure Allister was making the air vibrate around him. Allister spoke.

"Welcome to the Paxum!"

His voice boomed through the quarry. It sounded like he was speaking through a microphone. Lumen looked around for speakers but couldn't find any. Till tapped him on the shoulder.

"It's the air; he's knows a trick to make the sound amplified by vibrating the air. Pretty cool, ain't it?"

Lumen blushed again.

"Yeah, it is." He got a warm feeling in his gut.

The room erupted with cheers after Allister said this.

"Quiet down, quiet down. If you don't know already, I am Allister. I am the head of the Eauge group. I want to welcome everyone here; we are all very excited to get this new year started. I want to tell my fellow Eauge that we are known for our intuition and compassion. That is something we pride ourselves on. Let us not forget the longstanding traditions, but also let us not ignore what lies ahead. The two will meet in a time and space that requires both, and we must not be ill-prepared."

The people in Lumen's group started cheering and clapping. Lumen half-heartedly joined in. He was sort of put off by the statement and wasn't sure what that could possibly mean.

"Very kind of you."

Allister nodded toward the Eauge pillar.

"To my right is Janis. He is head of the Aeris caste."

Janis stepped forward and waved. A group of people standing near the cloud area erupted with cheer. There were more of them than there was in the Eauge group. Janis spoke without an accent.

"I look forward to working with you all! I can't wait to get a new year started. We have some exciting new individuals beginning here today. I look forward to teaching you all, as well as learning from you."

The group cheered again.

"We, as the Aeris, are intellectuals and curious of our surroundings. Let us remember that as we move forward to

143

always use our strengths to help ourselves, as well as those around us."

Janis stepped back, and the group by the cloud pillar of the Paxum erupted into cheer again. Allister put his hand out to the left of him, and Sasha stepped forward.

"Hello, my friends."

The group by the forest pillar erupted into cheer this time. Again this group was bigger than Lumen's.

"I am Sasha. I will be working with the Liros group for the most part. I want to remind everyone here that we are all friends. We are here to not only master our own abilities, but also to learn to work together and in harmony. We are practical and grounded individuals. We stay within ourselves to bring out the best. Let us have a great year."

Sasha stepped back, the group by the forest erupted in cheer, and the bald man stepped forward to speak.

"Hello all, I am Aiden." Aiden had some more flare than the other introductions and shot a few flames above his head by thrusting his fists upwards.

The group by the desert erupted into cheer, more so than the other groups. Lumen felt a wave of warm air come from their direction.

"Thank you, thank you. I want to reiterate what Sasha said. We are not only here to master your own skills; we are here to learn from one another, to work with one another, and to learn each other's past to keep us from repeating the bad while continuing to embrace the good. Let's not forget to have fun either. Us Ignous are full of enthusiasm and inspiration; we must use them for the greater good. Thank you." He shot another flame into the air. Lumen thought he was obnoxious.

The quarry erupted with cheers, and Allister signaled for them to quiet down.

"I want to introduce you to one more person before I let you go for the night."

An older gentleman, wearing an odd suit, stepped up the quarry to where Allister was standing.

"This is Pare Bant. He is on the board of Imperiums."

Pare thanked Allister and took off his top hat. The man had just a few wisps of hair and patted down the few remaining. He adjusted his tie, which appeared to be made of ivy. Lumen was confused if the man was from Bonumalus or just trying to fit in.

"Thank you, Allister. I want everyone here to give Al a round of applause. This is the fourth year the Paxum has been open. Allister came to the board about 11 years ago with the idea of opening a schooling center for the people of Bonumalus to teach right from wrong and how to use our power properly. He, Sasha, Janis and Aiden came together to form this, the Paxum, where we can all safely learn to use our power, as well as Bonumalus' past and present. You wouldn't be here without the work of these four. Let's give them all a round of applause for what this place has become."

Pare stepped back and clapped and the rest of the quarry followed suit. Allister and the others all put their hands up for thanks and bowed.

"Thank you, Pare. Okay, if you are staying here at the Paxum, please head to your quarters and unpack. If you are not, you can head back home whenever you would like." Allister waved his arm, and the air stopped vibrating.

Lumen went over to Alec.

"What is the Imperium?"

"They're like the governors of Bonumalus. They control what comes in and out of our world to yours . . . Have you seen Chester? He disappeared halfway through the introductions."

Lumen looked around at all the people moving.

"No, sorry."

"Okay, well everyone else in our group is staying at the Paxum, except for you and Lucy, so I need to find him and show everyone their quarters. You can get home right?"

"Yeah, I'll be fine. See you later."

Alec jogged away and yelled for the others to follow him. Lumen thought Alec was really in his element in Bonumalus. Same great looks and leadership without the sweating.

Lumen turned away. Most of the people had left. Allister opened a window, and the four leaders and Pare went through, presumably to Allister's cabin.

145

Lumen stood around until everyone was gone. They had all gone to their respective areas of the Paxum. It became quiet. Lumen looked around at his surroundings. This quarry was incredible. How Allister and the others were able to build these four sections around the quarry was incomprehensible to Lumen. How did they get the clouds to remain where they were in that section of the quarry? How did the snow not pour over into the forest, and how were the trees contained to just that parcel? It was beyond Lumen's understanding, but he didn't care. He felt like he belonged there. For the first time in a long time, Lumen felt comfortable where he was. Lumen felt his ring get warm again, and then someone tapped him on the shoulder from behind. He turned around, and there was Till.

"Hey, whatcha still doing here?"

Lumen was again perplexed at Till. She was beautiful. Her smile really caught Lumen's attention.

"Uh, I'm just, uh . . . looking around before I head home."

"It's amazing isn't it?"

Lumen nodded and gulped his saliva before speaking.

"Yeah, it's unbelievable that they were able to build something like this."

"Bonumalus' possibilities reach much further than that of where we are from. We are lucky enough to experience it."

"You're from Earth? Wait, is this Earth? Where is Bonumalus exactly?" Lumen asked curiously.

"Yes, a little town called New York City, not sure if you've ever heard of it. Bonum, I would say is between Earth and the heavens."

Till winked at Lumen. Lumen's heart dropped. He thought of another question quickly.

"How did you find out about the lights and your abilities?"

"Allister actually found me in a burning building. The building I was living in caught fire. I was the only one to survive. My family was gone just like that. . . Allister says I survived because I subconsciously covered myself with water."

Lumen's eyes widened. He wasn't sure how to react. He changed the subject.

"I'm sorry to hear that . . . What about the lights? They didn't bother you growing up? I was a diagnosed schizophrenic because of the way they distracted me."

Lumen wasn't sure why he told Till that.

"Oh yeah, they were there. I learned to ignore them at a young age. It's like your nose. You can always see it but your mind blocks it out when it processes what is in front of you."

Lumen focused for a moment on seeing his nose. He realized she was right.

"I wasn't lucky enough to learn that growing up," Lumen said as he rubbed the back of his neck.

"Well you're lucky enough to be here now. I'm glad you're here," Till said.

Till grabbed his hand. Lumen looked at her in confusion and turned pink again.

"Hey, what are you two doing?"

Lumen let go of Till's hand quickly and turned to see Alec walking toward them.

"Till you're supposed to be moving into your quarters. Go ahead now. You should get some rest."

Till turned to Lumen and waved as she headed back. Lumen waved back.

Alec waited until she was out of earshot.

"What the heck was that about?" Alec said as he pushed Lumen softly.

"What do you mean? We were just talking."

"I saw you two holding hands. What about Sofia, man? You can't have a girlfriend in both worlds, it's still wrong you know?"

"She's not my girlfriend yet. And I don't know what that was. She came up here and started talking to me about her house burning down, the lights. . .and then grabbed my hand. I hardly said anything."

Alec laughed at Lumen.

"I'm just giving you a hard time, man. But seriously, you should pick one. Big man now. Went from no friends and never ever speaking to a girl to having to choose between two."

"I don't have to choose between girls. I'm going to ask Sofia to be my girlfriend. I don't even know Till really. I met her an hour ago."

Lumen imagined for just a moment holding hands with Till and kissing her. His heart was racing.

"Good idea, man. I can tell Sofia really likes you anyway. Have you thought about how you'll ask her?"

Lumen's thoughts went straight to everything that could go wrong with asking Sofia. His date was on Friday. He needed to plan something out.

"No, I have no idea what I'm doing."

Alec laughed again.

"It's okay dude, she likes you. Don't freak out about it. Just be yourself."

Lumen gulped and told Alec he needed to go. He looked around one more time and waved to Alec.

"See you tomorrow."

Lumen imagined where he wanted to be, opened his eyes, and opened a window. He stepped through and was standing in his room. Wrigley was asleep on the bed. He looked at the clock.

10:17 PM.

"Let's go, Wrig. Bathroom time."

Lumen took Wrigley out and went to bed. He was exhausted from the day. Paxum was an incredible place, and he couldn't wait to return. He had a lot to learn and think about. He kept thinking of Till grabbing his hand. She had such a pretty smile. It was burned into his memory. Lumen tried not to think about it. When Till popped into his mind, he decided to imagine Sofia's smile instead.

He sighed. "This is way more stressful than having my head shoved in a toilet. You know what I mean?"

Wrigley turned his head sideways to try and understand but just trotted away and peed on the newly planted flowers.

"You know Mom would be upset if she saw you do that. C'mon, back inside."

Lumen had a hard time sleeping. Till and asking Sofia to be his girlfriend weighed heavily on his mind.

When he finally fell asleep, he dreamt of himself somehow standing between the Paxum and his home. In the Paxum, Till was pulling his arm to follow her to a deep and snowy expanse. Lumen looked in her direction and could see snow falling behind her amongst pine trees. The snow had a gray tint to it and Lumen felt an odd warmth in the air. In his home was Sofia pulling his arm to follow her to his living room. The TV was on and a puzzle was sprawled out over the coffee table. Wrigley lay on the ground, chewing on a block of ice, and his mom was cooking something in the kitchen. Lumen couldn't decide who to follow and ended up waking up in a cold sweat before falling asleep again to the same unfinished dream. The dream never led to anything, just two girls pulling Lumen's arms.

Lumen woke up to Alice yelling.

"Lu! Lumen! School starts in 5 minutes!"

Lumen jumped out of bed, threw on some clothes, ran to the kitchen, and quickly asked his mom why she was awake.

"I just got home. Sarah called in sick, so I stayed overtime."

Lumen took the banana out of her hand and ran out the door.

"Get some sleep!" he yelled before the door closed shut. He came back immediately after closing it.

"Actually, Can I get a ride?"

Lumen was 8 minutes late, the first time that had ever happened to him. The school counselor smiled when Lumen said he overslept. She handed him a tardy slip.

It was a typical day at school, and the day passed quickly. Lumen did get pushed into a wall when passing Blake, but no swirly. Lumen could live with that. The fire must be wearing off on the bullies conscious.

He saw Sofia twice. Both times they hugged and asked how their days were going. Both times Lumen felt guilty over Till. He wasn't sure why, nothing really happened. She grabbed his hand, he didn't do anything. Plus, he and Sofia weren't even technically dating yet.

The school day went by and ended, and Lumen headed home. He still wasn't sure about when he should return to Bonumalus; Alec hadn't told him a time to be there. He decided he would head back at 7:30 that night.

His mom was still sleeping when he got home. He decided to help around the house; he folded the clothes, washed some dishes, swept the kitchen floor, walked Wrigley, and planted one of the new flowers his mom bought. It was the same kind of flower that was left behind in the fire, a thistle.

"I decided to plant one to remind us of how lucky we are to still have this house," Alice said as she popped her head through the back door, wearing a robe with her hair up in a bun.

"Good idea. Maybe it will warn us of an intruder next time."

Alice laughed.

"Hopefully, there won't be a next time."

Lumen agreed in his head and finished planting the thistle. He poked his finger on one of the thorns and immediately yelped, "Ow!"

Alice popped her head out, laughing again.

"Can't get too close to them; the beauty will bring ya in, but it'll really bite ya once you get too close."

"Yeah, I see that now."

They both went back inside and Alice cooked some dinner for the two of them. Lumen had to figure out what to tell his mom tonight so that he could sneak off to the Paxum. She wouldn't be at work tonight.

"Hey, I, uh, think I'm going to go study at Alec's tonight."

Alice raised her eyebrows.

"Since when do you study? I'm not sure how you pass all your classes, but I've never seen you study."

Lumen thought quickly on his feet.

"It's to help Alec. Plus, this history class is kind of hard. I could use it."

Alice nodded in agreement.

"Okay, do you need a ride?"

Lumen thought of another lie.

"No, I think I'll run there. I haven't got a run in lately."

"Okay, whatever you say. Just be home by 10 please."

Lumen nodded. He never liked lying to his mom but had become good at it the last few weeks.

Lumen helped clean up the dishes and grabbed all of his school stuff, an extra jacket, and made sure he had his ring on.

He put on running shorts with a big jacket and a beanie. He had to at least make the lie look real.

"Bye, Mom!"

"Be safe please! Home by ten, don't forget! You better have your medicine handy!" Alice yelled from her room. She didn't even see Lumen walk out.

"So much for the shorts . . ."

Lumen jogged a few houses down the block. It was cold. The snow had already melted from last week, but it was definitely cold enough to snow again. The sky was full of dark, ominous clouds and looked poised to start snowing again any minute.

Lumen looked around when he was a block away from his house. The lights began to appear. He ran onto the side of a random house's yard, glanced around to make sure no one was looking, thought of the Paxum, quickly pieced together the lights, and opened a window. He stepped through.

Lumen landed in the quarry. It was very crowded again with what looked like even more people than yesterday. Lumen saw the man from the luxem shop in Entropolis, Nemo, talking to one of the new kids. He was showing the kid a watch, presumably a luxem. The man nodded towards Lumen. Lumen was still confused as to how this man knew who he was.

Lumen headed toward his group near the part of the Paxum where his training would be. He was nervous about seeing Till. Alec bumped into him.

"Hey man, you're on time."

"Yeah, nobody has told me a time to show up yet."

"Well now is good."

151

"Okay . . ." Lumen wasn't sure if that meant to show up at this time from now on.

Alec chuckled.

"Yes, 7:30 is good. Monday through Friday. Saturdays will be longer days. We'll start first thing in the morning and go until four or five. Make sure you get your story straight with your mom."

Lumen didn't answer as he thought about what he could possibly tell his mom.

"Also, have you set up your luxem yet? There will be a class regarding travel. It's a good idea to have that set up."

"I can't figure out where to set it to . . . It was going to be my house but that almost got burnt down, so I prefer to keep my mom and the house out of this," Lumen said.

"Yeah, man, I get that. Set it for Allister's cabin. He wouldn't mind that."

Lumen felt the ring warm up. He glanced down at it.

"Go ahead, man. Open a window to Allister's cabin; the luxem will know what to do."

Lumen didn't know how a ring would know what to do, but he listened to Alec. He focused on Allister's cabin, moved the lights and a window opened. Lumen looked at Alec, and Alec signaled for him to hold the ring in front of him. Lumen held his hand out in front of him. The window shimmered and funneled toward Lumen's hand. In a matter of seconds, the window had been swallowed by the ring and was gone from sight.

"What the . . . how do I get it out?"

"Don't worry; it will know when to open up for you. You're good to go now."

Lumen nodded but still wasn't sure how exactly this worked. He took the ring off to hold it up in the light. He didn't see anything on the ring that could possibly hold light. It didn't make sense. Then again, neither did any of this here. Lumen shrugged it off.

They walked over to the rest of the group. Alec and Lumen both said hello to the group. Till came up behind Lumen and jumped on his back.

"Uh, hello there."

"Hi, Lu!"

She jumped down and came around to hug Lumen. Lumen looked around the group, and everyone was staring at them. Alec had his eyes opened very wide and looked as though he was trying not to laugh at Lumen.

Lumen mouthed "shut up" to Alec.

"All right, group. We are going to head to the cabin right over there." Alec pointed to the nearest cabin in the snow.

"Why are there so many more people here today?" Yu asked.

Alec looked around him.

"Oh right, yesterday was mostly new students. The more seasoned students were not required to show up yesterday."

Lumen looked at his group, and he counted five people. Someone was missing from the group he met yesterday.

"Hey, are we missing someone?"

Alec turned around and counted five also.

"Lu, Lucy, Till, Yu . . . Where is Chester?"

At that moment a window opened in the middle of their group, and Chester fell through.

He gathered himself, fixed his zip-up jacket and wiped off his jeans. His white shirt looked to have a blood stain on it. Lumen didn't remember his head being shaved yesterday.

Chester looked around at everyone looking at him.

"What? I had stuff to do. I'm here now, aren't I?"

Alec regained everyone's attention.

"Great, let's head this way."

Everyone followed him up out of the quarry, into the snow. The snow wasn't that thick and was easy to walk through. Lumen was surprised. The trees leading to the cabin were covered in snow. Overhead, the clouds were a calming shade of gray. The group was in awe of the surroundings. The trees looked like pine trees on a postcard; they were picture perfect. Lumen kicked a pinecone that was perfectly square. He was awestruck by the perfectly cubed pinecone. Lumen caught up with Alec after Till attempted to grab his hand and missed.

"Dude, this place is incredible."

"Yeah, Allister is an artist when it comes to this stuff."

They walked into the log cabin. There was nothing inside except for a desk with a lady filling out some papers. She had bright red hair with lots of freckles, and was dressed like the rest of the people from Entropolis. Smiling, she stood up when the students started to file in.

"Welcome, welcome! We are very excited for you all to get started today! I am Gretchen. Nice to meet you all! It is my job to watch this cabin. We call the area down there the Genaqua. Before you go down to the Genaqua today, I would like to tell you that there is no light travel down here. Even if you were to try, it wouldn't work. You come in through that door and leave through that door. Me, or another watch, will always be here monitoring. Everyone understand?"

They all nodded their heads. Lumen was curious how they could limit light travel there and what she meant by "down there."

"Great, that's all I have for you guys! Have a great rest of your day!"

Lumen whispered to Alec, "How is it that no one can use light travel in here?"

"Allister is a genius, man. I don't know how he did it, but it's true. You can't jump from here."

Alec got the group's attention.

"Thanks, Gretchen. Okay, everyone over here." Alec signaled for them all to go to the back of the cabin.

"Everyone keep your hands and feet within the platform at all times," Alec said while trying not to laugh at his own lame joke.

Lumen and the other new students in the group looked at one another in confusion. Alec grabbed the chain hanging from the lamp and pulled it down. The light turned on, and the floor they were standing on descended down. Till came to Lumen's side and held his arm. He didn't know how to react but was more curious about where they were headed. He would deal with Till later, he thought.

The floor descended slowly, only lit by the small lamp Alec had used to start the descent. Lumen looked up, and the light from the cabin began to fade. He wondered nervously where they were headed. Eventually one of the walls opened up and they could see where they were going. They landed on the ground and stepped off the platform--Lumen noticed right away that there were many more Eauge pupils present there than in the Paxum. They landed on the end of a courtyard made of smooth, peppery stone. The courtyard opened up to a huge corridor with a large statue towards the end of the stone walkway. The statue was of a man Lumen did not recognize. There were large stone buildings on either side, each with several unopened doors and signs above them. Lumen peeked inside one as the group looked around. He observed what appeared to be a normal classroom with a chalkboard. The next room had nothing but a giant tank of water in the middle of it, extending from the stone floor to the ceiling. There weren't any desks or chairs inside; Lumen wondered what happened in there. On the other side of the corridor, Lumen guessed, was a convenience store, as students were walking out with bottled drinks. The corridor itself was at least a quarter mile long before it opened to a tundra. Behind the snow, that went on for at least a hundred feet, was a dense forest.

Lumen was confused about how there could be an area like that thriving underground. He got to the end of the enormous corridor and saw that the wooded area opened up. The entirety of forest wasn't covered by a ceiling like Lumen expected. Instead, it seemed to be clear from any walls at all. There was cloud cover above, just as there was in Entropolis.

"Wait, what? We went underground, how does that work?" Lumen asked, befuddled.

"I told you, man, Allister is a genius. Just appreciate it. The Illustra Forest," Alec pointed to the dense forest beyond the snow, "to the Genaqua, to the Paxum. It's pure art."

Lumen looked around once more and saw a group of kids having a snowball fight, only they weren't scooping the snowballs up from the ground. They were just holding their hands out as a snowball quickly formed in their hands. One of the girls involved hid behind a stone wall forming snowballs and creating piles for her team to use. Still observing in awe, Lumen laid eyes on a young man juggling three spurts of water into the air, only he wasn't using his hands. The three little spurts were simply moving about in a circular motion as the young man's head followed. He thrust his head down, and the three spurts of water immediately froze and slammed into the snow below.

Lumen couldn't wait to be able to do some of this stuff, all he could do then was make some water vibrate gently in a glass.

"It's amazing isn't it? I don't know how they created this place, but it's beautiful that people like us have a space to safely learn," Till spoke up.

"Yeah, I guess it is." Lumen looked at Till on his arm, suddenly realizing she had been there that entire time. She was smiling up at him.

Alec whistled.

"Alright, gang, over here. You guys will be starting in this classroom. This is your core class. You will all have this class together here every day to start. Your schedules may vary from there."

Alec pointed for them to head into the normal looking classroom. They all filled in, but Alec didn't follow.

"Hey, where are you going?" Lumen asked.

"I have my own classes to get to. Allister wanted me to help you guys out. Good luck, man. I'll see you in a little bit." Alec jogged off to the other side of the corridor, across the stone path between the two large stone buildings, near the statue, and into another classroom. Lumen watched all the other kids trot into their classrooms.

"Excuse me, Lumen. Could you close the door so we can get started?"

Lumen turned around to see a man standing at the chalkboard, wearing the typical Eauge attire. He had long black and gray hair tied up in a bun with a long gray beard with a massive scar over his left eye. Lumen thought he must have been getting hot in there.

"Yes, sorry." Lumen closed the door and looked for an open seat. There were more kids in there than there were in his group earlier. Till waved for him to sit by her; she saved a seat for him. Lumen looked around, but there weren't any other seats. He counted fifteen students in the room.

"Thank you. Okay, well, welcome to your first day for some of you! And to the others, welcome back."

Lumen looked around to see who may have been a returning student. He hoped to not follow their path.

"So, this is your core class. You will start each day in here. What we do here is go over Bonumalus' history as well as learn to use light travel properly. I will function as a mentor to you all in that. I will help guide you into a field of work that suits you. If you have any questions you can come to me. Now, let's get started."

The man was very serious in his tone. He did not seem to be someone who joked around. Still, Lumen found the man to be calming and welcoming. He felt he could go to the man for help. Till raised her hand.

"Yes, Till?"

"What do we call you?"

The class laughed softly. The professor didn't even crack a smile as he turned and wrote on the chalkboard.

Mr. Durum

"Any other questions before we get started?"

No one else raised their hand.

"Great. Take out your copy of *A History and Time of Bonumalus.*. I expect chapter one has already been completed. Take out your notebooks."

Lumen looked around. Everyone had a bag with notebooks and books already.

"Thanks a lot, Alec," Lumen murmured under his breath.

"It's okay. I have extra," Till handed him a notebook and pencil.

"Thanks."

Mr. Durum spoke up again.

"Does anyone know the four castes of Bonumalus?"

Lucy's hand shot up.

Lumen got through the rest of the week in one piece. His classes had started off well in Bonumalus. On Wednesday, he had Water Bending class. His teacher, Ms. Flecter, put on a

157

show of moving water in all different shapes and sizes. She tossed a bowl of water in the air towards the students and stopped it before drenching them. As the water hovered above, she formed it into the shape of a giant octopus that sprayed a mist at the students. The students clapped with awe as Ms. Flecter snapped and turned the octopus into steam. Most of the class that day was just a presentation of how well Ms. Flecter could bend water.

"Real show off, don't ya think?" Lucy told Lumen at one point during the presentation. They laughed together.

On Thursday, he had Pluviam class.

"What could Pluviam class possibly be about?" Lumen asked Yu.

"I'm not sure. Can't be as interesting as water bending though. Ms.Flecter was amazing," Yu said.

They learned that Pluviam was the ability to make it rain. There was yet another display for most of the class as Professor Jeremiah made miniature rainstorms appear. Professor Jeremiah did not come across as the humble type and was very stern.

"You will call me Professor Jeremiah or Professor J. Do not speak unless spoken to. Unpreparedness will be met with punishment. Understand?"

The class all nodded. They didn't dare speak.

"Good. You there. Tell me, why doesn't it rain indoors?"

He pointed at Chester who almost instantly turned red.

"Uh, there isn't enough water to evaporate indoors?"

Professor J snapped and made a tiny storm appear over Chester's head, which then proceeded to rain onto Chester. Chester ran out of the classroom immediately. Till was the only one laughing.

"Quiet! This should be an example to you all on the repercussions of being unprepared. You all must know the three commandments in Bonumalus. Can anyone tell me the three commandments?"

The class remained silent and no one raised their hand. J snarled as he tucked a black necklace under his garments.

"One, do not show your abilities to anyone on Earth. Two, do not create something that you cannot control. Three, do not use the elements with the intention to kill. These are to be followed by everyone in Bonumalus and on Earth. Even the most minor infraction can lead to severe punishment. Note that even the criminals of Bonumalus follow these rules. You will learn how important they are as time goes on."

The class went on with Professor J yelling at the class and creating tiny storms to scare or embarrass students who didn't know the answers to his questions. He seemed to get a lot of enjoyment out of it.

Friday came. Lumen was exhausted as he hadn't adjusted to his new life yet. He felt like he was constantly in school. His mom had been working unusually long hours, so he hadn't had to lie to her. He also had two tests that week and a couple homework assignments due in his normal school classes. He forgot to finish one of them and received his first zero ever-- he wasn't worried though, he had over 100% in the class. On Friday, he had a literature test. He fell asleep the second he sat down after turning the test in. The bell didn't even jar him awake. His teacher woke him up to let him know it was time to go.

He mumbled to himself on the way out.

"Crap, sorry Mr . . . thanks." The teacher just waved goodbye.

Lumen ran into Sofia on his way to his next class.

"Hey Lu, you okay? You seem tired or somethin'. You going to be able to make it tonight?"

Lumen completely forgot about his date tonight. He also forgot he had been planning to ask her to be his girlfriend. He thought of a lie quickly.

"Oh yeah, uh . . . I'm not sure. I'm not feeling too well. Can I let you know a little later?"

Sofia smiled.

"Of course. Don't worry about it if you don't feel well. I hope you feel better."

She hugged him tight, and they departed in opposite directions. Lumen wasn't sure why he didn't just tell her he couldn't. Not only was he exhausted, he had to go to

Bonumalus tonight for class. He was planning on taking a nap before class but decided that he could maybe hang with Sofia instead. He suddenly thought of Till. She had kept up her antics all week, somehow always ending up with her arm around Lumen or holding his hand when she was scared or surprised. Lumen never thought he would get annoyed of a girl giving him attention like she was, but Till managed to do so in a short amount of time. And the smile, it was burned into his memory.

Chapter 10 - Snow Day

Lumen stared out of a classroom window and the ground was covered in snow. The principal of Bromide High made an announcement over the intercom.

"We are going to continue to get heavy amounts of snow; it came a little earlier than expected today. I advise that you all call your parents or guardians to come pick you up. If you take the bus, it will be leaving in 15 minutes. Please get home safe. The storm should continue through the weekend. We will let you know about class next week."

Lumen wondered if someone from Bonumalus made it snow here. He deliriously decided to walk home because being Eauge meant he should be able to survive a measly snow storm. On his way out, he ran into Sofia.

"You're walking? Don't be crazy, you'll get buried out here. My dad is here, we can take you home or you can come over now if you're feeling better . . ."

Lumen thought for a moment. He could go there now and leave on time for Bonumalus. This was perfect, he decided.

"Yeah, I'll come over. I feel fine."

Sofia smiled and grabbed his hand.

"C'mon, my dad is right over here."

Lumen remembered his plans to ask Sofia to be his girlfriend. He wasn't sure how he would do it yet.

The snow was really coming down, and Sofia's father complained about not being able to see the car in front of him. Sofia held onto Lumen's hand tight during the car ride.

Sofia's dad dropped them off, mentioning he needed to take care of some things at work and would be right back.

"Don't do anything I wouldn't do," he said to Lumen as they got out of the car. Lumen nodded. He wasn't sure how to react.

They ran inside. Sofia decided they would make some hot chocolate and watch a movie. Lumen was perfectly fine with that. He sat down on the couch and looked around. He didn't realize Sofia's house was so big. She came back in with two steaming cups of hot cocoa.

"Here you go."

"Thanks. I didn't know you were rich," Lumen said.

Sofia giggled.

"I wouldn't say we are rich. My dad does well. He's never around though. You see, he went back to work even in this weather."

"Where's your mom?" Lumen asked.

Lumen saw Sofia's face turn white, and she gulped.

"She passed away last year. It's just been me and my dad since then."

Lumen felt awful for bringing it up. He never heard of that happening. It was quite surprising because news like that got around quickly in that town.

"Oh my gosh, I'm so sorry, Sofia. I had no idea," Lumen said, somewhat embarrassed.

"It's okay. We kept it under wraps. My dad didn't want the whole town to know. It was tough on both of us."

"I get that . . ."

They were both quiet for a moment.

"I never knew my dad. He left before I really remember anything. I know what it's like with a single parent . . . it's tough to say the least but it does get easier." Lumen added, hoping it would help.

"I just miss her mostly. My dad is trying, but he's just not the same. She was caring and loving. My dad is not so good with that stuff," Sofia said with watery eyes.

"Yeah, I bet that's tough . . ."

They sat in silence for a moment again before Sofia suggested a couple of movies to watch. They decided to watch *The Zombie Movie.*

The snow continued to pile up outside while they sat inside sipping on their hot cocoa. Sofia put Lumen's arm around her, and she snuggled up against him. Lumen could feel her body moving on his chest to get comfortable. *This was all I ever needed,* he thought as he smiled. They put in another movie when the zombie one ended. They cooked a frozen pizza that gave the house a pepperoni aroma, drank more hot cocoa, and talked. It was getting closer to having to leave for the Paxum. Lumen needed to make his move quick. He went to the bathroom to rehearse.

He looked in the mirror and said a few lines.

"Sofia, I really like you. Will you be my girlfriend?"

"Will you be with me?"

"Sofia, we should be together. Forever . . . No that's weird."

"I'm just gonna ask her. She likes you, Lu, don't worry." He wondered if they would kiss if she said yes. It made Lumen nauseous, and he sat on the toilet.

There was a beam of light, and a window opened in the bathroom. Alec poked his head through.

"Dude, come here."

Lumen stood up, eyes wide. He whispered.

"Are you insane? Get out of here. Classes don't start for over an hour anyway, it can wait."

He turned on the water so Sofia couldn't hear anything.

Alec's floating head rolled its eyes.

"No, dude, it'll be quick. Class is canceled tonight. Allister needs to speak with you."

Lumen was concerned. He didn't say anything and stepped through. They landed in the Paxum. There weren't any students there, just Allister, Janis, Sasha and Aiden.

"Hello, my boy. Glad to see you are well."

Lumen looked behind Allister. It was the Eauge area of the Paxum. Lumen looked up and saw three trees on fire.

"As you can see, someone set a flame to some of the trees in the Eauge expanse of the Paxum."

Lumen gulped. He wasn't sure what had happened or why Allister had summoned him there.

"We have reason to believe the perpetrator to be the same one that set fire to your house. We believe this person is targeting Eauge students now. You, Lumen, could be a target. You need to keep an eye out for yourself," Allister said calmly

Lumen was befuddled by this.

"A target for what? To kill? Why me?"

Allister looked at the others.

"Well, son, I don't know why you would be targeted--or if you are even being targeted, but we have an idea of what the criminal is trying to do. Follow me."

They stepped out of the quarry into the Eauge expanse and walked to the burning trees. As they approached, Lumen could see something burning on the ground. As he got closer, he could make out what it was.

"Join Us" was burnt into the snow.

"We believe someone is trying to mimic an old foe of the people of Bonumalus," Aiden said to Lumen.

"An old foe? Who?" Lumen asked.

The leaders looked at one another; they seemed uncomfortable answering. Janis looked at Lumen.

"Maldeus. He is the most notorious criminal of Bonumalus. He was killed about 11 years ago. He started a civil war amongst our people. He believed we should be ruling your world, not aiding it. Every once in a while, we get someone who wants to replicate what Maldeus did," Janis told him in his normal voice. Lumen was still confused.

"Why would they be after me? Are they trying to kill me?"

Allister spoke up again.

"No, as you can see from the message, they are trying to recruit for their cause. Why you? We aren't sure. It could be just a coincidence that they chose you to target first. This is probably a message for all of the students here. Luckily, Sasha was here early and caught it before any students did. We canceled today's classes to clean up. We don't want other students getting any ideas."

Lumen didn't know what to make of this threat yet.

"Okay . . . well what should I do?"

"Continue with your normal routine. We don't want the mimic to think they have caused a stir here. We certainly don't want them to think they are scaring anyone. Fear gives them power, remember that. Just be careful, and like I said before, if you see anything suspicious, report it to me immediately," Allister said. Lumen felt like everything would be okay.

"I can do that. How do we know if it is the same person or a group?"

Sasha stepped forward. She held out a flower to Lumen.

"This was left behind."

Lumen recognized immediately that it was a thistle.

"They seem to have a signature for their little stunts," Sasha stated bitterly.

Lumen grabbed it from her and looked at it. He didn't know what this could mean.

"You should get back now. We apologize for interrupting your date," Allister said with a smirk on his face. Lumen got that warm feeling in his gut again.

Lumen waved and headed back to the middle of the quarry with Alec.

"Will classes resume tomorrow?" Lumen asked.

"Yeah, no doubt, they will clean this up quickly. It will be like it didn't even happen. I'm sure they want the day off to try and figure out who is doing this," Alec said.

Lumen looked back at Allister and the others. He saw Aiden step toward the trees and clap his hands firmly above his head. The fires in the trees died out immediately. Sasha pounded her staff on the ground firmly three times, and the trees withered down to the snow. She pounded the staff three more times, and three more trees sprung up where the others were. Alec was right, it was like it never happened.

"Get back to your date now, I'm sure Sofia is wondering what is taking you so long," Alec said.

"Oh yeah, thanks. Keep me in the loop!"

Lumen opened a window quickly and jumped through. He landed in the shower of the bathroom in Sofia's house. Sofia was knocking.

"Lumen . . . Lumen, you in there? Are you okay? Are you sick again? It's okay if you are. I don't mind being around sick people . . ."

Lumen wasn't sure what to say. He didn't know how long Sofia had been there knocking.

"Uh, sorry. No I'm fine, I'll be right out."

"Oh okay . . ."

Lumen splashed some water on his face, unable to believe what had just happened. Someone was targeting him, or at least they might have been. How could Allister expect Lumen to act normal? What if his mom was in danger? Or Wrigley? Or Sofia? He wouldn't even know how to protect them. He turned off the water and walked out of the bathroom and sat back down on the couch.

"You okay?" Sofia asked immediately

"Oh yeah, uh, my stomach was upset for a second. Too much hot cocoa I think."

"That's okay, here is some water. Should I turn on another movie?"

"Sure, you pick again."

Lumen didn't even notice what movie they were watching. He was absorbed by the thought of someone after him. He hardly realized Sofia snuggled up against his boney chest. For just a moment, Lumen thought that maybe he should start working out. He went straight back to thinking about who the attacker could be.

Could it be someone he had met before? No one he had met so far seemed like a bad person though, and none of them knew the art of the Ignous--as far as Lumen knew, at least. It must have been someone from the other groups. But he hadn't noticed anyone following him. Maybe it was just a

167

coincidence. There was no reason anyone would be after him specifically. He had known for just a sliver of time that this world even existed. He could make water vibrate just slightly. What would anyone want with him?

Sofia looked up at Lumen.

"Are you sure you're okay? You haven't moved or said a word since you came out of the bathroom."

Lumen was staring off into space when Sofia asked him this, and he shook his head to come back to reality.

"Yeah, yeah. I'm okay. . . Hey, do you want to be my girlfriend?"

Lumen had no idea where that came from. One minute he was thinking about some person potentially targeting him and the next he was asking the girl of his dreams to be his girlfriend. The words just spilled out of his mouth. Sofia's eyebrows raised. Lumen messed up. He knew it. Why did he have to do this to ruin it?

"Of course, I thought you'd never ask."

Lumen couldn't believe it. His heart was racing and he couldn't help but cheesily smile. He felt his palms sweating. Sofia scooted up in her seat and went in for a kiss. Lumen followed suit and kissed her back. It was just one peck, but it was the most magical thing Lumen had ever experienced. His stomach flipped inside of him. It was the happiest moment of his life. Lumen's senses heightened. He didn't realize how musty the house smelled. It was as if nothing had been moved in the house for some time. He tried not to think about it and kissed Sofia again. Lumen's confidence was at an all-time high. His ring warmed again. For just a second, he saw Till's smile.

Sofia's father walked in shortly after the fireworks and offered Lumen a ride home. Lumen offered to call his mom first, but Mr. Chimera insisted.

They all hopped into the car and drove to Lumen's house. It took longer than it should have because of the weather. Everything was covered in snow. They passed *La Dernier Piece*, and saw Shari standing in the pouring snow, hitting the first *r* in *Dernier* with a broomstick, trying to get it to turn back on. For now, the diner was called *La Denier Piece*.

Lumen felt bad for her.

"Poor lady, she should really get back inside; nobody is going to go out to dinner tonight anyway," Mr Chimera said as they passed by the diner.

Mr. Chimera pulled up to Lumen's house. Alice was home. That also made Lumen excited. He could hang with his mom the rest of the night; he hadn't seen her much this week.

"Thank you, Mr. Chimera."

"Call me John. Not a problem, kiddo. Stay warm tonight, I don't think the storm will let up any time soon."

Lumen nodded. He was about to open the door and leave when Sofia pulled his arm and gave him an angry look.

"Right, sorry." Lumen leaned over and gave her a hug.

"What are you doing tomorrow?" She asked.

Lumen paused to think. Saturdays were supposed to be spent in the Paxum.

"I can't hang tomorrow. How about Sunday?"

Sundays would have to be their day. Lumen hoped that worked for Sofia.

"Yeah, I'm free Sunday. Call me."

Lumen nodded and jumped out of the car and sprinted to his house. He looked back and waved before entering the house.

He found his mom in the kitchen. He told her all about his day with Sofia. Alice yelled with excitement and hugged him tight when he told her about Sofia being his girlfriend now.

"I'm so proud of you, honey! Does she know about your . . . your sickness?" Alice asked genuinely concerned.

Lumen rolled his eyes.

"Yes, Mom. Everyone knows. But like I said, I don't see anything anymore. The lights aren't there anymore. I think, maybe, I was misdiagnosed back then. Maybe it was just my eyes or something."

Alice seemed concerned but nodded her head.

"Let's set up an appointment for next week. We'll see what the doctor says."

Lumen agreed. Maybe he can get the doctor to agree that he was misdiagnosed.

"Well anyway, you already ate, I assume, so I don't need to worry about dinner. Can you help finish covering the garden with the tarp? I almost finished."

Lumen looked out back and saw the tarp staked above the garden.

"Sure, let's do it."

They both put on heavy snow jackets and went out back.

Wrigley rolled around the snow. He loved the snow. He rolled upright when he saw Lumen and, with snow covering his face, ran and jumped all over him. Lumen fell into the snow. They wrestled for a few moments. Lumen realized he hadn't been giving Wrigley much attention this week.

"Sorry about this week, bud. I'll get better at this as time goes on, I promise. Oh, and Sofia will be around more often it looks like, you'll have another friend."

Wrigley turned his head at Lumen and put his ears back when Lumen mentioned Sofia. He walked away from Lumen.

"Hey, where you going? What did I say?"

Wrigley trotted into the house, ears back the entire time.

"Looks like someone is jealous of Sofia."

"That's not fair, he seemed to like her when she was rubbing his belly. I'm sure they'll like each other."

"I'm sure, hun, don't worry. Now get over here and hold the tarp while I put in the stakes. We just have to cover the thistles and roses over here." Lumen walked over. Something looked off with the thistles.

"Hey, are these dying, or did you cut some of them off?"

Alice looked down at the plant.

"Huh, that's odd. Looks like someone or something cut a couple of the thistles off. Maybe it was our friend that started the fire," Alice said jokingly.

Lumen forced out a chuckle, but he was truly worried about the missing thistles. Lumen counted and three thistles were missing. What if one was used for the stunt tonight at the Paxum? That would mean there could be at least two more fires if the thistle was actually used as a signature. He needed to tell Allister. Alice yelled at Lumen.

"Will you pull the tarp tight? I want to get inside before we get buried out here!"

Lumen waited impatiently until his mom went to bed so that he could jump to Allister's cabin. Alice was moving all throughout the house and was very talkative tonight. Lumen just sat on the edge of the couch the whole time.

"I have a date tomorrow just so ya know, Lu."

Lumen forgot about Allister for a moment.

"Excuse me?" Lumen said heatedly.

Alice had a little smirk on her face when Lumen turned to look at her in the kitchen.

"Yeah, you remember that cop who helped us?"

Lumen's tone expressed his displeasure.

"No, as a matter of fact, I don't."

Alice rolled her eyes at Lumen.

"Well he's really nice to me and asked me to go out tomorrow. I have the night off, so I figured why not?"

"What about me? Who is gonna cook dinner?"

Alice laughed loudly.

"Oh, don't be silly. You're fifteen for goodness sake. You can whip something up. Or you will want to go to that dang diner across the street anyways."

Lumen knew she was right but felt he had to keep showing his displeasure.

"This is not right. I'm going to bed."

"What? Come back here. Don't make me feel bad for going out!"

Lumen did feel bad as he marched to his room, but it was a good way to get this mom to go to bed. Five minutes later, he heard his mom retire to her room for the night.

Lumen opened a window as quickly as he could. Wrigley sat in front of him, ears still tucked back, as he was about to jump through.

"Fine, you can come this time. You can't stay mad at me though."

Wrigley's ears perked up and he jumped through the window. Lumen followed.

Lumen landed in the cabin. Janis was on top of the mantle above the fire looking down at Wrigley.

"Ey! Get the dog away! I 'ate when they a' this excited!"

Lumen wasn't sure what accent this was but understood enough to know to get Wrigley away. He laughed at Janis as he whistled for Wrigley.

"Oh weal funny isn't it? You watch yoozself, 'aaken"

Lumen furrowed his eyebrows, he wasn't sure what Janis had said. Allister walked in the room.

"Quiet down, Janis, Alec fell asleep. Long day for him. Ah, Lumen, you are here late."

Janis miffed at the comment and proceeded to lick his front paws while standing on his hind legs, all while on the mantle.

"Excuse our friend; it has been long days for all of us. What can I help you with?"

Allister looked at Lumen with his twinkling blue eyes. Lumen got that feeling again, his stomach warmed. He felt comfortable in Allister's presence.

He went on to explain the situation with the thistles, and Allister listened, hand going through his matted beard. They sat there in silence for a minute before Janis chimed in.

"You think tha' will be anotha' attack Allista? We need to act soon, this could get out of 'and. Chilwen could get a't. This isn't a joke anymo."

Lumen didn't fully understand, but he saw Allister nodding in agreement.

"Well thank you for this information, Lumen. You have done well."

Lumen felt as if that was the best compliment he had ever received.

"You should get back now. You have a full day tomorrow."

Allister created a small ice cube from thin air and handed it to Wrigley, who had been patiently sitting the entire time.

"Off you go." Allister opened a window for Lumen, and he and Wrigley jumped through.

Lumen didn't get much sleep that night. He was paranoid about someone coming to his house so he checked his backyard multiple times throughout the night. Every time he peaked out of his back door, all he saw was snow falling precariously onto the tarp. He decided he would get up early to see Allister before class.

Lumen's alarm went off at 6:30 am. He took Wrigley out into the brisk morning air to go to the bathroom, ran back in to feed him, and went back into his room. He needed to tell his mom where he would be for the day but wanted to get to Allister as soon as he could. He decided to come back later to talk to his mom.

He thought of the inside of Allister's cabin, pieced together a window, and jumped through. He touched down in a wooded tundra environment. Had he messed up? The lights led him to the wrong area. He looked around to try and figure out where he was and saw Allister's cabin in the distance. He thought for a moment, *how'd I end up over here? I haven't jumped out of place like that before.* He ran to Allister's cabin and walked up the steps. Lumen's hand wrapped around the cold door handle and was about to open the front door when he could hear someone talking inside. He paused for a moment, he didn't want to barge in on a meeting. His hand released the door handle and he stepped away when he heard Janis speaking. The catman sounded distraught.

Lumen crept to the open window.

"Do you think it is a good idea to be sending all these innocent and unprepared children to school? We do not know how serious these threats are, Allister."

Janis was speaking in his normal voice.

"Yes, of course, we do not want to scare them off a week in. The board would have a field day with this. It needs to stay between us, understood?"

It was silent for a moment.

"What about the boys? Lumen and Alec . . ." Sasha asked.

"I trust Alec. He is like a son to me. And Lumen, he needed to know for his own safety. We are monitoring him to keep him safe, but you never know," Allister said.

173

Lumen could hear them murmuring in agreement.

"Does he know? It could help him understand why someone would be recruiting him."

Lumen wasn't sure if they were talking about him still.

"Absolutely not. And he shall not know. Is that understood?" Allister said firmly.

Lumen heard murmurs of agreement again.

"Aiden, you're sure no one in your caste is acting strange or knows of anything?" Janis asked.

"I have been keeping a close eye on all my students. Nothing is out of the ordinary. I barely know the new students, but they are hardly capable of creating sparks, let alone full on fires."

"Okay, well, stay vigilant. We all know that whoever is doing this was welcomed here. We need to find this criminal before someone gets hurt," Allister said.

Aiden spoke again.

"Are we sure this isn't Maldeus? There have been mimics in the past, but nothing has ever gotten this serious . . ."

There was silence in the room. Lumen tried not to breathe in order to be as silent as possible. Janis broke the silence.

"Maldeus is dead, Aiden, we all know that. Don't be ridiculous."

Aiden interjected.

"What about Ja . . ."

Allister interrupted loudly.

"That is enough. We aren't here to speculate on the impossible. Off you all go back to the Paxum. Do a thorough check there before students start to arrive."

Lumen heard them shuffle around for a moment before it was silent again. He could tell it was just Allister there. He peaked in the window and saw Allister standing over the fire with a pipe in his mouth.

"You can come in, Lumen."

Lumen was startled. How did he know he was there? Lumen walked slowly through the front door.

"How'd you know I was there?"

Allister turned slowly. He smiled at Lumen.

"I heard the floorboards creak just a moment ago. What can I help you with, son?"

Lumen felt at ease.

"I was just coming by to see if there was anything I could do to help . . ."

Allister turned back to the fire and puffed on his pipe.

"Ah, I see. Well, you have been helping quite a bit already. There isn't much else to do right now."

Allister's rejection distressed Lumen deeply. Lumen wasn't sure why.

Allister turned around back to Lumen, the look on his face appeared as though he just had an epiphany.

"You know what, there is something. We are keeping this amongst ourselves; no one else knows about the latest attack. That thistle you found, look here."

Allister walked over to his desk and picked up the thistle. Lumen noticed there weren't any new drawings.

"Look here . . ." Allister pointed to a couple of the thorns. There was something that was dark red..

"What is it?"

"This, my boy, is blood. It looks like whoever is doing this, may have cut themselves when picking the thistles from your mother's garden. Don't be alarmed, but we have reason to believe that this is the work of a student."

Lumen scratched his head.

"A student? How is that possible?"

"Don't you worry about that part; I just need you to look out for anyone that may have a cut or a bandage covering a cut. Anything would help."

Lumen nodded. He felt good again.

"Yeah, I can do that."

Allister smiled.

"Good, off you go. Class starts soon."

Lumen felt great. He had a mission today: find someone with a cut.

Lumen and the Thistle

Lumen jumped home and landed exactly where he planned, in his room. He was nervous he would accidentally open a window and land in sight of his mom. Lumen couldn't let that happen; he thought she would probably lose her mind.

Lumen decided to tell Alice he was going to Alec's for the day to help him babysit. As he was lying to his mom, he realized that Alec lied to him all this time about what he did on Friday nights. Alice thought that was sweet of Lumen and reminded him of her date that night.

"I won't be home when you get back. I'll leave some dinner money for you."

Lumen rolled his eyes and yelled "Bye!" as he walked out of the house.

He went back to the same spot he jumped from before: on the side of a house about a block down the street.

He opened a window and landed in the Paxum. The students were walking to their respective cabins to drop down to class. Lumen ran into Till on the way to the cabin. She was wearing jeans, different from her typical sundress attire. They looked good on her, Lumen thought.

"First full day, you excited?" She asked.

Lumen nodded. He didn't want to talk to Till too much now that he had an official girlfriend.

They walked side by side to the cabin and down into the classrooms underground.

Till attempted to grab Lumen's hand on the elevator down. Lumen pulled his hand back.

"Look, you're cool and all, but I think we need to stay friends. I have a girlfriend now."

Till's face didn't change. She didn't seem to care.

"It won't last. How are you supposed to hide all of this? It's only a matter of time before you know what is right."

She smiled and walked away. It got him thinking. How would he keep this secret his whole life?

Lumen sat down, and the rest of the students filed in. Till still decided to sit next to him. Yu came in wearing his typical beat up baseball cap. Lucy wasn't far behind him, wearing a band shirt as usual; this band was called "The Coyotes."

Lumen jokingly wondered if the band members went to Bromide High. She waved to Lumen as she sat down.

It was 8:01 AM. Mr. Durum looked up at the class.

"Where is Chester?"

The class looked around at one another. Lucy spoke up.

"We haven't seen him, Mr. Durum. He kind of keeps to himself."

Mr. Durum frowned.

"His loss. Let's get started. Turn to page 19 in . . ."

The door burst open, and there was Chester, sweating profusely. He made his way into the classroom and took a seat in the open chair on the other side of Lumen.

"Thank you for joining us, Chester. Don't let it happen again. I don't like being interrupted."

Mr. Durum had the habit of scaring students, although Chester didn't seem fazed by them. He simply wiped the beads of sweat off his forehead and pulled a notebook out of his backpack. When his hand emerged from the bag Lumen noticed a bandage; it appeared to be newly wrapped.

Lumen didn't know if he could wait until class was over to tell Allister.

Chapter 11 – Hiding in Plain Sight

Lumen decided to wait until after class. He remembered Allister telling him not to start a commotion over anything. He also didn't want Mr. Durum making a big deal out of him leaving abruptly in the middle of lessons.

Lumen needed to find Allister to tell him about his suspicions of Chester. Class ended and he headed straight out to the foyer area where all the Eauge students hung out in between classes. He found Alec exiting his class. When Lumen peeked inside his classroom he saw a few students soaking wet from head to toe alongside an older woman that Lumen presumed was the teacher. Alec was smiling.

"Hey, Alec, where can I find Allister this time of day?"

"He should be in his cabin, what's going on?"

Alec could see the intensity in Lumen's eyes.

"It's about that thing . . . you know, that we aren't supposed to talk about . . ."

Alec looked around to make sure no one was listening. "What's going on?" he whispered.

Lumen leaned in and spoke in a whisper as well.

"I think Chester has something do with the fires, I need to let Allister know. Actually, can you keep an eye on him while I go?"

Alec nodded and walked in the direction of Chester, toward the back of the Genaqua to the forest.

Lumen opened a window to Allister's cabin and jumped through. He had no problem arriving there this time. Allister stood over the fire, one hand on the mantle and the other holding his smoking pipe.

"Hello, Lumen, what can I help you with?"

Lumen felt anxious with the information he knew. He regurgitated what he had just seen to Allister. Allister didn't move from his position as he took in Lumen's observations.

He puffed his pipe a couple more times. Lumen sat in silence for a few moments. He thought he may have said something wrong.

"Very good, Lumen. I want you to keep an eye on Chester. Stay close with him. He may be very dangerous, so if at any given moment that danger presents itself, you need to leave immediately. Is your luxem set up properly?"

Lumen nodded. He had it set for Allister's cabin.

"Good, I know this is a precarious position to be in, but we need all the help we can get. If the board were to find out the others or I were following a child around based off of limited evidence, they would have my head."

Lumen's eyes widened. He hadn't realized this world was so cut throat. That same feeling in his gut returned, the same one he felt when he did not know what had happened to his mother after the fire in their backyard.

Allister noticed the worried look on Lumen's face.

"Not literally, my boy. Just a figure of speech. You need to get back now. This stays between you and I. Tell Alec to come see me if you could."

Lumen nodded and opened a window back to the Genaqua.

179

He landed in the same spot from where he left and proceeded to run over to Alec. He was standing 30 feet or so from Chester who was sitting on a rock above the snow, playing with a Rubix cube.

"He hasn't done much except play with that cube. Some kids threw some snow at him. He didn't do anything about it, just wiped the snow off and kept playing with the cube."

Lumen couldn't help but think that that reminded him of himself; he also let that kind of bullying happen. With that, Lumen realized the people there were the same as the people where he was from, just with more abilities to torment each other.

"Allister wants to see you. I'm going to keep an eye on him for now," Lumen said nodding in the direction of Chester.

Alec patted Lumen on the back.

"Okay, man, be careful. Once this is all over, we should celebrate. I feel like you haven't been able to fully appreciate all of this yet. I've got to show you *The Danse.* It's a good time."

"The Dance . . .?"

"Yeah, it's a hall to hang out in. There are some games, good food, just a good time. It's back in Entropolis."

Lumen nodded.

"Okay, sounds good, man."

Lumen wondered if Till goes there.

Alec jumped to Allister's cabin. Lumen sat down on a bench and glanced over at Chester every once in a while.

Chester didn't move too often. He played with his Rubix cube, put in some headphones, and wiped some more snow off that was tossed at him.

Their break period ended. Lumen had the same class as Chester again: Pluviam. Lumen followed Chester in and found a seat behind him toward the back of the classroom. As they walked in, Professor J was sitting at the front of the class reading a book. Lucy came in and sat to Lumen's left; when Till arrived she sat on the right. She smiled and waved. It was like she had already forgotten about Lumen telling her to leave him alone. Maybe Lumen could convince her to just be friends with him.

Professor J went over how to control water in clouds .

"I'm not asking for you all to make this water and cloud appear in the classroom; I'll do that for you easily," Professor J said smugly.

"I just want you to be able to hold the cloud above without letting the water pour down. Let's get a volunteer up here to show us how it's done."

Professor J conjured a small cloud at the front of the room. It was dark, just like the clouds one would see before a major storm is about to hit, only the size of a plush pillow. Nobody raised their hand to volunteer.

"Fine, I'll pick . . . You, Lucy, come up here."

Lucy got up nervously, made sure her black and red checkered flannel was tied around her waist securely, and walked to the front. She took off her fanny pack.

"Stand here," Professor J pointed underneath the cloud.

"I assume you did the reading assigned?"

"Yes, professor." Lucy said as if that was a given.

Professor J nodded with approval.

"Good, I am going to relinquish control of this cloud in just a few moments. All you need to do is keep the cloud from releasing all of the water held within. If you don't, well, let's just say I hope you have a change of clothes." He said all of this with a little smirk on his face.

Lucy seemed nervous but determined. She had a new band shirt on today, "Goofproof", with a clown face sticking its tongue out and X's for eyes. Lumen thought it was cool.

"Are you ready?"

Lucy nodded and stood as if she was preparing to fight.

"Okay, here we go . . . and it . . . is . . . all . . . yours . . ."

Professor J stepped back. Lucy stood there, looking at the cloud above her, hands above her head as if she were literally holding the water within it from falling.

Nothing happened. The cloud remained as it was, no water fell onto Lucy. The class remained silent. Professor J's smirk slowly disappeared as time went on.

He waved his arm in the air quickly, and the cloud disappeared.

"Very good. Back to your seat."

The classroom clapped as she walked back, and Lucy had a smile on her face.

"Nice job, that was awesome. I think he's is a bit disappointed you succeeded," Lumen whispered to her. Lucy chuckled.

"Yeah, that was my main concern, not to fail in front of him for his entertainment." They both laughed quietly before Professor J spoke again.

"Alrighty, thank you, Lucy. You all are going to pair up and do the same thing. The pair that can manage the biggest cloud will get a small prize. Let's get started."

He split everyone off into pairs. There were 26 of them in class. Lucy and Lumen were paired together, Chester was paired with Till.

"Okay, I will be making your clouds slightly bigger after a few moments. It will be harder to control as more water accumulates in the clouds. Last pair standing gets a prize. Here we go . . ."

Professor J conjured thirteen clouds, one above each pair. These clouds were a little bit bigger than the one Lucy managed in the front of the class. Lumen was nervous. He needed to keep an eye on Chester while helping to keep his and Lucy's cloud afloat; luckily, it looked like Lucy had been practicing.

"Here . . . we . . . go . . . it's all you."

Professor J relinquished control of each of the clouds. All of the students bent down, as if they were holding something heavy above their heads, trying to prevent it from crushing them.

Chester and Till failed almost immediately. The cloud rained down on them and they were soaked.

"Way to go, Chester! These are my favorite jeans!" Till yelled. Chester looked flustered and scurried out of the classroom. Lumen watched him go and almost followed when a few drops fell onto his head. He immediately stepped back into stance and refocused on the cloud; he needed the other groups to fail. Professor J added water to each cloud every thirty seconds or so. After a couple of times of adding water, there were only two groups left, Lucy and Lumen being one of them. Lumen found himself sweating. *Nothing in the textbook explained how difficult this would be physically,* Lumen thought. Professor J added just a little bit more to each cloud and the other group collapsed to the floor, drenched in water. He then waved and the cloud above Lumen and Lucy disappeared.

"Lucky Lucy not getting wet at all today. Very good. Lumen's lucky to have you as a partner. I want you all to know that I could dry you all quickly by removing the water from your clothes but that wouldn't teach you anything. Read chapter three and four by next class. Go dry off and study. Oh, Lucy and Lumen, you will receive an extra five percent boost on the first test."

Lucy high fived Lumen.

"Great job! We kind of killed it in there. We should partner up for all the group activities. We can avoid getting wet most days, hopefully."

Lumen laughed quickly and awkwardly as he regained focus on Chester.

"That sounds great. I got to run, I'll catch you later."

Lumen ran out of the class in desperate search of Chester. He looked toward the end of the Genaqua where the snow and trees were. He saw the last bit of Chester heading into the forest. *Gotcha.* Lumen took off running toward him.

From the looks of it, Chester seemed to be in a rush. He frequently looked over his shoulder to, Lumen assumed, see if anyone was following him. Lumen wasn't far behind and tried to stay hidden so that Chester couldn't see him. Chester disappeared into the trees.

Lumen ran to catch up to him, and suddenly he was nowhere to be found. Chester was gone. He must have jumped where Lumen couldn't see. Lumen thought he may have got too close.

Where could he have gone? I thought it was impossible to jump from the Genaqua? I need to tell Allister.

"Back so soon, are ya? What'd you find out?"

Lumen was still panting from chasing Chester.

"Well, he left class early after failing to hold a cloud with Till . . ."

Allister laughed.

"Oh Jeremiah, he loves that stuff. Great teacher, bit of a sadist though. Good guy overall."

Lumen felt like Allister wasn't taking him seriously.

"Yeah, great guy," Lumen said sarcastically. "Anyway, Chester took off right after he failed. I chased after him once class was finished but he disappeared into the woods. I think he jumped somewhere."

Allister stopped smiling and scratched his chin under his coarse salt and pepper beard, adjusting the goggles on top of his head. The straps appeared to be getting worn.

"Interesting . . . good work. Nothing you can do for now. When he returns, back to watching him. Thank you, Lumen. This has been very helpful."

Compliments from Allister felt very good to Lumen. He wanted to impress him for some reason. *Alec thinks highly of him, maybe that's why I feel that way*, he thought.

"How could he have jumped? I thought it wasn't possible down there?" Lumen asked.

Allister scratched his chin again. He eyebrows furrowed and seemed to struggle coming up with an answer.

"I thought so too. The lights will present themselves when needed most, regardless of measures taken to avoid that. . . Back to the Paxum. We will meet again soon."

Lumen finished up classes for the day. His first Saturday was complete and he was exhausted. He didn't have to rush home as Alice was going on a date. Afterwards, he went with Lucy and Yu to the Genaqua's food hall for the first time. The hall contained all sorts of food and drinks, but Lumen chose to stick with the food he knew he would like. The hall didn't have any drinks he recognized. There was bottle after bottle lined up on the beautifully carved wooden shelves. Finally, Lumen grabbed a classic Hutchinson style glass bottle. The label read "Whistleberry Juice." Lumen thought it sounded interesting. He kept the bottle and walked out with Lucy and Yu, following with their own juices and pockets.

"Why is it called whistleberry?" Lumen asked.

Lucy pulled an odd shaped red flower from the ground. In place of the usual flower center was a berry. Lucy proceeded to squeeze the berry and it made a loud whistling noise.

"Ah, makes sense now," he said as he uncovered his ears. Yu giggled as he washed down the last of his pocket with the juice. Lumen thought it tasted like orange and cranberry juice mixed together. They all sat together and ate and drank and laughed. Yu asked about Pluviam class.

"How'd you guys keep that cloud up for so long? I felt like I really had a hold but my partner was useless," Yu said.

"We both did our part. It's nice having a partner that can hold their own. All my life, peers have jumped on my back for help and answers. It was nice to see the effort reciprocated for once," Lucy said as she smiled at Lumen. Lumen blushed from the compliment.

"That was mostly you, I had no idea that would be so hard," Lumen replied.

"Well you two are lucky. You don't have to walk around with wet clothes. You know how much colder it is when you're soaking wet?" Yu asked. They all laughed together.

Lumen was happy to be making friends there.

When Lucy went back up to the Paxum so that she could jump home and Yu retired to his dorm, Lumen stayed behind. He sat down and glanced around the Genaqua; it was littered with students walking around with bottles of juice discussing their classes.

He saw a pair of students practicing some of their new skills. One conjured up a small rain cloud, and the other held it in the air, intermittently letting water pour down. They were definitely more advanced than Lumen. He wondered what was next after he completed school. Would he just have these skills to use if need be, or are there jobs he could do? He decided he should ask Alec about it.

Lumen walked over to the statue from the food hall that was at the end of the corridor, between the two stone

185

buildings. He looked up to see a muscular, shirtless man who reminded Lumen of the Greek god Poseidon. Lumen looked down at the nameplate and read "Maredeus."

That's similar to Maldeus, wonder if they're related.

Lumen thought that maybe Poseidon was based off of this guy. He also thought that maybe all of the Greek gods were based off people from Bonumalus. He could imagine the average human thinking the people from Bonumalus were gods. Lumen liked the idea of being considered a god, and he wondered what the Greeks would have called him.

He turned away from the statue and started making his way back at the elevator when he saw him. Walking back toward the foyer area from the elevator was Chester, covered in mud. It appeared that Chester couldn't use the lights jump back into the Genaqua. Lumen decided to stay put to watch where he was going. Coincidentally, he seemed to be walking in Lumen's direction. Lumen was worried Chester would see him so he looked away and acted as though he was practicing things he learned from Pluviam class. He got in stance as though he was trying to hold a cloud above him when Chester walked right by him.

"Don't practice too much, it won't help you," Chester said as he strolled by.

He kept walking into the food hall, covered in mud and all. Lumen was perplexed by what Chester meant by that. Was it a threat? He wanted to run it by Alec before telling Allister. Lumen checked on Chester one more time from the door of the food hall as he perused all the juices on the shelves. Lumen thought Chester seemed in higher spirits.

Lumen took the elevator back up to the Paxum. Gretchen wasn't at the top in the cabin. Lumen had never not seen her there. He walked out of the cabin and into the Paxum where he found a large crowd of people.

This is odd, why is everyone up here? Don't they have class or homes to return to?

Lumen noticed everyone looking toward the Liros expanse of the Paxum and followed suit. He could see smoke starting to plume above everyone's head. He wove quickly through the crowd to get a better look up front.

Lumen began to smell a pungent, smokey aroma, one that reminded him of a meal his mother set ablaze in the oven. As he got closer, he could see the flames, but he couldn't tell where it was coming from. The air was opaque and made his eyes water, his nose singed. He reached the front of the crowd and he saw it. Many of the trees were on fire near the Liros cabins. The crowd was silent behind Lumen, so much so that he could hear the crackling of the wood and brush burning. A tree branch broke off and fell to the ground. Embers flew up into the air. Lumen looked around at one of the cabins and saw something written on the side:

"JOIN US NOW B4 IT'S 2 LATE."

Lumen squinted to better see the written message. The writing looked like it was done with mud or dirt. As that observation crossed his mind, Chester walked up from behind Lumen. He was holding a whistleberry juice and a wetchop sandwich, chewing loudly.

"Wow, that's crazy. Who would do something like that. . . Join who now? " Chester said as food spilled from his mouth.

Lumen turned and looked at him, anger filled his face.

"Don't act like you don't know!" Lumen said, louder than he intended.

Chester stopped chewing mid bite and looked back at Lumen with a puzzled look. He was about to say something when Professor J walked in between them from behind. He stood in front of them for a moment, looking at the fire. He opened a window to the left of him, waved his hand in front of it and made it shimmer. Lumen had never seen that done with a window and wondered what he was doing. J turned back to the fires and raised his arms. Clouds suddenly appeared above the forest as rain began to pour down. Three figures emerged from the shimmering window J had created. Lumen was enamored by Professor J's ability to forcibly and quickly create such a large rain cloud. Lumen was so impressed with the skills shown by Professor J that is took him a moment to realize that it was Allister, Janis, and Sasha that came through the shimmering window. Lumen was fascinated. The shimmering window must have been a call of some sort to Allister. Just then Till walked up and grabbed his arm. She was wearing fresh clothes and jeans again.

"Oh my goodness, who would do such a thing?"

Lumen looked at Chester again who was staring at the now dwindling fire. He continued drinking and eating. Lumen could see the dying fire reflecting off of Chester's eyeballs.

Chapter 12 - A Surrender?

Allister spoke to the filled quarry in the Paxum. He stood with the trees smoldering in the background with Janis, Sasha, and Professor J behind him working to put out the fires quickly.

The air vibrated like it had before and Allister's voice boomed.

"None of you should be alarmed. This was merely a publicity stunt by someone who thinks it is a joke to set things on fire. I want you all to know that the Paxum will be on 24-hour surveillance until this criminal is caught. If anyone has any information, please do not hesitate to come and see me or any of your teachers."

The quarry went quiet for a moment before a girl near the back spoke up.

"What does the message on the cabin wall mean? Sounds like a recruitment for something."

Murmuring erupted in the quarry. Allister spoke a little bit louder this time.

"I know what some of you are thinking, so I will address the elephant in the room. Maldeus is not alive. He has not been for some time now. If you think this is Maldeus recruiting to rebuild his army, you are a fool. At best, this is a mimic who is seeking some attention. Are we all clear here? There isn't anything to worry about at this time. I would like for all of you to return to your dormitories or homes. By Monday, this will all be sorted and classes will continue."

Most of the students began to disperse, evidently satisfied with Allister's answer. Chester nodded after Allister spoke and headed to his dorm. Lumen saw him get pushed to the ground by a group of students. He felt bad for him but quickly changed his mind when he got a whiff of smoke and thought he deserved it after this stunt. Lumen turned back towards Allister when he saw Sasha hand him something; Lumen squinted to get a better look, it was a thistle.

Lumen met with Allister and Janis back at the cabin shortly after. Lumen told them every detail he observed about Chester, from the bandage on his hand, to the mud on his clothes, to being a loner among the Eauge. Janis interjected after Lumen finished, and spoke in his normal voice.

"Maybe we should act now. All the signs are pointing to this boy. We could send him to the juvenile Vincula and ban him from learning here . . ."

Allister adjusted the goggles on his head, as he so often did when he was thinking hard. Lumen noticed he was flushed in the face; he was clearly struggling with this decision.

"No . . . not yet. We still aren't 100% sure, and we can't ban a child from learning the correct methods. If he is the one doing this, he has just been misguided by someone... or by our history. We can turn him around. I think the bigger issue is how did we overlook his innate Ignous ability? He clearly doesn't belong with the Eauge-- *if* he is the one doing all of this. Maybe that is why he is acting out."

It fell quiet again, and Lumen thought of something.

"He doesn't do very well in class. He was the first to fail in Professor J's group exercise today, with Till."

Janis looked at Allister, as if this could change Allister's mind about acting now.

"That still doesn't mean he is the one. He could be adjusting slowly to this life. It's the first week," Allister said.

Lumen thought again about what he had noticed about Chester.

"Well, I think he was able to jump while within the Genaqua. I thought that wasn't possible?"

Janis turned quickly to Lumen.

"How do you know that?"

Lumen explained how he followed Chester into the forest, how he disappeared and how he came back in through the elevator in the Paxum, covered in mud. Janis again thought this was enough to convict Chester.

"C'mon, Allister. This is getting dangerous. Whatever the motive is, someone can get seriously injured. I mean look at Lumen's mother, she could have been killed!"

Lumen gulped. The feelings of not knowing if his mom was okay returned in his gut.

Allister put his hand up at Janis to signal for him to stop talking.

"No, it doesn't feel right. We need to catch the boy in the act. Lumen, keep an eye on him. If he leaves class, you follow. I will speak to your teachers if they give you a hard time. I want everything to go on as normal. Understood?"

Janis rolled his eyes and nodded as he began to clean his paws. Lumen nodded as well.

"Alec will keep an eye on him tomorrow. Monday night, it will be all you. Report back to me immediately if you see anything."

Lumen nodded. He felt a lot of pressure but was up for the task. He wondered why Allister would give him so much responsibility. Lumen felt that Allister had put a lot of faith in someone who hardly had any abilities. Lumen had one more question.

"What is Vincula?"

Janis answered.

"Somewhere you don't want to go. It's where the worst of the worst go when they get caught. There is a juvenile facility connected that isn't nearly as harsh, but it could whip a young man or woman into shape if need be."

Lumen remembered reading about one of the harshest prisons on Earth, Guantanamo Bay, in class last year. He knew it was a place for the worst of the worst criminals. He knew what criminals on Earth must have done to land there. He couldn't imagine what the criminals of Bonumalus were capable of.

Lumen went home with a lot on his mind. Luckily, Alice had picked up a couple of new puzzles before her date and had also taken out all of the Christmas decorations. Lumen almost forgot that Christmas was coming up in just a week and a half and that he would have a few weeks off from his normal school.

Lumen always helped his mom with the decorations. He loved that time of the year.

Christmas wasn't usually a special day as his mom often worked all of Christmas day or the night before, and they would hardly get to spend time together. However, Alice always tried her best to make it feel as much like Christmas as possible in the house. She tried to get presents for Lumen but was often short on cash in years past. Lumen didn't mind. He liked the ambiance the lights and decorations provided to his home. He felt the holiday spirit in the air and always did his best to reassure his mom that she didn't need to stress about it.

Alice came home a bit earlier than expected.

"Hey, hun. How was your day?" Alice asked as she walked in.

Lumen sighed.

"Longer than expected. You're home earlier than I thought you'd be."

"Charles had to get home to his daughter," Alice said with a smile.

Lumen rolled his eyes.

"The cops name is Charles, huh? Shouldn't he be patrolling or something?"

Alice rolled her eyes this time.

"Shall we get a tree?"

Lumen had been feeling so stressed from his new schedule that the trip to the Christmas tree lot was even more welcomed than usual. Once home with a tree, they turned on some Christmas music and made hot chocolate to decorate, their Christmas tradition. After two and a half cups of cocoa, and with the tree all lit up, they turned on a movie. Alice quickly fell asleep. Lumen took Wrigley out; it had stopped snowing and the ground was covered with fresh powder. Lumen thought of Bonumalus and wondered who was responsible for making it snow in his hometown. When he went back inside, Alice was still fast asleep on the couch. Lumen turned down the TV and decided to work on a puzzle--it had been a while. He picked up the one nearest him; it was of an overhead shot of the Amazonian rain forest. He had a feeling it would be difficult based on all of the green. The second was of a mountain range in the Antarctic, with most of the puzzle being white. This would be just as difficult. Lumen decided to go with the Arctic, in honor of his new life as an Eauge-in-training. He ripped it open and dumped the pieces out.

The thoughts of Sofia, then Till's perfect smile, and Chester's peculiar behavior drowned his thoughts for a moment.

He took a deep breath, cracked his knuckles, took one more sip of his hot chocolate, and dove into the puzzle. He hadn't felt this at ease in some time now.

Lumen finished up the puzzle in a couple of hours and felt refreshed. He decided to eat some dinner. His mom had woken up and had already heated up a frozen pizza.

"So, what are you going to get Sofia for Christmas?"

Lumen hadn't even thought about getting her a present. *So much for feeling at ease,* Lumen thought.

"Uhh, I have no idea. What do you get a girlfriend for Christmas?"

Alice chuckled and grabbed Lumen's cheek gingerly.

"Oh, hun. I can't tell you what to get. It needs to be from you!"

Lumen shrugged.

"I mean, you technically will be the one to buy it, so it's kind of from you. I don't have a job, remember, Mom . . ."

They laughed and then tried to brainstorm some gift ideas.

Lumen went to Sofia's house the next day and helped her and Mr. Chimera with Christmas decorations. It snowed lightly when they were putting lights up outside, and Sofia snuggled up under Lumen's arm. Things like that happened repeatedly throughout the day, and Lumen couldn't have been happier about it. He had almost forgotten about the ordeal in Bonumalus until he was briefly distracted while they were watching a movie.

"Did you hear that?" Lumen asked

Lumen stood up, ready to act if there was an intruder in the house. He looked around and thought he saw something moving in the backyard. He began to notice the lights around him as he continued to the back door, taking a few deep breaths as he approached. Lumen had no idea what he would do if there were an intruder. His clammy hands slowly turned the handle and pulled open the door; it creaked as he pulled it back. He stepped outside and looked both left and right with his arms crossed. Nothing. No one was there except a branch hitting a window on the second floor of the house. He turned back to join Sofia. The lights were gone again, he missed seeing them sometimes.

They hung out until dinner time. Lumen mustered up the strength and gave Sofia a kiss before leaving. They both blushed and kissed one more time before Lumen trotted out of the house to his mom waiting outside in the station wagon.

The week went by with ease. Lumen became adjusted to his new schedule, and he had three weeks of winter break to look forward to once Friday passed. He did follow Chester as Allister requested, but he didn't see him do anything too out of the ordinary. He played with his Rubix cube often and was bullied just as much. When he got frustrated with the bullying, he would take the elevator up to the Paxum and hang out there or go to the back of the forest and somehow jump from there; Lumen was never able to catch him. Whenever Lumen thought he jumped from the forest, he always came back muddy. Lumen relayed this all to Allister, just as before.

Saturday came again, and it was more of the same from Chester. He was reprimanded by Professor J for falling asleep during the lesson on why it is important to not freeze rain too high in the sky-- apparently it could become dangerous, softball-sized hail that could wreak havoc and harm the people of Earth.

"Chester, could you tell us when you should freeze water if you want it to snow?"

Chester lifted his head up and wiped the drool from his chin.

"Uh, at the top, right?"

Professor J shook his head as if he was disgusted.

"What is wrong with you, boy? The top of what? Hm? Pay attention in my class! Don't make me send you to Allister!"

Chester straightened up in his seat. He seemed uncomfortable with the thought of having to be face to face with Allister. Lumen sympathized for Chester for a moment; he got picked on by his peers and teachers. However, Lumen still thought it wasn't an excuse for the crimes he had potentially committed, especially the one aimed at his house, but could see why he was led to do it.

195

"Hi, Lumen."

Lumen sighed as he turned to look at Till.

"Hi, Till," he said in a monotonous voice.

Lumen noticed that Till was back in her floral sundress.

"Do you have any notes on this last chapter? I forgot to do the reading."

Lumen didn't say anything and handed her the notes he had taken.

"Thanks! Don't wanna get called out by J; I'm sick of getting rained on."

Till's face turned red with anger. Lumen had never seen her get angry and was curious what had triggered her. *Professor J is mean to her, but no more than he was to other students.*

"You okay?" he asked.

Till looked down, closed her eyes and took a deep breath.

"Yeah, just a lot going on with these new classes. A lot of pressure to do well. I could use some fun. . . Will you hang out with me sometime soon?"

Lumen knew he should say no, but he felt bad for her.

Maybe J does pick on her a little more than some of the other students. Now that I think of it, she does get rained on daily and hasn't really made any progress. . .

"Uh, yeah sure. How about next week sometime?"

Till's face lit up.

"Sounds good!" Till turned back to look at Professor J with a huge grin on her face.

Lumen felt like he had committed a crime. He told himself that this was just as friends, and it wasn't a crime to be friends with a girl. As a matter of fact, Lucy and Lumen had become good friends. Why didn't Lumen feel guilty when he was with Lucy? Lumen couldn't figure that part out.

Lumen went shopping with his mom on Sunday, just a few days before Christmas. He had saved some money to buy his mom a gift and used some money from his mom to buy Sofia a gift. Lumen found a book on flowers for his mom that listed the most popular in each state in addition to each country outside the US. As for Sofia, he and his mom agreed that she would like a green scarf they saw while passing a boutique window. Lumen felt it was the perfect gift; he wanted to get her something she could use every day. He still had money left over after the purchases. He felt like he should get something else. He had some ideas.

On their way home, Lumen and Alice bought some wrapping paper. Lumen wrapped up the presents he got for his mom and Sofia before putting them under the tree. He also wrapped the new chew toy they found for Wrigley while they were out. Wrigley was very curious about the gift, and Lumen had to tell him multiple times to stay away from the presents. He thought it was very important for everyone to open their gifts on Christmas day, and that included Wrigley.

Sofia came over that night for dinner. Alice cooked them up some chicken and rice with some vegetables on the side. Lumen found himself missing the food he experienced in Bonumalus.

"Whistleberry juice would be good with this . . ."

Sofia looked at him confused.

"What kind of juice?" She asked.

Lumen forgot where he was for a moment.

"Orange juice-- I said orange juice would be good with this. Hey Mom! Do we have any OJ?"

Lumen smiled at Sofia and turned the same red color as whistleberry juice.

Alice came to the table with two glasses of OJ and sat down.

"What about you, Sofia? What was your favorite gift you ever received?"

Sofia was silent for a moment. Her face went long and sighed before answering.

"Honestly, the best gift was just having my mom there. I don't think Christmas will ever be as good as when my mom was alive. My dad tries to make it the same, but it's just not . . . My mom would cook all day long, and the house would smell

197

so good. We would open gifts from one another throughout the day, and my mom would bake some cookies. Now, I'm sure my dad will give me a nice gift, but that'll be it. He isn't much of a cook."

Sofia stared off into space, clearly saddened by her memories.

Lumen and Alice looked at one another. Lumen gave her an angry look for asking the question.

"Oh, I'm so sorry, hun. Look, you can come here on Christmas if you would like! You and your dad! I can cook up something nice and bake some sweets."

Lumen took a bite of his chicken and immediately tasted how burnt it was. He looked at his mom as if she were crazy to say she would cook for more people.

"That sounds nice. I'll talk to my dad," Sofia said as her face brightened.

Sofia smiled and took a bite of her food. She too realized the chicken was burnt. Lumen could see her force it down with some OJ.

"Mom . . . you burnt the chicken . . ."

Alice sighed.

"I know, I didn't think it would be that bad. Is it that bad?"

Sofia said no, and Lumen said yes at the same time.

Alice laughed.

"Well don't worry, I won't cook this on Christmas. Maybe we'll order in then. Anywho, should we go to *La Dernier Piece* now?"

Lumen got up and went to get his and Sofia's coats. Sofia smiled.

"Thank you, Miss Haaken. I thought it was just fine."

Alice smiled back at Sofia.

"Thank you, hun. And call me Alice please. I sound like an old woman if you call me that."

They both laughed for a moment. Lumen sounded desperate

"Mom, Sofia, are we going or what? I'm starving."

Sofia got up, and Lumen helped put on her coat. He rushed to the front door and held it open for them both. They walked down to the diner and enjoyed a hot meal. Shari was their server as usual and had a booth ready for them before they even walked in. Lumen ordered the usual, Sofia ordered a sandwich with fries, and Alice got the soup du jour. They spoke about their winter break plans.

After dinner they walked around the neighborhood, looking at Christmas lights as it snowed lightly. *Another perfect night*, Lumen thought. They strolled around the neighborhood for about an hour before heading back home.

They walked in, and Lumen stepped in a wet spot on the carpet.

"Great, just great. Wrigley! Where are you?"

Lumen thought Wrigley had peed on the carpet. He looked around, and he wasn't in the living room or kitchen. Alice and Sofia headed to the kitchen to make some hot chocolate. Lumen rushed down the hall and opened his bedroom door quickly. Standing in the room was Allister with his long, green trench coat and his musty goggles on top of his head. Wrigley was on the bed wagging his tail. He had an ice cube in his mouth.

Lumen shut the door abruptly.

"Very nice home you have here, Lumen. Much more cozy than my cabin."

Lumen's eyes widened as he put his finger to his mouth to indicate to Allister to be quiet.

Lumen whispered.

"Are you crazy? What if my mom or Sofia walked in here before I did?"

Allister scratched his chin to think.

"I am only here to check on you. I apologize for showing up unannounced. This was left in my study."

Allister handed Lumen a thistle.

"Is this the one from the Liros fire?"

Allister shook his head.

"I am afraid not. This was left in my cabin. I have spoken with the others and nobody has seen anything particularly out of the ordinary. I wanted to check on you personally to make sure everything is alright . . ."

Lumen grabbed the thistle and looked at it closely.

"Maybe the person is surrendering. Maybe Chester gives up. Too much pressure to keep up what he was doing. It was silent all week," Lumen whispered.

Allister scratched his chin again. He seemed perplexed.

"Perhaps you are right . . . I hope you are right. So, nothing out of the ordinary then?"

Lumen shook his head.

"Okay, I'll be heading back. You better get back to that hot chocolate, smells delightful."

Allister opened a window, but Lumen grabbed his arm before he could step through.

"Hey, one more thing. What did I say about the ice for Wrigley? It's bad for his teeth."

Allister nodded and put his hand up to apologize.

"I just love dogs, and Wrig loves ice . . . I'm sorry."

Lumen nodded and let go. Allister smiled, and Lumen felt the warmth in his gut again.

When Lumen returned to the living room, Sofia and Alice were already covered in blankets on the couch with mugs of hot cocoa.

"Were you talking to someone in there?" Alice asked.

Lumen panicked for a moment.

"Uh, was just talking to Wrigley. Can't believe he peed on the carpet again . . ."

Lumen scurried off to the kitchen to grab paper towels to clean up the pee, which wasn't pee after all. Lumen joined Sofia and his mother afterward to watch *All Out Lie,* an intense action movie.

"What's up with the movie? Thought we were going to watch something a bit more, oh I don't know, Christmas-y?" Lumen asked.

Sofia and Alice shrugged together and continued to watch the movie. Lumen sighed reluctantly but couldn't help but enjoy the moment.

Chapter 13 - Christmas

Lumen was off from both schools Monday through Wednesday. After Christmas on Wednesday, it was back to the Genaqua on Thursday. Lumen enjoyed his days off spending time with Sofia, Alice, and even Alec for a bit. Alec was so busy those days that he was no longer required to keep an eye on Lumen. Lumen missed their friendship, but it was like nothing changed when they hung out.

Alec came over on Christmas Eve to have dinner with Lumen and Sofia. He sweat profusely throughout the entire dinner; Lumen forgot that happened to Alec on this side. He wondered if that would happen to him once he became more in tune with his abilities.

Alice handed Alec a gift after dinner and insisted that he open it.

"Do you like it?" She asked before he was done unwrapping the gift.

Alec ripped the bright blue wrapping paper off the present and there was a water bottle that, according to the wrapper, could keep liquids cold all day. There was also a card. The card contained a free-entry pass to a rock climbing gym.

"I know how sporty you are and didn't think you ever tried rock climbing. You'll have cold water to bring with you," Alice said merrily.

Alec smiled and gave Alice a big hug.

"Thank you, Miss Haaken. It's great. I can't wait to go."

Alice smiled back.

"Oh, I forgot. I got you something too . . ."

Alec reached into his basketball shorts and pulled out a small envelope.

"Here . . ."

Alice smiled and said, "Oh, Alec you didn't have to."

She opened the envelope, revealing a small package. Lumen peered over at Alec and Alec winked.

Alice peered down at the front of the tiny package. On the front, written with a dark green cursive, was "Marble Rose Seeds."

"It's seeds to plant in the garden. I figured this would help get the flowers going again, you know, once it stops snowing here . . ."

"Marble Rose? I've never heard of that flower . . ."

"Yeah, it's rare. Every rose that blooms will look unique from all the others."

Alice's mouth dropped open as if she had just learned she had won the lottery.

"Oh my goodness, Alec. Thank you very much. That was very thoughtful of you. I cannot wait until spring to see them!" Alice gave Alec another hug. Alec's eyes teared up.

Lumen rolled his eyes.

They finished dinner with some hot cocoa and conversation, then Alec took off. They met in Lumen's room before Alec departed.

"You just had to get her the most amazing flowers, didn't you? How is my lame gift going to look now? Where'd you get those seeds anyway? I've never heard of those before."

Lumen crossed his arms as he awaited an answer from Alec.

"I got them at a market in Entropolis. Don't worry, dude, I'm sure she'll love the book. Have a good Christmas. I'll see you Thursday?" Alec asked.

Lumen smiled.

"See you Thursday. Wait, take this. Open it tomorrow though. I don't like when gifts are opened before the day."

Alec laughed and nodded, taking the wrapped present from Lumen.

He opened a window and stepped through.

Lumen brought gifts for Lucy and Yu as well. Lumen decided to put the gifts by a tree in the cabin that held the elevator to the Genaqua; he saw others living in the dorms do the same, so he figured it was a safe spot.

It was snowing lightly in the Genaqua, the perfect ambiance for the students staying there. Lumen thought that Allister had out-done himself. Lights dotted the trees and on the cabins. It was nice for everyone to have this place to stay in if needed. Lumen placed the presents under the small tree in the cabin, noticing the cozy fire going in the fireplace.

Lumen stepped out of the cabin into the center of the Paxum. He looked around in awe. Each expanse had its own version of decorating for the holidays. Even more striking, Lumen thought how it looked like nothing had happened last week. Allister and the others had really done a good job cleaning up after the fires.

Lumen was about to jump back home when he heard someone call his name. He turned and looked back, Till was jogging toward him.

"Hey, Lu!"

She was wearing her floral dress with a cardigan.

"Don't your legs get cold?" Lumen asked, genuinely curious how she could always wear a dress.

She shrugged.

"Eh, not really. They kind of stay warm on their own. How's your Christmas?"

Lumen smiled.

"It's been great so far. How about yours?"

Till sighed.

"It's been alright. Thought I would be in a different spot by now, but I think I'm progressing. It'd be more joyous if there wasn't so much pressure."

Lumen was confused by what she meant.

"You mean with school? Like in Pluviam class? You get poured on almost every class. I'm sure that's rough. I know what it's like to get wet at school almost every day."

Till squinted as she was thinking. She seemed confused with what Lumen was saying.

"Oh right, Pluviam class. Yeah, it sucks. J is a real piece of work. At least I can sit next to you every day."

Till reached for Lumen's hand. Lumen pulled his hand away.

"What's up with you always doing this? You know I have a girlfriend. Why can't we just be friends?"

Till smiled at Lumen.

"I don't do well with friends, typically. I like you, Lu. I know you like me too. I've seen how you look at me. You should just come with me. It'd be best, for both of us."

Till tried to pull Lumen. He noticed how soft and warm her hands were, but pulled away again.

"No, stop. Enjoy your Christmas, Till. I hope you find what you're looking for. It's not me though."

Lumen opened a window and went back to his home. He never slept well on Christmas Eve. After his interaction with Till, tonight would be no different. Lumen decided to do another puzzle.

It was Christmas morning. Lumen, Alice and Wrigley gathered in the living room to open presents. Lumen got mostly clothes and puzzles; he was at the age where those kinds of gifts would become more prevalent. He gave his mom the gift he got her, the book of flowers. Alice seemed just as excited about that gift as she was about the gift from Alec, Lumen was relieved. He also gave Wrigley his gift. It was a new squeaky toy in the shape of a dog bone. Wrigley ripped the toy out of the bag and trotted away. Lumen and Alice laughed.

They cleaned up the torn up paper, and Alice went to go get donuts. While she was out, Lumen washed up for the day; Sofia and Mr. Chimera were coming over later. When Lumen returned to his room after his shower, Alec was sitting on his bed with Wrigley. Lumen jumped and almost lost his towel.

"Will you stop doing that? I'm going to have a heart attack one of these days!"

Alec laughed.

"I just wanted to stop by to say thank you-- for the gift."

Alec held up the gift Lumen had given him. It was a book on the history of the prominent Eauge families.

"Means a lot to me, man. Thanks."

Alec almost seemed teary eyed. Lumen had no idea the book would mean so much, he just thought it was a cool idea. Alec walked over and hugged Lumen while Lumen stood there, making sure his towel didn't fall off.

"I think our friendship is on another level after that hug."

Alec laughed at the comment.

"I'll see you tomorrow, man. Have a great Christmas."

Alec opened a window and walked through. The window closed and almost immediately reopened. Alec stepped back through.

"I almost forgot, here."

Alec handed him a small gift. Lumen looked at it for a moment and ripped off the bland, brown paper.

It was a small glass ball. It seemed to be filled with some sort of dark smoke.

"It tells you what the weather is going to be like. It's showing dark clouds right now, which means a storm is probably on the way. It'll rain inside of there when it's going to rain, clear up when it'll be sunny out, snow when it's going to snow, you know, just the weather in general . . ."

Lumen's mouth dropped as Alec explained it.

"Wow. Thank you. This is probably the coolest gift I have ever gotten. Thanks, man. This is awesome."

Alec smiled and nodded.

"No problem. Now have a great Christmas. See you tomorrow."

Lumen waved and Alec stepped back through the window and left. Lumen placed the glass sphere on his desk while he got dressed. When he came around to take a closer look at the ball he saw it was starting to drizzle inside. Lumen thought it was fascinating and wondered how it worked.

Just then, Alice returned with the donuts.

Sometime after breakfast, Alice and Lumen began prepping for their future guests; Alice was making a baked ham and Lumen cleaned up around the house. Sofia and her dad arrived shortly after noon, hauling along a bottle of wine for the adults and pumpkin pie. All four of them hung around in the kitchen, drinking and snacking on small appetizers. Mr.Chimera and Alice got to talking about their work lives, and Sofia and Lumen snuck away to take Wrigley on a walk. They returned to find John and Alice laughing loudly.

"I'm glad my dad is having a good time. He didn't want to come at first, said he felt it was betraying my mom."

Lumen shrugged.

"Well, I'm glad you both came. This is really nice, having a full house. I've never had this before."

Sofia grabbed his hand and kissed him on the cheek. Lumen blushed.

The two exchanged gifts before dinner. Sofia loved her scarf and proceeded to put it on immediately. Lumen was relieved that she liked it. Sofia gave Lumen a puzzle and card that said "One FREE Chicken Pot Pie." *La Dernier Piece* was written on the bottom of the card. Lumen told her it was a perfect gift. They hugged, and Alice yelled that the food was ready. When they all sat at the table Lumen couldn't help but feel elated. To Lumen's pleasant surprise, Alice didn't burn the food this time. Instead, the ham she made was baked perfectly. They ate and drank for a while, not one of them wanting to leave the table that brought them together. They finished their meals and ate the pie the Chimera's brought. Alice found some whipped cream in the fridge to go with it.

They all helped clean up, then John decided it was time to go. Alice had to work the night shift and he wanted to give her time to rest. Alice insisted that they didn't have to leave, but John insisted that they should go. John gave Alice a kiss on the cheek and sincerely thanked her for having them over.

"Anytime, John. Thanks for the pie, it was delicious."

"It's from the bakery down the road. We should get some coffee and pie next week, if you have time . . ."

"I would like that; give me a call."

They smiled at one another for a moment before John walked out.

Lumen and Sofia looked at each other with worried faces, they didn't like the sound of that. Sofia hugged Lumen and thanked him for the scarf. As John and Sofia were walking to their car, Lumen could hear Sofia say, "Don't you have stuff going on next week?"

"Nice man. I'm glad they came over," Alice said.

Lumen rolled his eyes.

"He's alright. He ate a lot of our food."

Alice gave Lumen a look.

"We invited them to eat, hun, I hope he ate as much as he wanted."

Lumen rolled his eyes again and walked to the kitchen to finish cleaning up.

Alice got ready for work. She and Lumen hugged before she left.

"I hope you had a good day, hun."

"Yeah, Mom, it was great. Thanks for everything."

Lumen kissed her on the cheek, and Alice took off for the night.

With a free night ahead of him, Lumen decided to head into Bonumalus; he wanted to find Lucy and Yu to make sure they got their gifts. Lumen was about to take off to the Paxum when Wrigley began to cry.

"Fine, you can come. You're lucky it's Christmas."

Lumen put on a jacket. He looked at the sphere on his desk. It was very dark in there. He thought that there must be a big storm on the way.

Lumen opened a window to the Paxum and jumped through with Wrigley.

He found Yu hanging out near the cabin. He was wearing the gift Lumen got him.

"Hey! Thanks for the hat-umbrella thing man. I'll definitely wear this in Pluviam class! Here, I got you something, too."

Yu handed him a big pack of whistleberry juice.

"It's a twelve pack. Should last you a little while, right?"

Lumen laughed and thanked him for the juice. He asked if he had seen Lucy. Yu told him she was studying down in the Genaqua at the food hall.

Lumen took the elevator down and found Lucy. She was sitting by herself, headphones in with a cup of some juice Lumen had never seen and a book titled *A History of Music in Bonumalus*. Lumen tapped her on the shoulder. Lucy lit up and stood up to give Lumen a hug.

"Thank you so much for the book! I had to come here to start reading; my house is crazy right now. Too much family there. Hold on a second . . ."

Lucy opened a window, just stuck the upper half of her body through, and then came back to where she was sitting. She held a basket in her hands.

"I know how much you like those pockets, so here is a basket full of them. I found this stuff that will keep them fresh . . ." She said as she handed him the basket. She pulled something out of it.

"And this paper, you just fold the edges and rub them together, it will heat up. You can place the pocket on top of it, and it will heat up the pocket in no time. Cool right? I think it's called calor paper . . ."

Lumen grabbed the paper and rubbed it together like Lucy had explained. He set the paper down and held his hand above it; he could feel the heat coming off of it. He placed a pocket on it and it began steaming after just a few seconds.

"Wow, that's incredible! Where'd you find this?"

"I have a friend in the Ignous caste. I saw her use it to heat up her lunch once. Asked where she got it. Apparently it's only available in a market down by their classes. I asked her to get one for me."

Lumen gave Lucy a hug.

"Thank you, this is awesome."

"Be careful with it, if you rub it hard and long enough, it can start a fire."

Lumen nodded and assured her that he would. They sat and talked about their day for a few minutes before Lucy had to get back to her family. She said bye to Lumen, gave Wrigley a hug, and headed up the cabin elevator so that she could jump home.

Lumen walked around with Wrigley in the Illustra Forest of the Genaqua for some time before he decided to head home. Before he got to the elevator, he saw a hooded figure jogging into the forest in the back of the Genaqua. Lumen thought it could be Chester. He instinctively decided to follow. Wrigley stayed close behind Lumen as they jogged into the forest. Lumen lost the figure in the trees. He saw a flash of light, presumably a window opening, and then the light was gone. Lumen knew the person had jumped from the Genaqua again, most likely Chester. Lumen decided he needed to tell Allister.

Lumen and Wrigley jumped into Allister's cabin. Allister was sitting on his couch, fire burning, chalice in one hand and a scroll-like paper in the other. He was wearing glasses to read. Janis sat across from him, legs crossed. He had a small tobacco pipe in his mouth and also had a scroll-like paper in hand. There was a small tree in the corner, decorated with lights and a few ornaments. Neither flinched upon Lumen's arrival. Lumen stood there a few moments before clearing his throat.

"Ehem . . ."

Allister and Janis both turned to look at Lumen.

"Oh hello, my boy, Merry Christmas! Sorry about that. Janis and I don't often get time to read the paper. As you can see, we got a bit carried away in it."

Wrigley trotted over to Janis.

"Niet, Niet! You brrrought dog? Niet!"

Janis stood up on the edge of the couch. Lumen was pretty sure he was speaking with a Russian accent this time.

"Oh, don't be such a baby, Janis, he just wants to say hello."Lumen said with a smile.

Janis shook his head.

"Don't you know cats and dogs have been enemies forr all time? He vants to eat me!"

Lumen shook his head.

"No, Janis, he just wants to say hello. I think he can tell you aren't a normal cat. Tell him to sit. I'm sure he'll listen."

In almost a whisper, Janis told Wrigley to sit, and he did just as Lumen said.

"Good boy, Wrig. Come over here and leave the scaredy cat alone," Lumen said.

Allister chuckled.

"What can we help you with on this lovely Christmas evening? Shouldn't you be with your mother? Or Sofia?" Allister asked.

Lumen turned pink when he mentioned Sofia. He didn't know Allister knew about her.

"Uh, well, I was with them earlier. My mom works the night shift, and Sofia went home with her dad. I went to the Paxum to find Yu and Lucy. That's why I'm here, actually. Lucy was down in the Genaqua, and after she left I saw a hooded figure go into the forest. I followed it, and saw some lights flash, and it was gone."

Allister looked at Janis. It was like they were speaking telepathically.

"Did you see who it vas?" Janis asked.

Lumen shook his head.

"No, but it had to have been Chester, right? I have seen him do that before."

Allister nodded his head and stood up. He walked over to the fire and leaned on the mantle. Lumen and Janis waited for him to say something.

"Though it is against the rules to jump from the Genaqua, there wasn't a serious crime committed. Nothing we can do right now."

Lumen disagreed with Allister.

"What? What if he is planning another attack right now? Wherever he goes is where he must be planning out these attacks. We should catch him. Can't you tell where the lights led him anyway?"

Allister shook his head. Janis spoke for him.

"Ve checked arrea, zere is no flaw in Allister's vorrk."

Lumen had to replay what Janis said in his head to fully understand.

"Then how is it possible for him to jump?"

Allister turned back toward Lumen.

"The lights . . . some consider the lights to be a fifth element. You can become a master of the lights just as you can become a master of fire, or water. The difference with the lights is they're impossible to fully control. It is as if they are their own being. They can present themselves at opportune times, in a time of need for example. Chester must have been presented in a time of need, and he seized it."

Lumen looked at the ring on his finger. He often forgot that it was there. Allister took notice.

"Not like your luxem. Your luxem is used in a time of danger, to a designated area. Most people are never presented with lights like Chester presumably has. There is no telling what prompted the lights to help Chester. This phenomenon is called Incipiam. Some believe it to even be a myth."

Lumen had a million questions buzzing in his head.

"Have you ever witnessed it before?"

Allister and Janis looked at one another again.

"Not firsthand, my boy, but I can assure you that it is no myth," Allister stated.

Lumen felt like he touched a sore spot. Janis seemed uncomfortable. Lumen decided he would talk with Lucy about this later.

"Well, what do we do now then?"

Allister came toward Lumen and put his hands on his shoulders.

"Next time you see Chester going to the back of the forest, you follow and try and make the jump just as he does. The window should remain open for a second or two after Chester jumps. You'll have to time it perfectly."

Lumen gulped and nodded as Allister smiled at him. He did not want to let him down.

"Great, any questions?"

Lumen nodded, he had one.

"What do I do when I get through? Do I apprehend him?"

Allister smiled again.

"No, no, of course not. Watch him for a moment to see where he is and what he does. Do not put yourself in danger. Once you take note of where he is and what he is doing, you come straight here and get me. Janis and I will take care of it."

Lumen had one more question.

"What will happen to him if he is the one causing all of this? Does he go to jail? He is . . . is he sentenced to death . . ."

Both Allister and Janis shook their heads.

"We are civilized people here in Bonumalus, Lumen. We will decide punishment based on what we find. Though his crimes have been serious, and could have resulted in serious injury or death, I always believe we can help, especially children and young adults. We don't want to subjugate a child to the horrors of Vincula. You let us worry about that part."

Lumen nodded. He had a lot to think about and decided he should head home to rest up.

"All right, happy Christmas then . . ." Lumen said as he went to leave.

Allister waved and then hollered for Lumen to wait.

"I almost forgot, open it when you get home. Read the note before doing anything with it. Merry Christmas, Lumen."

Allister handed Lumen a cube-shaped box that fit in his hands. Lumen had no idea what it could be. He was overjoyed by the fact Allister gave him a Christmas gift, so much so that he couldn't even manage to say thank you before he jumped from the cabin.

Chapter 14 - The Jump

Lumen tossed and turned for the next few nights. He didn't want to let Allister and Janis down, especially after receiving a gift from Allister. Lumen opened it the same night he received it and found a ball of water sitting in the box. The water was not bound by anything other than the air around it, yet it stayed in a perfect sphere shape. Lumen picked up the water, and its form remained. He picked up the accompanying note.

STICKY WATER - in case of a fire , throw this at the flames. It will "stick" and put out the fire immediately. Once the fire is out, just ball the water up again. Use with caution. Has other uses as well. - AA

Lumen had no idea how it worked but was excited to have it. He set it down gently in one of his desk drawers and covered it with some papers in case Alice came around.

Classes in Bonumalus commenced the next day. Lumen made a point to follow Chester around whenever he wasn't in class. However, Chester did not seem up to anything out of the ordinary as of late. Lumen followed him for a couple of weeks and found nothing relatively odd. He found Chester liked to lay on the rocks near the forest on his off time, play with his Rubix cube, and listen to music. Every once in a while someone threw a snowball at him or have a tiny storm rain on him. Chester would look toward the forest in those instances, but never actually took action. Lumen was becoming impatient. He wondered if he could entice him to go and decided to enlist Yu and Lucy for some back-up. He asked Alec to help as well, but he declined.

"I got midterms, man. It's no joke for us second year-ers."

Lumen understood. He asked Yu and Lucy to meet him in the food hall to discuss a plan. He broke down everything that had been happening with Chester and explained that he needed to follow him through his secret window.

"Let's just throw a couple of snowballs at him, he seems to get overwhelmed pretty easily," Yu suggested.

"No, Yu, I just explained that he has been ignoring stuff like that, we need something else . . ." Lumen said as he put his head down to think.

Lucy seemed to be thinking deeply and was nodding.

"You got an idea, Lucy?"

"Yeah, I think so. I think Chester doesn't really like Professor J. We have a quiz tomorrow, maybe we can do something then . . ."

They all nodded and got to work on a plan.

Before Pluviam began, Lumen, Yu and Lucy went over their plan one more time to make sure they had it right. They knew the test would be on drizzling.

Professor J had a habit of making each student test in front of the entire class so that everyone could see their shame when they failed. Chester had been much better as of late and had not failed after the incident with Till.

Yu was the first student to test. Professor J conjured up a tiny cloud, and Yu had to control it to make it only drizzle. It couldn't be a mist or a rain, but a drizzle. Yu passed easily, he had become one of the best students in this class. Lumen,

Lucy, and most of the other students all passed as well. Chester was last to go.

When it was finally his turn, Chester strolled up to the front of the class with his hoodie on over his head, seeming determined.

"Do you have no respect, boy? Hood down in my class."

Chester took down his hood, unphased by Professor J's last attempt to scare Chester into failing as he had in the past. Lumen thought for a second that Professor J was just a little bit evil with his antics and joy for seeing students fail.

Professor J began to conjure up a cloud. Lumen looked at Lucy, and they both nodded.

Lucy screamed loudly. The entire class looked at her, except for Chester who was solely focused on the cloud above him.

Professor J seemed irritated.

"What is it Lucy?"

"There is a fire under my desk, please, help!" Lucy yelled.

Professor J sighed and told Chester to hold the cloud there. He walked over to Lucy's desk, and there was indeed a small fire.

"A fire? Are you sure, girl?" Professor J walked cautiously to Lucy's desk. There was in fact a small fire under her desk, but he put it out with a bit of water with the snap of his fingers. At the same time, Chester had managed to make it drizzle ever so lightly. He was smiling. Lumen and Yu nodded at one another and both focused on the cloud. They put pressure on the cloud to release a downpour of rain. Chester was very obviously struggling to keep the cloud at just a drizzle.

Professor J found what had caused the fire.

"Calor paper? How did you get this? It's dangerous if not used properly, young lady."

Lucy shrugged.

"It's not mine, I've never seen that before."

Professor J shook his head.

"We will speak after class. Don't take off right away."

He then turned around to go back to the front of class. He smiled when he saw the drizzle coming from the cloud.

Chester was really struggling at this point. Lumen and Yu turned up the pressure. The cloud poured down onto Chester.

"You insolent boy! The only one to fail! When will you learn? Maybe this life isn't meant for you. Maybe you should consider a life on the board. The board is full of people like you who can't tap into their innate abilities. Fools, just like you."

Drenched in water, Chester ran out of the class. Lumen ran after him.

Chester headed straight for the forest in a sprint. Lumen tailed him but tried to keep a distance so that he didn't notice. Chester didn't look back once as he headed into the trees.

Lumen thought he saw Lucy for a moment running to the left, but when he glanced that way nobody was there. He looked behind and could see Yu and Lucy looking on from a distance as Lumen had told them to not follow. They were into the thick of the trees and Lumen was having a hard time keeping his eyes on Chester.

Chester stopped abruptly. He glanced behind him, pacing back and forth for a moment before stopping again. Suddenly a window was opened. Lumen didn't see Chester do anything to open it, however. Allister was right, the lights could present themselves if needed. Lumen thought that the windows must not be biased against good or evil if they were helping Chester.

Lumen moved up to the closest tree; he needed to time this perfectly.

He positioned himself in a way where he could take off in a sprint. Chester glanced around once more and stepped through. The moment Chester lifted his leg to step through, Lumen took off running. Chester disappeared through the window. Lumen only had a second or two to make it before the window closed. In the midst of a full sprint, he fell flat on his face. He looked behind and saw his foot caught on a tree root. He slammed his fist into the ground in frustration, thinking only of how he let Allister and the others down.

But, before he could beat himself up even more, Lumen looked up and the window was still open. He was confused but didn't have time to question it. He sprinted to it and jumped through.

Lumen tumbled into some bushes as he landed on the other side of the window. He looked up to see trees all around him. He was in another forest. Lumen looked around and recognized a kind of familiarity. His attention was directed towards a flower on the ground. He remembered seeing the same flower the first time he came into Bonumalus. This had to be the same island on which the Liros resided, Mighty Falls Island. Lumen remembered that it floated in midair.

He heard some leaves crunch and turned to look in the direction of the sound where he saw Chester jogging through the trees. Lumen got up feverishly and followed in his direction. He kept a safe distance in order to make sure Chester made it to his intended destination.

Lumen followed him for a few minutes when he realized that the island was coming to an end, and if he kept running, he would run right off of a cliff.

Lumen slowed down. *He can't go much further*, he thought. When he could no longer see Chester he picked up the pace again until he was through the trees. Then, suddenly, there was Chester, sitting on the edge of the cliff. Lumen didn't know what to expect. Definitely not Chester simply sitting on the edge of a cliff. There were no thistles around, no fires, no master plans-- nothing except open skies in front of him and a forest behind. It was silent. Lumen could hear the slight breeze rustling the trees behind him.

Lumen cleared his throat.

"Uh, Chester, the scheme is up. I've found your secret window. You need to come back with me."

Lumen realized Allister had told him to alert him when he found Chester. Lumen had to finish the job himself now; he couldn't leave.

Chester jumped in his seat, quickly looking back with a look of fear in his eyes.

"What the . . . how'd you get here?"

"I followed you. Took some time to find the window you were using, but I finally was able to follow you through. The jig is up, we all know you're the one starting the fires. It's time to turn yourself in."

Chester didn't respond. He scratched his head and furrowed his eyebrows.

Lumen got a little angry.

"I mean, for goodness sake, you almost killed my mom! You could have seriously hurt so many others too. I can't believe anyone could do such a thing. Lucky for you, Allister thinks he can help people like you. You won't have to suffer in Vincula like most the other criminals."

Chester put his hands up toward Lumen as Lumen poised himself into a fighting stance.

"Whoa, whoa, I didn't start any fires, Lumen. I can't even handle a little rain cloud, you think I can handle learning both?" Chester asked, desperately.

"No, I think you're actually an Ignous trying to infiltrate the Eauge caste. . ."

Chester shook his head. He didn't move from his position. His legs were shaking.

"No no no! I swear Lumen! I had nothing to do with those fires. I am really sorry about your mom, but it wasn't me! You heard Professor J, I should plan on going for a board job. I can't handle this."

Lumen was confused. He took notice of Chester's shaking.

"This isn't where you go to plan your attacks? Where you find your thistles to leave at your crime scenes?"

Chester shook his head.

"No, I come here to get away from everyone! Day after day, I fail in class. Day after day, the other students pick on me. . . What's a thistle anyway?"

Lumen shook his head. He couldn't decide if he should believe Chester or not.

"So you just come out here to get away?"

Chester nodded his head as his legs continued to tremble.

218

"But why would the lights present a window to you in an area where you can't travel from? The Genaqua is supposed to be jump-proof. I don't get it."

Lumen paced back and forth while he mulled over his thoughts.

"You wouldn't understand, Lumen. You do well in these classes. You have friends. Allister works with you personally. I came here with nothing and still have nothing. I've been trying to figure out why the lights brought me here also . . ."

Lumen stepped toward Chester to listen.

"I thought it was to just have a safe place, away from everyone else. But the more I come here, the more I think I was brought here to disappear."

Chester stepped back and looked over the edge of the cliff. There was no end in sight as Chester peered past the roots dangling from the side of the cliff.

"What? No, Chester, the lights wouldn't do that," Lumen retorted.

Chester looked back toward Lumen.

"How do you know that?"

Lumen wasn't sure why he thought that, but he firmly believed it.

"They just wouldn't. Look, I understand where you're coming from. The town I'm from, I was bullied almost everyday. There's this one kid, Blake, he really has it out for me. He used to give me swirlies every day."

Chester was listening closely.

"Seriously? I've never gotten one of those . . ."

"Yeah, it was pretty bad. And for a while I just accepted them. It was part of my life, and I let him and his buddies do it."

Chester stepped closer to Lumen.

"What changed?"

Lumen realized how great it was to have a friend like Alec. Alec, in a way, saved him from a dark life.

"I had some help. A newfound friend came to my side and guided me through everything. That gave me the courage to not let it happen anymore . . ."

Chester put his head down.

"What it means, Chester, is that you should seek someone to talk to. By no means is it your fault that you're bullied. People are terrible to one another. But if a few of us can stick together, we can really help one another."

Chester looked up and had a little smile. Lumen thought it might be difficult at first, but he could convince Yu and Lucy to let Chester join their group.

"So, I guess we are back to square one. For a while now, we thought you were the one starting all of the fires . . ." Lumen said as he sighed.

Chester shook his head.

"No way, man, I can't even make it drizzle. You expected me to be capable of starting full on fires? I come here to be alone. I sometimes climb up these trees and end up falling into the mud. I can't even accomplish that."

They both laughed. Lumen felt bad about making him fail the quiz in Pluviam class. Chester was doing just fine until he and Yu intervened. Lumen decided to keep that to himself.

"Well, we should head back then. I should let Allister know you're not the one."

Chester nodded in agreement. He stepped toward Lumen when his jacket started smoking. The jacket went up in flames. Chester fell to the ground in a panic and started yelling. Lumen panicked for a moment before realizing he was able to create a small rain cloud. It took a few moments to conjure a small cloud but was able to rain down onto Chester.

Chester managed to get the jacket off.

"Are you okay?"

Chester patted himself down to check for any injuries. He stopped and smelled his forearm.

"Yeah, I think so. Just my forearm hairs were burned off, smells awful . . . thanks for the rain."

Lumen nodded.

"Where did that come from? You sure you're not an Ignous?" Lumen asked, half joking.

Chester gave Lumen a stern look.

"Are you kidding me? And set myself on fire? How does that make sense?"

Lumen shrugged.

"Well, where did it come from?"

A rustle came from the trees. They were both suddenly aware that they were not alone, although they couldn't tell from where the sound came. The pair looked around frantically for someone to show themselves. They heard a clap. And then another. Someone was applauding them.

They heard a loud crack, and a large tree came tumbling in flames. The tree that was once covered in a plethora of green life was now burning to ash on the ground near them. The tree laid a short distance away from them, the leaves crackling loudly as they burned. Lumen could smell the smoke. Chester coughed as he tried to clear the smoke around him with his arms. Lumen was sweating now. His heart was racing, and his mouth was dry. He had no idea what to expect.

The person emerged slowly from the trees and smoke, still clapping.

"Bravo, bravo. Quick thinking, Lumen. You. . .you are one of the best Eauge students. You looked so cute while you managed to create the tiny, little cloud to help Chester . . . Poor Chester couldn't help himself."

Till laughed as she stepped closer to Lumen and Chester.

Lumen's first thought was of relief and then of confusion.

"Did you really follow me here Till?" Lumen asked

"Oh yes, of course. I've been following you for some time now," Till said with a smile--the same smile Lumen couldn't forget.

"Allister would be really upset if he knew you followed me here. This is serious stuff we are dealing with."

"I know," Till said as she continued to smile.

Lumen became aware of the fire again.

"Did you see anyone back there? I think we were followed by someone else," he said as he looked at the burning tree; half of it had already turned to ash.

Lumen looked at Till, the odd smirk still on her face.

It was starting to come together.

"Till . . . it's been you this whole time?" Lumen said.

Till moved closer towards them as she created a fireball and tossed it between her hands.

Lumen realized it made a lot of sense. She was one of the worst students in his classes thus far, maybe she was an Ignous after all. Till was in one of her classic sun dresses. Lumen just then saw the scars on her legs. Till took notice.

"Yeah, those thistles can be really painful if you're not too careful. Scratched me really good on a dark night . . ."

Till continued towards Lumen and Chester. Lumen raised his hand to try and open a window.

"I wouldn't do that if I were you."

Till pushed her hands down. Flames surrounded the three of them with no way out, their backs were against the cliff.

"Open a window and Chester won't be so lucky next time. I'm afraid your little rain clouds won't be able to put out these flames."

Lumen and Chester glanced around. She was right, there was no escaping. Lumen peered over the side of the cliff.

"Why are you doing this, Till?" Lumen asked.

Till started to pace slowly. She was basking in the moment.

"I'm here to recruit, to show you our power. We need more people to join our movement. It'll be easier that way."

Lumen and Chester looked at one another. They didn't know what she was talking about.

"Maldeus, of course, is back. He is going to build up his army, not that he really needs it if you ask me, and take back control."

"Control of what?" Chester asked.

"Of what is rightfully ours!"

Till stamped her foot down, and the flames rose just a bit higher.

"We have an entire planet that we gleefully manage for those pathetic humans that live there. We provide them with everything they need, everything, and what are they all doing?"

Lumen and Chester shook their heads.

"They are turning it into a dump! They tear down the trees, they waste water, and they pollute the air! It is time for us to take it back. They don't deserve it!"

Till was breathing heavily.

"I thought Maldeus was dead?" Chester said in a whisper. Till laughed.

"Of course not. Allister was too weak to finish the job. He made a mistake. Maldeus retreated to a place he could not be found. It's been twelve years. Twelve long years of planning and now he has seen enough. He is stronger than ever and ready to begin."

Lumen remembered that Allister had found Till in a burning building.

"I thought Allister rescued you? How could you betray him?"

Till laughed again.

"Saved me? Don't be ridiculous! I burned that building down, along with the feeble humans in it. I used sticky water to 'protect myself' and make it look like I had Eauge ability. Allister didn't even question it, that fool."

Lumen gulped. This was it, he thought, there was no way out.

His ring warmed his finger.

"What is supposed to happen here, Till?" Lumen asked as he was thinking.

"Pledge yourselves to our cause, to Maldeus, and I will take you back to our camp."

"And if we refuse?" Lumen asked as he moved in front of Chester.

"I guess I will have to start the cleansing now, which would be very unfortunate. I really like you, Lu."

Lumen looked at Chester and could see him trembling. Lumen glanced over the edge of the cliff again. He touched his ring.

"Well, alright, if you say so."

Lumen turned and pushed Chester off the side of the cliff. Chester grunted and then screamed as he fell from the cliff's edge. He clawed for the sides of the cliff, missing with each swipe. Lumen looked over the edge and saw Chester fall through the window he opened with his ring. Lumen turned back to find Till still, eyebrows raised and a smirk on her face.

"Well then, I knew I could convince you. I was going to extreme lengths to show you our might. I just got back from Sofia's, as a matter of fact. You won't have to worry about her any longer. It'll be difficult to say goodbye to your mother, but it gets easier with time," Till said as she resumed playing with the fireball in her hands.

It took everything in Lumen's body to not react to what she said about Sofia. He didn't know what that meant. Was she dead? Lumen tried to stay calm.

"Good" is all Lumen could manage to say. He was breathing heavily but tried his best to not show it.

"Great, I'm glad you understand. I really think you're special, Lu, there is something about you. You're going to be powerful. I can promise you that."

Lumen nodded. Till walked toward him.

"Come here, give me a hug. I feel like we are on another level now, Lu."

Lumen stepped away quickly.

"Don't be shy. We are a team now. Look what you just did for me. You pushed Chester off this cliff for me. It's a long way down, I bet he is still falling. Poor kid probably isn't smart enough to open a window on the way down to save himself."

She looked down and saw a window close. Lumen's hand pulled away from his ring. Till looked at Lumen, eyes wide. She shook her head in disappointment as she smiled again.

"Ah, the good ol' luxem never fails. That's too bad. I had a lot of hope for you. Maybe in another life . . ."

Till raised her hands. A ball of flames quickly formed in her palms. Till chucked it at Lumen. Lumen dove in an effort to avoid it, if only just barely. The flames hit his leg, burning his pants. He couldn't tell if his leg was burned or not, his adrenaline was pumping.

"Just let it happen, Lu, you don't have the skill to fight me. . . Last chance, join us, or perish."

Lumen stammered to his feet. He could feel that his leg was in pain now. The flames surrounded him; they had risen slightly and he could barely see over them. Smoke was rising from the fallen tree, making the air coarse and difficult to inhale. Lumen took a deep breath before answering.

"No."

He put his hand on his chest and felt his heart pounding. Even so, he felt calm. He was ready for whatever was about to transpire.

"I have one question: why a thistle?"

Lumen's curiosity never failed him.

"They were used as a warning to invaders back in medieval times, thought it was a cool signature. Was going to use it just the first time but your mom replenished my supply."

Lumen nodded his head; despite everything he thought, that was pretty clever.

Till created another ball of fire in her hands. She stepped back and threw it at Lumen as if it was a fastball. Lumen closed his eyes and braced for contact. He wondered what dying felt like. He thought that if at least he saved someone's life then it would be worth it--it wasn't for nothing.

When Lumen looked up he saw the fire coming at him; everything was in slow motion. He put his arms up, a natural instinct, to block to flames. Just when he thought he was about to feel the fury of the fire ball, the flames seemed to have hit something in front of him and continued around him.

Till was just as confused as Lumen. Her smile disappeared as she geared up to throw another.

The same thing happened. Lumen was even more befuddled. It was like an invisible shield was directly in front of him. He looked beyond Till and could see a trio walking behind the flames. There were Allister, Janis and Sasha. Lumen's face lit up and he thrust a fist in the air in excitement.

Till took notice of the trio and threw a flame at the group. Allister put up his hands and put the flames out with little balls of water. Till tried to run. Sasha hit the ground with her staff, and the ground under Till rose up. Till tried to open a window, but Allister clapped and the window closed immediately. Till was trapped. She attempted to throw another fireball, but before she could manage to, Sasha hit her staff on the ground again and roots underneath her entangled her limbs. The roots wrapped around Till until she was completely immobile, and only her head was showing. Sasha stomped the staff down a third time and the roots set Till down near her, detaching themselves from the ground. Janis raised his hand, and Till's root-wrapped body floated in mid-air.

Lumen was beyond relieved to see the three of them. He was sweating profusely and could feel his burned leg even

225

more so now. He was light-headed. The last thing he saw was Allister approaching him and felt Al's hand under his head.

Chapter 15 - Summer

Lumen awoke in a room he didn't recognize. He rubbed his eyes as looked around this unfamiliar room, trying to figure out where he was. It smelled like grass. On his left, he saw a table filled with jars of what appeared to be herbs and roots of some sort. To the right was a nicely carved rocking chair. There were two windows in the room, opened wide, and a doorway without a door attached. The room looked like it was covered in bark. Lumen began to get up when Allister and Lucy walked into the room.

"Hold up there, Lu. Take it easy," Lucy said.

"Where am I?"

"You're in a tree," Lucy said. Allister chuckled.

"Indeed you are. This is a hospital on the Mighty Falls Island, best in Bonumalus. They really have a handle on all these natural medicines. You're going to be just fine." Allister said matter-of-factly.

Lumen remembered his leg had been badly burned. He took off the covers and saw that it was wrapped in some bandages.

"My leg . . ."

"Was burned badly, but like I said, the Liros know medicine better than anyone. A couple drops of fickleberry and frigograss and your leg will be back to normal in a couple of days."

Lumen was relieved.

"It looked pretty bad when you came in," Lucy said. "Sasha knows the best doctors though. They were all really nice, Lumen. Everyone is here to see you . . . Guys, come n! He's awake!"

Sasha, Janis, Yu, Aiden, Alec, Chester, and Wrigley all came into the room. Lumen was overwhelmed to see them all, including Chester.

"Chester explained what happened and how you saved him. That was incredibly intelligent and selfless thinking, Lumen," Allister said. Chester approached him.

"Thank you for everything back there. I don't know how I can ever repay you."

Lumen shook his head.

"Don't worry about it, just make sure you come study with us from now on."

Chester smiled and stepped back. Wrigley jumped on the bed and began licking Lumen's face uncontrollably.

"Okay, okay! I missed you too, buddy. Don't worry, I'm alright." Wrigley laid by his side. Alec approached the bed.

"I'm sorry, man. I should have been there with you," Alec said somberly.

Lumen shook his head.

"No way, man. You've been there enough for me the last couple of years. I was prepared to handle something on my own . . .What did you tell my mom to get Wrigley?"

"Oh, I told her you were badly injured in this world called Bonumalus, and I wanted to take Wrigley to comfort you. She passed out after I said all that, so I figured it was okay to take him."

Lumen's mouth dropped.

"I'm just kidding! I told her you were caught up studying and asked me to drop by to help her. She didn't question anything."

Lumen sighed in relief.

"What about Sofia? Is she okay?"

Alec broke eye contact with Lumen.

"Just relax for now," he said as if he did not hear Lumen's question.

Allister asked everyone to give him and Lumen a moment alone. He allowed Wrigley to stay.

"What you did was incredibly brave today, Lumen. You stopped a very powerful young lady from hurting others. We cannot express our gratitude enough."

Lumen smiled.

"Don't worry about it, I would have been dead if you guys hadn't showed up at the perfect time and put that shield up."

Allister eyes squinted and he seemed confused.

"Shield? I'm not sure what you mean . . ." Allister said.

"You know, Till threw that fireball, and there was, like, an invisible shield in front of me that blocked it."

Allister shook his head.

"What you're explaining is an advanced Aeris move, an auraclip. Neither Janis nor I performed it."

Lumen scratched his head.

"Who did then?"

Allister smiled.

"I think you know the answer to that. You weren't wondering why you passed out? That was an advanced move that you performed innately. Your body was exhausted from doing it."

Lumen's eyes widened.

"Does that mean I should be an Aeris instead of an Eauge? I like the Eauge. I don't want to switch. I'm already a few months in, and I have learned so much--"

Allister put his hand up.

"Relax, kiddo, you are going to stay with the Eauge. We can talk about this at another time."

Lumen nodded, but he had a ton of questions buzzing in his head.

"What happened to Till?"

Allister sighed.

"Well, Janis and Sasha believe she should be sent to Vincula. I believe she is too young for that. I think we can still help her. She'll be sent away for some time," he said, seemingly disappointed.

"How did she get like that? Does it mean Maldeus has returned?"

Allister hesitated to answer.

"No. She probably just read about him and thought what he did was the right thing. Maldeus had a lot of followers in his time. I suppose I need to find out her true origins. Maybe her parents were followers. I am not quite sure," Allister said as he looked away.

Lumen nodded.

"How'd she know where I was? And the window, it stayed open for me. . ." Lumen said curiously.

"As I have said before, the lights can present themselves in a time of need. You needed to find Chester. It's possible she followed you through the same window," Allister said calmly.

"I'm just glad this is over. I feel like so much has been happening since I've come here. It's almost like she was targeting me, right?"

Allister hesitated again for a brief moment.

"I think she just liked you. Don't take it to heart. She was talented and could see the potential in you as well, just as I do."

Lumen blushed.

"What now?"

"Now, you rest for a little while. Sasha's people will look at you one more time and then discharge you. After that, you can go home and rest. No more school for you for the rest of the week. I spoke to your teachers already, don't worry. I also spoke to Alec and the others, they will stop by to bring you homework and keep you up to date."

Lumen smiled but was a little disappointed he still had to do the homework.

"Thanks, Allister. I have one last question that I've always wanted to know the answer to. . ."

"What's that?"

Lumen laughed a little before asking.

"What's up with the goggles? You always have them on, Janis too."

Allister smiled.

"That, my friend, has been wagered on by the students of Bonumalus for some time now. I don't think it would be fair to tell you. I think you'll have to do more to earn the right to know."

They both laughed. This only made Lumen more curious.

"Well, off I go. I'll leave you to rest. See you soon."

Allister petted Wrigley's head and exited the room. He said bye to the others outside. Janis popped his head in to give his well wishes and they both opened a window and departed.

Sasha's people checked on Lumen one last time, just as Allister said. They unwrapped his bandage and applied a couple more droplets of medicine. The drops tickled Lumen but he could feel his skin healing quickly. When he examined it himself, the marred skin almost looked normal, just hairless. He decided he'd wear jeans until the hair grew back. The rest said their goodbyes and left. Alec stayed behind to help Lumen get home.

Sofia was alive and well, her father too. However, their house was not. Sofia came over the next day.

"We have to leave. My dad thinks it's best after the fire. Says we need a fresh start after my mother. . . and now the house. . ."

Sofia explained that their house had burned down the day before. There was no explanation for how it happened; the fire department came up short, but Lumen knew the cause.

"I'm so sorry, Sofia, that's horrible."

Sofia cried into Lumen's arms.

"I don't want to leave, Lumen. Most of my memories are here."

"I don't want you to leave either." Lumen sighed heavily as his eyes teared up. He did not want Sofia to leave, but also knew they had been through a lot. He did not want to make it harder on her.

"But maybe your dad is right. It could be good for him. For you, too," Lumen said as he wiped snot from his running nose.

232

Sofia nodded, "Maybe . . ."

"I guess this is it then . . ." Lumen said, choking up. Sofia kissed him on the cheek.

"Maybe one day, hopefully, we will come back. We can write each other, and when we are old enough, we can travel to see one another."

Lumen nodded in agreement but knew he would most likely never see Sofia again. They hugged one more time before Mr. Chimera came to pick her up. And just like that, Sofia was gone. Lumen was saddened to see her go, their time together had been everything Lumen could have hoped for. Despite his feelings for her, he did think it was best for them to pack up and go. His life as an Eauge would only become more time consuming. The Chimera's had too many poor memories in this town. Lumen didn't want her to leave but thought it would be selfish to not think it was for the best. There was relief in his heart knowing she would not be targeted by someone from the exotic world of Bonumalus.

Alec came by shortly after.

"Dang just like that, you're girl-less again. Sofia moves away, and Till ends up being some supervillain. What are the chances?"

Lumen gave Alec a foul look.

"Shut up, Alec. Do you have any school work for me?"

Lumen focused on getting through regular school for the next few months until summer vacation. Bonumalus did not have a summer vacation, so once high school was out it would be a good time for Lumen to focus even more on becoming an Eauge.

During a routine doctor's visit Lumen and Alice got some unexpected news: Lumen was not a minor schizophrenic after all. The doctors he had been dealing with had been misdiagnosing hundreds of patients just to sell medicine. Alice threatened to sue them before storming out of the office.

"I'm calling my lawyers! How dare you give a child drugs that he does not need! What is wrong with you people! Have you no morals?" Alice was fuming, yelling profanities as she stormed out of the office.

Lumen was just happy not to have to lie to his mother as much now. He also figured word would get around town that he was not a "skitzo" and, hopefully, the bullying would calm down a bit. It would be less of a problem if he could convince his mom of something else.

"Mom?"

"Yes, dear?"

"How would you feel about me being homeschooled? Like you teaching me or assigning stuff for me to learn. . . "

"Homeschool? Are you sure? You would be on your own a lot. I work a ton, Lu, I'm not sure I could help you much," Alice said concernedly.

"I know, but I figure it would be a good way for me to get more prepared for college. School is too easy, Mom. I feel like I'm not learning anything at Bromide. Maybe I can get into college earlier if I do homeschooling. I can work at my own pace."

Alice nodded. She was happy that Lumen was looking ahead to his future.

"Let me think about it, hun, I'm sure we can work something out," Alice said.

Lumen thought it would be ideal to focus all of his time on learning to be an Eauge. It was challenging and he was excited about the possibilities. He knew he was leading his mom astray, once again, but eventually she would have to find out what he really was. Now wasn't the time though, Lumen decided, especially after the fiasco at the doctor's office.

Lumen finished up the year of school with straight A's. Alec returned for the remainder of the year; it would be his last at Bromide as well. They met in Entropolis after their last class at Bromide.

"Yeah, I am going to go full throttle in Eauge training. I want to be a part of the LOT. You have to be top notch to join, " Alec said.

"Lot? What's that?" Lumen asked.

"Leveraging Out Traitors. LOT. They basically work to catch our people working for the wrong side. People trying to cause havoc on Earth. The LOT work to catch these people, stop their storms, and sometimes even rehabilitate the criminals to do some good in Bonumalus. I'm surprised you have never heard of them. They are well known and respected around here. That's why I'm so focused on my studies. They only accept the best," Alec said proudly, as if he was already apart of the group.

Lumen nodded. He thought that sounded amazing. He didn't know if he would ever have the abilities to do that. He never even thought about a career there, and he had no idea what direction he would take if he did.

"What else is there to do here, like for a career?" Lumen asked.

Alec laughed.

"Dude, I have a feeling you'll be able to do whatever you want. Don't worry . . . We're almost there. I hope you're ready for a good time," Alec said as he pointed ahead.

Lumen was a bit confused. Alec hadn't told him what they were doing there. They walked through the snowy terrain to a large hut with the words "The Danse" engraved on a placard of wood. Lumen could hear live music inside. Someone tapped him on his shoulder.

"Hey, Lu!" Lucy gave Lumen a big hug. Yu wasn't far behind and joined in to make a group hug. Yu's baseball cap kept hitting Lucy in the forehead.

"Okay, that's enough, I don't want a concussion on the first day of summer . . ."

Around the corner, Lumen saw someone lurking.

"Chester?"

Chester looked up and waved. He walked over slowly.

"What are you doing over there, man?"

Chester shrugged.

"Was letting you guys have a moment or whatever, didn't want to intrude . . ."

"Don't be ridiculous, you're a part of this group too."

Chester smiled. Alec walked over.

"Alright guys, and lady of course, I got a table in there and a free dessert for everyone."

Lucy gasped.

"How'd you get us in so fast? And free dessert? It's usually an hour wait! And there's a good band today!"

"I know a couple guys that run the joint. Don't worry about it," Alec said.

Alec and Lucy smiled at each for a moment. She turned red.

Lumen, Alec, Lucy, Yu, and Chester walked in together to kick off their summer. Lumen couldn't have been any happier.

Epilogue - Channel 6 News

An older gentleman woke up at 6:45 am as he usually did. He stared at the ceiling for a few minutes before groaning dramatically as he rolled out of bed. The man's wife had already been up since 6:00 am. The man brushed his teeth, showered, combed the little bit of his white hair that he had left, and got dressed. He had been retired for some time now, but he always dressed nicely: slacks, a polo shirt or button-down, with some shined shoes. After preparing for the day, he went to the kitchen, as he always did, to eat breakfast with his wife. Per usual, the wife cooked up some eggs and bacon for her husband. They asked each other how they slept the night before and what they had planned for the day. The man told his wife that he was thinking about golfing. She said that she would be doing some shopping with her friends and would probably get some coffee after with their daughter.

"You said you might golf today? You should check the weather, I believe it's supposed to be a scorcher," the lady said.

The man sighed. They had a TV on the kitchen counter. He picked up the remote and turned it on. The channel was already set on Channel 6. The commercial break was just ending.

This is Channel 6 News. Let's go to Stormy for this week's forecast.

Thanks, Sherman. I hope you have your sunscreen, folks. Today is going to be a hot one. We are looking at temperatures in the upper 90s today, breaking a local record high on this day. Stay in an air-conditioned building, if possible, and try not to walk your dogs during the day; you could really hurt their paws. Looking ahead, we will have a bit of a cool down Tuesday and Wednesday, but we are going to climb into the triple digits over the weekend, again projecting to break local record highs. Be careful out there, folks. Stay hydrated and cool. Back to you, Sherman.

Thank you, Stormy. Stormy has a big story she has been working on the past few weeks on Global Warming, right Stormy?

That is right Sherman. Without giving away too much, I will just tell you that I have found some pretty astounding effects in this area alone. This town has been warming each and every year for the past 17 years. You'll have to tune in next week on Wednesday at 7:00am to hear the rest.

Thank you Stormy, we look forward to hearing more. Now let's go to Ruben for sports . . .

The wife turned to look at her husband.

"You can't golf today, hun, you'll have a heat stroke," she said firmly.

The husband shook his head in disappointment.

"It's been getting warmer every year, you heard the lady. There's only so much time left for me to try and enjoy these days before it turns into a wasteland out there. I'm going!"

The wife shook her head.

"I really wish you wouldn't, but you're right. The summers are too hot, and the winters too cold. I feel bad for the future. Everything is going to be burnt to a crisp!"

The husband nodded his head.

"Me too, this world is trying to tell us something. Hopefully, society can step up and make some sort of change, we sure as heck didn't!" They laughed together as they agreed with one another and went on with their day.

Lumen and the Thistle

Made in the USA
Las Vegas, NV
28 February 2021